Forbidden War

The Intern Diaries Series- Book 3

D. C. Gomez

GOMEZ EXPEDITIONS

Cover design by Christine Gerardi Designs

Edited by Cassandra Fear

Proofread by Michelle Hoffman

ISBN: 978-1-7321369-3-9 for Paperback Editions

ISBN: 979-8-9857369-0-8 for Hardcover Editions

Published by Gomez Expeditions

Request to publish work from this book should be sent to: author@dcgomez-author.com

For my parents, Jose and Altagracia.
Thank you for believing in me and not letting me stop.
I love you both so much.

Chapter One

"Eugene, you really know how to show a girl a good time," I told Eugene as I followed him down the old path.

"Oh, come on Isis! What better way to spend a Saturday night than collecting specimens." I was sure Eugene was trying to be charming, but considering we were crawling around a cemetery at night in the middle of Texarkana, his charms weren't working for him.

"Do you know how suspicious we look wandering around here four days before Halloween?" I asked him softly as I looked around the place.

"Oh, Isis, this part of town is deserted on the weekends. Besides, of all people, you should be used to cemeteries," Eugene told me without looking my way. "Remember, you work for Death."

"Eugene, I see dead people. That doesn't mean I hang out in cemeteries during my free time," I said.

Eugene was right about one thing: I did work for Death. I was Death's Intern in North America. Normally, that statement made most people panic. We terrified the poor souls who knew about us. We did have a terrible reputation, after all. Especially me. Death's Interns had a reputation of being a menace to society. Honestly, it wasn't our fault. For some strange reason, trouble had a way of finding us. For those who were blessed with not knowing about the supernatural world, they still believed

Death came to take their lives, and that just wasn't the way it worked.

The truth was completely different than what most people believed. Death was in the business of transporting souls to their final destination. Depending on the individual's beliefs of their after-life, Death would deliver them there. In other words, Death was the UPS for souls. Anything that interfered in the delivery of the souls was the Intern's job to find and fix.

Death was unique, appearing to each person according to their own belief. For some people, Death appeared in the shape of a monster or their worst nightmares. Others saw Death as a long-lost friend or relative who came to guide them to their next journey. For me, Death was always a tall, beautiful lady with long, silky, brown hair who dressed impeccably. She often resembled my dead mother.

I always wondered which one I resembled the most, my mom or my dad. I was five feet nine inches, with long, black hair and a mocha complexion. In the twin cities of Texarkana, I was considered exotic to the point of attractive. Unfortunately, my parents had named me Isis Black. In the age of terrorism, my name was a constant topic of painful discussions and explanations. I wasn't sure why I didn't consider a nickname. It wasn't like people ever remembered the Egyptian goddess when the name Isis was brought up.

"Isis!" I heard Eugene say my name. I didn't know how, but he whispered and yelled at the same time. "Are you listening to me?"

Oops, I guessed I tuned him out for a while.

"Sorry. I was thinking," I said, looking around the area. We were at the Sacred Heart Cemetery, located on Texas Boulevard across from the T-Line station. And I still didn't understand why. "Tell me again why we are roaming around this cemetery at night."

"Easy. Because we would probably get arrested for poking around the cemetery during the day," Eugene told me, planting his feet in a wide stance as he folded his arms over his chest. A smirk lifted the corners of his mouth.

"Thanks, Mr. Smarty-Pants. Now, think you can explain the cemetery part?" I replied as I waved my arms around to emphasize the setting.

"You have a lot of questions today," Eugene told me with a frown.

"Yes, I do, but normally you aren't this shady with your information. Stop changing the subject and spill it, or I'm not moving." I put my hands on my hips and stopped walking.

Eugene wouldn't meet my eyes, instead his gaze drifted everywhere but to me. I had to admit he looked extremely cute when he was nervous. He was a very attractive black man in his early twenties. He looked like a young Will Smith. I'm talking about the Will Smith in Independence Day.

"Stop pressuring me, Isis. I'm not supposed to talk about it."

I raised my eyebrows. If Eugene was keeping secrets, it could only be for one person.

"The Mistress said this was a classified mission," Eugene confessed in a whisper.

I knew it. The only one Eugene was this loyal to was his Horseman, Pestilence. While I was Death's Intern, Eugene was the rookie Intern for Pestilence. Pestilence was also Death's sister, and one nasty lady. The sisters were polar opposites. While Death was warm and motherly, Pestilence was Queen B. Pestilence even made her ten Interns call her Mistress. She didn't bother learning their names. They all went by numbers, which was completely insane. The poor guys worked and lived underground in a state-of-the-art lab. It was a good thing they were chemists and enjoyed their living conditions. Because if it was me living there, I'd be terrified.

Constantine, the five-thousand-year-old talking cat that served as the guardian and trainer for all of Death's Interns, explained how all the Horsemen had interns. We all had different purposes and modes of operations. Normally, Interns did not interact with each other. According to Constantine, that piece of information—and so much more—could be found in my Intern manual. Who read manuals anyway? I was pretty sure my manual was MIA—missing in action and not coming back. To Constantine's pain, I never read it. It wasn't on purpose. It just didn't look that important since it was so tiny.

"Eugene, talk. We don't need another zombie apocalypse," I told him sternly. That was how we first met, trying to stop a zombie apocalypse that Pestilence's poor hiring practices instigated. Afterwards, Death convinced her sister to keep the partnership, and now we get to spend every weekend with Eugene.

"Fine, just don't tell Constantine." Eugene looked around like he was expecting Pestilence to appear. He cleared his throat before continuing. "I'm supposed to bring back these little white flowers that are only grown by gnomes. Pestilence is researching a new strand of the whooping cough."

"What gnomes?" I asked as my gaze roamed the area. What was he talking about?

"Seriously, Isis. That's what you are concerned about?" Eugene pressed his lips together.

"Your entire team is in the business of killing humanity," I told Eugene. "Why should I be shocked that you're developing a new strand of some deadly virus? That is standard procedure for you. But the gnome thing, that's new."

"You got a point there," he agreed. "According to the mistress, now that Texarkana is a Haven, gnomes will be moving in everywhere." Eugene looked at me like that made any sense.

"Okay, Einstein, slow it down. What's a Haven?" I sucked today. I could barely follow this conversation, and I definitely wasn't understanding it.

"You really need to read your manual," Eugene told me as he crossed his arms.

"Don't you start with that," I replied in a firm tone. I knew the only reason he read his manual was because Pestilence had a mandatory test on it. I prayed Constantine never heard about that. "Just tell me, please. I really don't want to ask Constantine." And I didn't. He was known for instilling fear in the hearts of everyone.

"That would be a painful lecture." Eugene gave me a soft look. "Havens are a sanctuary for the supernatural communities. They are places where every creature is protected and treated fairly. In North America, Texarkana —both the Texas and Arkansas side—and even a few of its surrounding communities are the new Haven."

"Why? Of all the places to have a sanctuary, why here?" I wanted to know who made that decision. Why wouldn't they pick San Diego or Cancun since those are tropical areas, larger cities, and have a lot more to offer? It made no sense to me.

"I don't know. Why did you pick Texarkana to move to?" Eugene asked me.

"What does one thing have to do with the other?" I wasn't in the mood for reminiscing on how I landed in Texarkana running away from my past. The funny thing was, my past came knocking at my door anyway, only in the shape of Death.

"Everything." Eugene rubbed at his sleeves. "Havens are the territory of Death. The locations are based on the places where the Interns live. Which means, Isis, you now are the town sheriff."

"Sheriff!" I yelled, and the sound echoed through the cemetery. I couldn't help it. I did not like the sound of that.

"Unfortunately, you are responsible for keeping everyone safe and enforcing the law." Eugene looked at the ground when he spoke. "The good news is, everyone knows the reputations of the sheriffs, so everyone behaves." I knew he was trying to make me feel better, but it wasn't working.

"Eugene, what are the punishments for crimes committed in Haven?" I asked as a sick feeling tossed back and forth in my stomach.

"The usual, I guess." He shrugged. "Banishment, beatings, and even death to all violators."

"Great," I mumbled, my shoulders slumping and my whole face falling. I didn't have the stomach to kill anyone. "I'm not sure why we have intern rules if I have to violate them to do the job."

As Death's Interns, we had five simple rules we had to follow. Luckily, I could recite the rules in my head. One: you couldn't tell anyone you worked for Death. Two: you couldn't kill anyone unless it was self-defense. Three: you couldn't contact Death unless you were actually dying. Four: being Death's Intern was your primary job and other jobs couldn't interfere with it. Five: any romantic relationship couldn't get in the way of the job.

"Eugene, why is this happening now? I have been an Intern for over a year," I asked him, hoping there had been a mistake.

"What I gathered from Fifth, because of the short life of Death's Interns, Havens can only be established after your one-year anniversary," Eugene explained. "So, congratulations, you made it to Haven status." Eugene gave me two thumbs up when he finished.

I blinked at him, not nearly as excited as he was. "Thanks. We can celebrate later. For now, let's get out of here." I had information overload and needed time to process it.

"Great. Look for a small white flower. They grow near the headstones," Eugene said as he leaned down, almost crawling over the tombs.

As I watched Eugene, something caught my eye. I glanced to the left, sure I'd seen something moving, but there was nothing there. Maybe it was just a branch from that big tree in the back. But then the whole tree moved, and I knew it hadn't been my imagination.

"Oh God. Eugene, the trees are moving!" I tried to whisper, but it came out as a squeal.

"What?" Eugene turned around to stare at me. "Trees moving? What are you talking about?" he asked, the words rushing out of him in confusion.

I pointed in the direction of the nine-foot-tall tree coming at us.

"Isis, that's not a tree," Eugene said, his voice way higher than normal. "That's a troll, and he is coming for us. Run." Eugene took off, grabbing my hand and dragging me along.

"Eugene, let go of my hand. We need to split up." I had never seen a troll before, but I knew survival tactics. "He can't chase us both. That will give us a chance to knock him out." After several instances of people trying to beat me up, I was a bit paranoid. I never left the house without taking certain precautions. Thanks to Eugene, I now carried a paintball gun. The paintballs were filled with the formula Eugene had created; they knocked people out without killing them.

"Unless you have a fifty-pound barrel, you don't have enough." I looked over my shoulder and realized Eugene was right. That thing was huge.

"Whatever. We are trying this. You go left, I'll head right," I told Eugene as I pulled away. He didn't look happy, but he moved with a purpose. Eugene looked like one of those people you see at the mall powerwalking.

I, on the other hand, took off at a full sprint. At the beginning, I was doing great, weaving through the tombs and moving quickly, until I heard Eugene scream. I looked back and somehow managed to slip on some grass, landing flat on my butt. I didn't have time to nurse my pride, not when I stared into the eyes of two very strange creatures, a male and a female. They looked like ten-inch dolls that were mixed with flowers. They had petals coming out of their heads like little hats, and branches sticking out of their bodies in different places.

"What are you?" I asked the two little creatures as I reached to touch them. They looked so cute and delicate.

"Oh no, she can see us. Get Godzilla to squish her," the male said.

"I need to ask Constantine if our insurance covers being squished by a troll." I giggled like a little girl. Surely, I must have a concussion if I was giggling.

"She said 'Constantine?'" the female said as she sprayed me with sparkling dust. "We killed the Intern. We are dead."

"It might be a different Constantine," the male told her.

"Do you know another five-thousand-year-old talking cat?" I asked them as my head started spinning.

"Oh, we are so dead," the female repeated.

"Nobody is going to die," I said, trying to get up, but failing. "What are you guys?"

"Oh yes, sorry," the female said as the little couple tried to help me stand up. They had worse luck than I did. "I'm Trish and this is Trey. We are the new gnomes in town."

"Hi, nice to meet you," I said when I managed to sit up. "Why do I feel this way?" I asked the little gnomes.

"Sorry about that, Isis." Trey's voice shook when he spoke. "It's our, you know..." He couldn't finish the sentence.

"I have no clue, but I'm probably too stoned to get it." After several visits to the hospital in the Army, I knew what good narcotics felt like. Whatever this was, it was out of this world. "Is that tree-troll thing with you?" I asked the cute little couple, pointing toward the troll.

They glanced in the direction I pointed. "He is our security guy," Trish said so softly I almost missed it.

"Great. Could you call him off before he kills my friend?" I couldn't turn my head without feeling nauseous.

"Of course." Trish let out a loud whistle. I couldn't focus very well, but I did see the tree-troll retreating. "Please don't tell Constantine."

I giggled. That cat had everyone terrorized. "Not a problem; he will be fine." They both took a few deep breaths. "Could you do us a favor please?" I asked, giggling again.

"Sure, anything," Trish said, but Trey was biting his lips and looking around the place.

"Could we get some of your little, white flowers?" I asked the gnomes and they looked at each other, then raised their leafy eyebrows. "My friend works for Pestilence and he needs to bring some back."

"That crazy witch is back to her old tricks," Trish said, shaking her head. "Sure, but only this time. This stuff is dangerous."

"Thank you so much. You two are so cute," I said as I leaned my head against a headstone near me. The world started spinning around me.

"She is so cute and so polite. I hope she lasts." I heard Trish talking, but could hardly focus on her.

As soon as my eyes closed, everything went dark.

"Isis. Isis, wake up!" Eugene screamed in my ears as he nearly shook me to death.

"I'm awake. I'm awake. Stop that," I mumbled to Eugene. My head was still spinning, but not as much. Still, I just wanted to sleep, but I forced my eyes open slowly. I hoped I wasn't drooling.

"Oh, thank God. You scared me to death." Eugene hugged me so tight I couldn't breathe.

"Sorry, just don't strangle me now," I said, and Eugene released his tight hold.

"We need to get you out of here now," Eugene said, pulling me up.

"Don't forget your flowers. The gnomes left them for you," I told him, still giddy.

"Great." That was all he said as he struggled to pick up the flowers and keep me up. "You need fresh air and a slushy."

I smiled happily at Eugene as he led us out. I loved slushies.

Chapter Two

My head was still fuzzy by the time we made it to Reapers. That was after an hour of Eugene driving us around and feeding me Sonic's slushies and fries to clear my mind. I was a little jealous of Eugene today. The gnomes' narcotics didn't affect him. As one of Pestilence's Interns, he was immune to any form of virus, bacteria, or any type of drug. That was a blessing with his job. Last thing anyone needed was the scientists dying from their experiments.

Reapers Incorporated—as the red Gothic letters in front of the metal building read—was our headquarters. We were located in Nash's Business Park. From the outside, Reapers blended with all the other buildings in the park and was just another metal building. If I had been driving, we would have pulled around the back towards the vehicle entrance. Constantine had a rule that only Reapers' vehicles were allowed in the building.

Eugene parked his company car, a hearse of all things, by the front door and we walked in the front entrance, then moved through the security system.

Any other day, this would not bother me. Today, it was a painful experience. Reapers was a giant bomb shelter with every kind of security installed. The scanning system in the building was more precise than any you would find at an airport. It scanned for metal, explosives, and even spells. Unfortunately, the crazy blue light was giving me an aching headache. By the time we passed all the securities, I was in no condition for the climb up the stairs. In fact, it made me wonder why we didn't have an elevator.

Reapers had a first floor and part of a second floor. The first floor housed our shooting range, personal gym, car shop, and Bob's apartment. The second floor was a combination of bedrooms, kitchen, and central control area. The front of the second floor we called the Loft, since it served as our common area and Command Center. You could see the Loft from the first floor, since the inside wall was made of glass.

I was still feeling loopy from my interaction with the gnomes. My balance was still off, so I braced myself for climbing the stairs, afraid if I didn't, I might tumble back down them. Eugene grabbed me by the waist and guided me, making sure I didn't kill myself.

"I'm pitiful," I mumbled to him.

"I'm actually very impressed," Eugene whispered in my ear.

"Impressed about what?" The words sounded wrong to me, which made me think I wasn't enunciating properly.

"Most humans are knocked-out cold for at least twenty-four hours due to the narcotics of the gnomes." Eugene looked me up and down as he spoke. "I can't believe you are walking." He gave me a sweet smile.

"I wouldn't call this walking," I replied in a dry tone, but I still smiled back.

By the time we made it to the second floor and into the loft, I was exhausted. I did a quick check of the area. Constantine and Bob were on the opposite side of the room, watching a movie on the large-screen TV that doubles as our teleconference screen. We had the most comfortable leather couch on that side of the loft. Around the TV, we had tons of monitors, which Bartholomew used to hack into the city's security systems. I had no idea how he did it, and I didn't want to know.

Bartholomew sat in front of his computer station across from Bob and Constantine, and I assumed he was playing a video game. In the last five months, Bartholomew had grown another two inches. He was now only an inch shorter than me at five feet eight inches. His curly brown hair was its usual mess and his hazel eyes were glued to the screen.

Bartholomew was only twelve, but he was a certifiable genius. Last May we made a pact and I verbally adopted him as my little brother. No paperwork was required, but everyone knew he was my family. Neither of us had blood siblings, so it worked out perfect. Bartholomew's parents had died when he was young, and Death had become his guardian. A part of me wanted to give him a normal life—as normal as I could while working for Death and chasing souls around. I just hated how fast he was growing.

The first one to notice us was Bob. Bob was my first friend in Texarkana, and like me, he was prior military. I wasn't sure how old he was, but I guessed in his forties. Bob was six feet tall, with sandy-blond hair and sea-green eyes. He looked like a rugged Daniel Craig. While Bartholomew was our resident arms dealer and supply sergeant, Bob had become our in-house chef and getaway driver.

"What happened to you?" Bob shouted when he finally realized Eugene was carrying me. He rushed across the room and before I could explain, he grabbed me from Eugene's arms and sat me down on one of the kitchen chairs.

"Isis inhaled quite a large amount of gnome dust," Eugene said in a soft tone. "Don't worry, though. She is going to be fine. I got her out before the hallucinations started."

I was glad Eugene had failed to mention that to me earlier.

Constantine sprinted from the couch and was sitting on the table in less than two seconds. It impressed me how fast he was for a fifteen-pound cat.

"Gnomes? They found us already?" Constantine hissed as he spoke. "Who was it? I'll take care of this." I couldn't tell for sure, but it looked like Constantine was glaring.

"Relax, Constantine, they didn't do it on purpose," I managed to say, but not very loudly.

"They? So, it was more than one?" Constantine's claws were retracted, but he still tapped the table as he spoke. "Great. We have a plague of gnomes in town." He looked around like the gnomes had invaded Reapers and we hadn't noticed. "Explain how you looking like hell is not their fault, and why your clothes are dirty." Constantine demanded me as he took a closer look.

I took a deep breath before starting, a nervous habit I'd never been able to shake. "Technically, we were trespassing on a cemetery. I tripped and landed at their feet." I was a little embarrassed to admit the last part, even under the influence of all the narcotics.

"Why were you guys at a cemetery?" It had taken Bartholomew longer than I expected to join the conversation, but when I glanced over at him and saw the headphones around his neck, I understood why.

"That is a really good question. Please explain," Bob insisted as he walked over to the kitchen and faced the fridge.

"Eugene, how about you do us the honor since this was your idea."

Fine, so I was a chicken, but I was not going down alone for this little adventure.

"This better be good," Constantine told Eugene as he crouched into his favorite Sphinx pose.

"You see, what happened was..." Eugene trailed off. He was in trouble. I knew it because he always was when he started a sentence that way. His eyes searched the room, as if he wanted to bolt out the door. Eventually, he gave up looking for a way out and slumped into a chair. "It isn't my fault. The mistress made me do it. She didn't tell me the gnomes were going to hire a troll as a bodyguard."

"Hold up. What troll?" Bob shouted, leaning against the open fridge door, probably looking for something to cook.

"He was huge," I told Bob in a serious tone. "I was sure a tree was attacking us." I spread my hands wide for emphasis.

"Are we supposed to have trolls in town?" Bartholomew asked, glancing at Constantine.

"Unfortunately, it was only a matter of time." Constantine answered, shaking his head. "I probably don't want to know what Pestilence sent you to get," Constantine said, his eyes landing on Eugene.

"Some weird flower that only grows around gnomes," I told him, rolling my eyes. I started giggling for no reason, and the boys stared at me as if I had turned into a crazy person. I guessed I was still high, so I tried to regain control by rubbing my face. "So, this Haven stuff, do we take a head count of who's moving in? I would like to know which areas might get me killed the next time Eugene wants to trespass."

"A head count?" Constantine asked me.

"Yeah, like a census," I answered. That made perfect sense to me in my current condition.

"That's an interesting idea," Constantine said as he eyed at Bartholomew.

I raised my eyebrows at the boys. "Okay, what am I missing?" I was hoping it was the narcotics affecting my thought process, but I feared I was a little slow today.

"Most Interns avoid Havens like the plague. The fact you want to be involved is unusual," Bartholomew told me. "They move around every six months to avoid establishing one," Bartholomew finished with a sad tone to his voice. That sounded like a lot of work just to avoid people.

"Is this another one of those Intern duties nobody wants to do?" I asked.

"Isis, like I said earlier, you are now responsible for all the citizens of Haven," Eugene jumped in. "That's a huge responsibility on top of everything else you do."

"Guys, I don't like the idea of enforcing random laws or killing anyone," I told them. "But I'm not planning to run away from my responsibilities because they aren't fun. I joined the Army to serve and protect those I love. This is not any different. Since I'm in charge, it means you are all coming along with me. Starting today, you can consider yourselves deputies."

Their eyes went wide with excitement.

"Yes! I'm a deputy." Bartholomew bounced with anticipation.

"Oh Lord, wait till Shorty hears about this," Bob said with a smile. Shorty was our resident informant to the Underground—the large network of transient citizens in Texarkana.

I looked over at Constantine and I swore he winked at me.

"Sorry, Isis, the Mistress won't let me moonlight," Eugene told me with a frown. "But can I still get a badge?" He looked like a five-year-old waiting for a present.

"Of course, Eugene," I told him. "Bart, sounds like you need to order us some badges and proper IDs." I giggled again.

"Bartholomew, add developing a registry for the Haven to your list of things to do," Constantine told Bartholomew. With a salute, Bartholomew ran to his computer, and Constantine turned to me. "And you need a shower."

I looked down at my clothes. He was right. I was filthy. I wasn't sure how I had gotten this dirty since I was pretty sure I had fallen on my butt. Maybe when I blacked out, I rolled around in the dirt or something. Either way, I saw no reason to argue with Constantine, so I stood from the chair and headed towards my room.

"Here, drink this." Bob handed me a glass filled with a strange, green liquid. "It's an Eric shake to clear your head." Eric was Reaper's martial-arts trainer, wizard on retainer, local cop, and hunk extraordinaire. The last part I would never have said to his face, of course.

Eric's shakes were never bad, they just looked weird. He had an ability to blend magical ingredients with super foods. My first six months at Reapers, I was on a diet of his shakes. It was the only thing that helped me make it through my training sessions, plus it ensured I didn't die. So, there was that. Needless to say, I didn't hesitate to chug the drink as I made my way to my room.

When I turned on the light switch, big-band music filled the room. Bartholomew had rewired my room so when I flipped the lights on, the stereo would play. Death's Interns had certain powers that would affect the dead—also the living, but that was neither here nor there. My powers came through music. Thankfully, my room was sound proof.

As I walked inside and shut the door, my eyes were pulled to the new guitar I had purchased. It stood against the wall by my dresser. My goal for the weekend was to practice playing that beautiful instrument. Death's gifts enhanced my natural abilities, and lately, I had been able to pick up and play any instrument with very little training. I was dying to see how good I could get. Though, due to my little Eugene adventure, practice was cancelled for the rest of the evening.

With a soft sigh, I headed towards my bathroom for a long, hot shower.

By the time I entered the loft again, the boys were sitting at the kitchen table playing a Dungeons & Dragons game. Bartholomew was asked to join a gaming group at Texas A&M after last May's zombie apocalypse. Unfortunately, he came home and converted the rest of the tribe. Imaginary mission to save or attack some random group always felt too much like work for me, so I just watched from the side.

"Isis, why didn't you tell me your birthday is November second, the day of the dead?" Eugene asked me from the table. His eyes were on the game, so he didn't notice how mine had bugged out.

"I don't do birthdays," I said.

Constantine opened his mouth to respond, but the front door burst open then, saving me from an explanation. Death walked through, looking radiant in a black-and-white Armani suit. I was pretty sure Eugene didn't see the same thing. He looked a bit pale in the cheeks.

"Constantine, did you give my brother my number?" Death asked Constantine as she crossed the room.

"Brother? What brother?" If I didn't know any better, I could've sworn Constantine's voice cracked a bit. "Death, what are you talking about?"

"Constantine, I'm not playing. He has called me twenty times already." Death pulled out her cell phone as she spoke.

The only sibling of Death's I had met was Pestilence. If the other two, War and Famine, were anything like that crazy witch, I would rather skip the reunion.

Constantine wouldn't meet Death's eyes. Everyone else pretended to be busy with something else, and I made my way to the fridge to look for food. It wasn't like we were cowards, but Death and Constantine had a special relationship—one the rest of us didn't get involved in.

"Isis, your dinner is in the fridge," Bob told me as he walked in my direction. I almost rolled my eyes since I was already standing in front of the fridge.

"Death, honestly, why would I do such a thing?" I heard Constantine say. Bob and I were now hiding behind the fridge door. "Hey, what's that sound?"

At first, I thought Constantine was stalling for time, but then I heard it. Bob and I met each other's eyes before I closed the fridge and faced everyone. It was our teleconference system, and it was ringing.

"Constantine. Do not pick that up," Death said, her tone more than serious.

Unfortunately, her words came too late because Constantine had already sprinted across the room and pressed the button. It wasn't his fault. Constantine was a sucker for blinking lights.

Death took a deep breath as a broad-shouldered man with an olive complexion and jet-black hair came on the screen, wearing a military uniform.

"Guerra, what's up my man?" Constantine said to the stranger with a huge grin on his face.

"Constantine, is that you?" the man asked as he stared at Constantine. How many talking cats did he know?

"Hey, don't hate," Constantine replied. "This is my North America camouflage. Taking a few pointers from you," Constantine finished, putting his pointy fangs on full display. I almost laughed out loud.

Everyone else had a different reaction to the mystery caller. Bob looked a little pale, Eugene was mesmerized by him, and Bartholomew looked like a kid in a candy store. Death, on the other hand, was glaring at her brother. She had her arms crossed and her foot was tapping furiously.

As for me, I wasn't too impressed, so I focused on eating my food.

"Good call, easier to fit in," the mystery caller said. "Have you seen Muerte? He's not answering my calls. I really need to talk to him." The mystery caller's gaze roamed as if he could see around the screen.

"What did you say?" Constantine asked the mystery caller. "Guerra, I think I'm losing you." Before he could reply, Constantine hit the off button, then he turned to face Death. "Sorry, boss."

"Constantine, I'm not in the mood for this," Death replied as she headed out the door. "Fix this."

"Death, you know he is just going to keep calling until he finds you," Constantine told Death.

"Not today." That was all Death said as she walked out the door and left us all staring at the spot she had just been standing.

"Oh wow, please tell me that was War!" Eugene broke the silence.

"Who else would it be?" Constantine asked as he made his way across the room.

"Yes! Wait until I tell the guys." Eugene bounced off his chair and ran out the door. During his weekend visits, Eugene stayed downstairs in Bob's guest bedroom. I guessed he was heading towards his room.

"Pestilence's Interns really do need to go out more," Constantine said as he stared out the glass wall and watched Eugene run across the first floor.

"Bob, are you okay?" Bartholomew asked Bob. I turned around and noticed Bob had a greenish hue across his face.

"I think it was something I ate. I'm going to bed." Bob was out the door before we could say another word.

"When I think my days can't get any weirder, I'm always surprised," I said out loud. "I'm heading to bed. I don't think I can process any more today. Goodnight." I wasn't sure if I was still suffering the side effects of the narcotics, but whatever just happened had been odd, so before anything weirder happened, I went to bed.

Chapter Three

For most of the residents of the Bible Belt, Sundays were days of rest and worship. That was not the case for me. I was a Christian, technically Catholic, so I did practice my faith. As long as I was in town, I went to mass on Saturdays at five p.m. I even volunteered for the Saturday morning services of the Church Under the Bridge. That was one of the most moving experiences of my life. A dedicated group of volunteers ministered to the transient population and shared a meal together. Even for those who don't believe in magic or God, they could feel the power.

With my Saturday church schedule, Sunday became another training day. This was like being back in the military. If we were not at war, we were training. As Death's Intern, I trained all the time. Most of my training consisted of running, hand-to-hand combat, firing range, and of course, music. Nobody could deny I didn't have a diverse life. I could qualify for a musician spy. Fortunately, I was far enough in my training that I could pick my own routine.

Today, I planned to do a long-run, at least fifteen miles. After my little episode with the gnomes, I wanted to make sure my head was completely clear. I had been running six days a week and doing two long-run days. On average, I ran between a five-and six-minute mile. I wanted to take all the credit for that, but I had a feeling Death's gifts played a part. The plan was simple. Head west for seven and a half miles on Highway 72, and then turn back.

I tiptoed down the stairs before sunrise. I didn't have to be quiet at this time of the day. The boys were night owls and there was no way I'd wake anyone up. Still, I enjoyed the silence.

I left Reapers using the pedestrian entrance. Our doors were opened by hand-scanners, which made it easy to run and not worry about keys getting lost. I did a quick stretch outside and took in the warm, fall air of October. After one last look around, I set my watch and took off.

It was almost eight by the time I made it through the security door. The weather was so perfect when I had started that it inspired me to run a couple of extra miles. I hummed out loud by the time I entered the first-floor training area. The lights were on, and I heard someone talking. As I went further inside, I found Eric on the phone, pacing the length of the work-out area. God sure had blessed that man with some good genes. He was six-feet tall and muscular, with brown hair and gorgeous brown eyes. He was also one of the most focused, no-nonsense kind of guys I had ever met. Today, he looked upset, though.

I waved at him, but he didn't even notice me. It was not like Eric to be distracted and unaware of his surroundings.

"Honey, please let me explain," Eric shouted into the phone.

Obviously, Eric was having a private conversation and it had nothing to do with me, so I jogged to the stairs. I knew he'd been dating a hot blonde, and there must be some trouble between them. Maybe that wasn't the best way to describe the girl. Texas was full of hot blondes, after all, and between the big hair and the accents, the women there made quite an impression. It wasn't fair how one state could have so many good-looking people.

I put those thoughts out of my mind as I rushed up the stairs, hoping Bob was up and had made breakfast. I was one of the few non-meat eaters in Texarkana, so breakfast used to be fairly boring, at least until Bob had come along. I couldn't have been happier when he'd become our resident chef, going as far as taking culinary classes at Texarkana College.

I wasn't expecting Bartholomew or Constantine to be up when I got to the loft, but they were, along with everyone else, including Death. Bartholomew still wore his pajamas while he worked in his computer area. Death paced the room, wearing a path in the floor. Constantine did the same, only on the kitchen table. It would have looked funny if the tension wasn't so thick. In fact, Bob even looked on edge. Every burner on the stove was covered with pots. I wasn't sure if he was cooking or sacrificing ingredients to some secret god.

"Morning, everyone. Did I miss the world domination meeting?" I asked, trying to break the tension.

"Not yet," Bob replied, glancing at Death and Constantine. "I'm afraid it might happen soon, though." He pointed at the TV with his spoon.

"In that case, I'm glad I made it back in time," I joked, trying to entice a grin, but I failed. So, I gave up the humor and focused on the important issue—food. "What are you making? It smells amazing and I'm famished."

Just like that, Bob's shoulders relaxed and a smile brightened his face. "I got a cheese casserole with sautéed onions and peppers. The veggie quiche is in the oven with the extra bacon for Constantine and Bartholomew." He was a pro and made sure he addressed everyone's preference from my non-meat-eating to poor Bartholomew's gluten intolerance.

"Do you think anyone would care if I eat now?" I pouted my lips and tried to bat my eyes, hoping to inspire a bit of sympathy.

"I doubt it," Bob said. "However, you smell like road-kill, so you might want to take a shower first." The way he spoke told me his suggestion wasn't really a suggestion.

No matter. He was right, and I had sweat dripping from my head down to my toes to prove it.

"I get no love around here," I told him with a glare. Bob ignored me as he pulled fresh fruits from the fridge. I grabbed a piece before he could complain, then stuck out my tongue as my victory salute.

"So mature," Bob teased as he tossed me a few more pieces of fruit.

I caught them all. "By the way, what is going on with Eric?"

"I'm not sure," Bob replied as he looked out the glass window towards Eric. "From what I gather, his girlfriend wants to move their relationship to the next stage. Whatever that means." Bob shrugged a shoulder. I did the same, since I really had no clue what that meant.

"Constantine, I don't have time to deal with War's little feud," Death shouted from the other side of the room. Bob and I looked at each other, confused.

"That's my cue to hit the shower," I told Bob as I headed towards my room.

"Catch." Bob threw me a bottle of water and I barely turned in time to catch it. "Hurry before your food gets cold." My stomach growled in response to the word "food."

I gave him a quick salute and proceeded out the door. I had mixed feelings about the situation because I wanted to know what could ever make Death aggravated like that, but I also had a horrible feeling this wouldn't end well for me. If something bad was happening, it was the Intern's job to do the dirty work and investigate, after all.

My curiosity won in the end and I took the fastest shower of my life, then rushed back to the loft in less than fifteen minutes. Death sat on a chair, drinking coffee with Bob. Bartholomew was gone, and Constantine was laying on top of the leather couch. Nobody was saying anything. It was like the calm before the storm.

"Hi, Isis. Sorry for not greeting you earlier," Death told me as she put down her cup. "How was your run? I see you are getting faster." She smiled at me when she finished. Death had a way of being soothing and strong all at once.

"Relaxing," I replied as I grabbed the plate of food Bob had left for me on the kitchen island. I took a seat next to Death and Bob. "By the way, did we get our trees cut for some reason?" I asked the room.

"What?" Constantine asked from across the room.

"The really tall trees around Reapers are gone," I told them in between bites. It might have made me look a bit rude to be chomping on food and talking at the same time, but I was too hungry to care.

"Are you sure?" Death asked, her brows etched with concern.

"Hard to miss. I used to lean on one to stretch every day." I took another bite before talking. "It's weird, though. I couldn't even find a hole for the trunk or the roots. I'm pretty sure ours are not the only ones missing. The whole area looks emptier." That was saying a lot. Texarkana was located in the piney woods of Texas, so we were packed with trees. Especially tall pines.

"Constantine, I guess it's time to talk to my brother." Death let out a deep sigh.

"What's going on?" I aimed my question at Death, who stood up and started walking towards Constantine.

"I have a feeling we are about to find out," Death said as she smoothed her shirt. "Constantine, do me the honor and call your favorite General," she said, not even a hint of humor in her tone.

"I'm going to do some laundry," Bob said as he sprang up out of his chair. Come to think of it, his face looked rather pale.

"Are you okay?" I asked him. I'd never really understood what had happened to him yesterday.

"Yeah, I'm fine." I couldn't tell if he was lying to me. "Eugene left early this morning, so I'm going to organize his room." Bob took Death's empty cup to the sink as he spoke.

"Did something happen to him?" I asked, my voice a little high. Eugene had a military schedule at the lab, so on Sundays when he was over, he slept in. I figured he was still sleeping. He had parked around the back, so I didn't notice the Hearse missing.

"Relax, Isis, nothing major," Bob told me with a tight smile. "Pestilence just wanted her plant as soon as possible. Now, finish your food and make sure Bartholomew finishes his." Bob was out the door before I could ask any more questions.

"Are you sure about this?" I heard Constantine ask Death from across the room.

"Just call him before I change my mind," Death snapped.

Since I had no intention of moving any closer, I leaned in for a better view. Anyone that made Death that miserable deserved my undivided attention. Constantine did his magic and in less than a minute the teleconference system was ringing. I expected there would be a long wait, but that didn't happen.

"Muerte! Have you been avoiding me?" War asked from the other side of the screen.

"Yes, I've been avoiding you, War," Death replied. I was impressed. I didn't think Death would admit to that. "Every time you call, some horrible catastrophe is happening. What is it this time?" Death shifted and placed her hands on her hips.

"I have nothing to do with this one," War replied, sounding like a mischievous little boy. "The elves and the vampires are planning to go to war without my consent." He narrowed his eyes. Of course, he'd be mad. How could any being have the nerve to go to war without his permission? I almost burst out laughing at his outrage.

"I don't get it. What's the problem here?" Death moved her hands from her hips and crossed her arms over her chest.

"I'm in the middle of planning a huge conflict between the world and Korea." War's voice was getting louder as he spoke, and he'd almost reached the point of shouting. "I don't have time for petty family feuds over star-crossed lovers."

"I still don't see how this applies to me," Death told her brother with an intense glare. This time, War impressed me because he didn't flinch.

"Simple. Vampires are your expertise." War flashed Death a brilliant smile and she looked like she was going to punch the screen. "If the elves and vamps go to war, you know the vamps are going to start recruiting again. Only way to beat those shady-trees, no pun intended. I would hate for the treaty to be broken and for us to have another dark age."

I had no idea what War was talking about, but Death started pacing and it looked like steam might fly out of her ears. Obviously, she must know exactly what he'd meant.

Constantine jumped off the computer area, not stopping until he made himself comfortable beside me. Nobody said a word for a few minutes.

"Fine. I'm listening," Death told War as she took several deep breaths to settle herself.

"What just happened?" I angled my head towards Constantine.

"War is good," Constantine said, shaking his head. "He found all the right buttons and pressed them. Did you know he invented psychological operations?"

I heard of psychological operations, or PsyOps as the Army called it. I had a few friends that did that job when I was in the military. Their training was to discover the enemy's psychological and emotional weaknesses and exploit them.

"Oh, don't look so mad. I promise it is no big deal." War's lips stretched into a big grin. "It's not like the zombie apocalypse you had to clean up for Pestilence. You helped that violent nut, so why can't you do your brother one little favor?" War actually batted his eyelashes, looking as innocent as he could, while he waited for Death's response.

"War, get to the point now," Death demanded in a harsh tone. "What do you want?"

"The elves and the vamps are having negotiations that the witches are facilitating. I want your people to attend and make sure all goes well," War said in a nonchalant way, as if he had just asked us to pick up a gallon of milk from Walmart.

"You want my Intern to attend a treaty? Isn't that your Intern's specialty?" Death gaped at War as if he'd grown horns and turned red. "Aren't treaty talks and peace summits your areas of expertise? What exactly are my people supposed to do there?" Death threw her arms up in the air and started pacing again.

"Katrina is under a lot of stress lately," War shot out. "We just need a third party to make sure the witches don't screw this up. You know, someone from the outside. It won't take more than three hours. What do you have to lose?" War asked with another brilliant smile.

"You do know this is a horrible idea. The vampires don't trust us, and the elves avoid us at all cost," Death told War. "I don't like this."

"Three hours. That's all. You help Pestilence and Famine all the time," War said in a whiney tone. "Please." He stretched the word out for a solid twenty seconds. He was definitely whining.

"Fine," Death agreed, stopping in front of the screen. "When is this treaty?" Her words came out in a growl. She was definitely not happy.

"This afternoon, and it's here in Kansas," War replied.

Death held her hands in front of the screen in a strangling motion.

"Send the details to Constantine and you'd better be quick," Death told War, and before he could respond, she turned the system off.

"This is going to suck," Constantine whispered to me.

"Isis, you heard my brother. He needs your help on this," Death told me. "I don't like it, either, so be careful." She turned to Constantine with a glare. "You are taking everyone. Brief them on the plane, and don't forget to take some overnight clothes. Everything takes longer than War expects."

I had no clue what had just happened, but the bottom line was, we were all headed to Kansas.

Chapter Four

Talk about change of pace. We went from a slow Sunday morning to full combat mode. According to War's instructions, the negotiations were taking place at 2:30 p.m. near Manhattan, Kansas. That meant we had less than five hours to make our way there. I was wondering why the elves and vampires would have their negotiations so close to a military installation. Fort Riley was less than twenty minutes from Manhattan. It was a post I always wanted to visit because the Big Red One was stationed there.

It was probably a blessing we were used to short notices and preparing in a hurry. In less than an hour, we had Bob's baby blue Ram 2500 Heavy Duty work truck, Storm, fully packed with our gear, clothes, and weapons. We were all silent on the way to the tiny Texarkana Airport located on the Arkansas side. I had no idea how we were going to find a flight at this time. The airport only had three departing and arriving flights each day. Even if we could get a flight, I had a bad feeling TSA was not going to let us board with all our weapons, especially since Bob had added extras just for this trip.

"It might be a little late to ask, but how are we going to get all of our stuff through security," I finally asked as we were pulling into the airport entrance.

"We are not," Constantine replied from the front passenger seat. Yeah, that was right, Constantine always rode shot-gun. Go figure.

"What do you mean?" I asked, meeting Bartholomew's eyes. He sat next to me in the backseat, but only shrugged his shoulders at me. I guessed he didn't know the answer either.

"We don't have time to lose today. We are taking my private plane," Constantine replied, directing Bob towards the executive terminal of the airport. The separate terminal was away from the commercial area.

"Huh?" My mouth fell open. Had I heard him correctly? "You have a plane?"

"Of course, I do," Constantine said in a tone that depicted his words explained everything, when in fact, they explained nothing.

I'd been all over the country this past year, and he had never mentioned he owned a private plane. The thought made me say, "Wait, if you have a private plane, why am I always flying commercial?"

"Simple. You are supposed to blend in. You can't blend in with a private plane landing everywhere," Constantine told me. "Besides, you are flying first class, so why are you complaining? If I travel commercial, they want to shove me in the cargo area. Is that even fair?" Constantine peered around the seat to look at me as he spoke.

"Good point." I couldn't argue with his facts.

"Besides, I thought you like to people watch," Constantine said with a smirk.

"That is true. I wouldn't get to see anyone from a private plane." I did enjoy watching the strange things people did and airports were the best places to watch. "I take it back. I'm sticking to first class," I told him with a smile.

"Oh wow. The horror of first class," Constantine mocked.

I rolled my eyes but couldn't hide my smile. He was right. The job had spoiled me, and it was the first job I'd ever had that paid me really well. I received a paycheck every month, but I also had a clothing allowance and every other expense was covered as well. We joked that Death paid really well since the life span of Interns was really short. Normally, you had to die to be replaced, which made the person that killed you the next potential Intern. We needed to work on our recruitment process.

Bob drove around the executive terminal and went straight onto the runway. I was expecting a small plane with enough seats for maybe five to seven people, but boy, were my thoughts wrong. I hadn't prepared myself for Constantine's plane. It was bigger than the American Eagle planes that normally flew into Texarkana, which had three rows of seats and only held about thirty people. So, not only was Constantine's plane bigger than American Eagle Airlines, it was also stylish, painted black with gothic red letters that read Reaper 1. The man had a sense of humor.

"Constantine, do you really own that plane?" I asked him before getting out of the truck.

"It's a little dated now. It was brand new when I got it," Constantine told me with a shrug, and it sounded like he was thinking of trading it in for a new one. "It's the Embraer Lineage 1000 Private Jet. Wait until you see the inside. It's customized. Only reason I haven't gotten a new one." Constantine jumped out of the truck as soon as Bob opened the door.

"Bart, did you know he had a private plane?" I asked Bartholomew, hoping I wasn't the only one blown away.

"It's Constantine. I'm sure he has one of everything," Bartholomew said without an ounce of surprise inflected in his voice. "Come on. I can't wait to see the inside. I bet he has a gaming station." I shook my head. Bartholomew was a genius, but he was still a twelve-year-old boy. His priorities were always a little skewed.

"Isis, hurry up. We don't have all day!" Constantine yelled when I finally climbed out. He was right, though. I did need to hurry.

The crew of the plane unloaded our gear and had already started loading it in the plane. I guessed if you could afford a private jet, you could keep a crew on standby, too.

"Good morning, ma'am," a very friendly crew member said to me. I smiled at him but widened my eyes as I realized his eyes were cat-like. He winked at me and got back to work, leaving me standing with my mouth hanging open. I had a feeling I didn't want to know who was flying the plane.

If the plane was impressive from the outside, the inside was out of this world. I wondered if Air Force One looked this good. The plane had leather seats, a leather couch on one side, a large screen TV on the back wall, and of course every gaming system imaginable. This was luxury. I thought I was spoiled, but I had nothing on Constantine.

"Boss, we will be ready to take off as soon as all the bags are secure," a tall, handsome man in a pilot uniform said to Constantine. I glanced at his face and he had blue cat-eyes as well, and he gave me a wink just like the last one had. What was going on today?

"As soon as you are ready, get us in the air. We are on a tight schedule, George," Constantine told the pilot.

"It will be our pleasure, sir," George told Constantine before he headed to the cockpit.

Constantine stepped towards the middle of the plane. He jumped on a leather chair and made himself comfortable.

"Isis, take a seat. We need to talk." Constantine pointed to the chair facing him. There was a small table between the two chairs. Bob took a seat on the other side of the plane. Bartholomew went straight to the back towards the gaming area and started playing.

"Why do I have a feeling this is not going to be a good talk?" I told Constantine as I took my seat.

"It's not a bad talk," Constantine said as he licked his paw and wiped his face off. "But since you refuse to read the manual, I need to catch you up on our history."

"Oh, come on. That isn't fair," I mumbled. "Besides, that manual can't have that much stuff in it. It's too small." My protest sounded weak, even to my own ears. Bob shook his head and smiled at me.

"You're right. This information is located in your year two manual," Constantine told me. "But considering you didn't read the first, there is no reason to give you another one. So, here is your audio version." I was pretty sure Constantine was making fun of me, but I didn't care.

"Finally. Why didn't you do this from the beginning?" I told Constantine as I made myself comfortable.

"Everyone, please buckle your seat-belts. We are about to take off," a sweet female voice said over the intercom.

"Really? No demonstration on how to buckle ourselves. Shouldn't they at least point out the fire exits?" I asked Constantine as I looked around.

"Are you serious?" Constantine said, his tone dripping with sarcasm. "If you haven't figured out how to buckle your seatbelt at this stage in your life, we have other issues to worry about. Now focus." Those last words came out in a hiss.

I frowned. Perhaps it wasn't the best time to mess around. "Sorry. I was just joking."

"Have you heard of the Dark Ages?" Constantine asked me.

"Of course. Everyone has," I replied.

"Do you know how it started?" Constantine asked.

"It's been a really long time since I covered world history," I answered, scrunching my forehead as I tried to remember. "Was it after the Crusades, or some plague that hit Europe?" I wasn't sure. That time period was not my favorite and honestly, it never came up in conversations.

"It was a crusade but not the kind you are thinking," Constantine said, posing like a Sphinx and staring out the window as the jet started moving. "We are not proud of this part of our history, but hard choices had to be made." Constantine met my eyes. "It was a time of chaos and humans were hungry for power. They were disorganized and vulnerable, easy prey for most predators. Vampires took advantage of this, multiplying their numbers. It wasn't enough for them to be able to turn the willing, they wanted to take over the world, so they turned everyone they could, whether they were willing or not. You know what that means?" Constantine paused, watching me hard, as if I held all the answers he was seeking.

It took me a minute to process all that information. "I'm guessing it means Death wasn't happy?" She couldn't have been. She hated vampires because the process to become one destroyed the human soul.

"That's an understatement," Constantine told me before he gazed out the window again. "It started slowly at first, so we didn't notice right away. When we did, Death called a meeting with the vampire leader and demanded him to stop what he was doing. Of course, they refused. In their minds, they had found a way to beat death. Hundreds and hundreds of souls were gone and more each day. Death's fury only grew hotter, and soon she gave them an ultimatum: stop taking souls by force or we would destroy every vampire." Constantine took a deep breath, but still didn't look my way.

"Let me guess, they refused," I said.

"Of course, they did. We had no choice, then. We went to war with the vampires," Constantine almost whispered. "We started recruiting Interns because we needed more people. We were losing bodies each day. Then Death had an idea. What if the Interns had more of her powers? So, she gave them a choice, refusing to force any. Many took the leap, and the Interns became Reapers, bound to Death with superhuman powers and immortality." His body drooped and he frowned as he finished.

"That doesn't sound like such a bad deal," I told Constantine. "Did it help?"

"Oh, it helped," Constantine said in a positively somber tone. "The Reapers turned the war in our favor. Unfortunately, we learned a little too late that this transformation was not perfect. Like with Death's gift, the power enhanced the person's true nature. Some became like guardian angels to humanity. But others became worse than the monsters we were fighting. To stop them, Death had to kill off her own children." He paused again, and the room grew so quiet I was afraid to move, let alone breathe.

After several seconds, he continued. "The pain was unbearable." He cleared his throat, like there might be a lump stuck in there from him holding back his sadness. I didn't know if he spoke of Death's pain or his own. "In the end, Death asked War to facilitate a peace treaty with the vampires. We would stop hunting them if they stopped turning humans against their will. The vampires agreed, and they went underground. We made a point to avoid them." Constantine's eyes were glued to his paws.

"If we promised to avoid them, why are we getting involved?" I asked.

I glanced over and saw Bob leaning against the leather couch he was sitting on, not paying any attention to our conversation.

"The only thing vampires' fear is Death, and her Reapers of course," Constantine answered. "With us there, it will ensure that everyone keeps their word." He didn't sound very convincing.

"Constantine, what happened to the Reapers?" There was a hesitation in my tone. Truthfully, I wasn't sure why I asked the question because I didn't think I really wanted to know the answer.

"The good ones that were left went to sleep with the rest of our Interns," Constantine said with a smile. I sure hoped sleep truly meant sleep. "An army ready for judgment day."

"I'm sorry, Constantine." That was all I could think to say, but even those words felt empty.

"That was a very long time ago," Constantine said, his eyes meeting mine once more. "Besides, Death swore she would never make another Reaper again." Constantine wiped his face with his paw. If I didn't know any better, I could have sworn he was tearing up.

"That's good, right?" Maybe this horrible story would actually have a happy ending.

"Yes, it is. Unfortunately, now the rumors will start again," Constantine told me.

"What rumors? Constantine, what are you talking about?" I wanted answers, not all these weird riddles.

"Bartholomew, bring me the case please?" Constantine called back to Bartholomew. "Bob, you might want to get dressed." Bob jumped out of his chair at the sound of Constantine's voice.

Bartholomew walked over from the gaming area and placed a sleek, silver briefcase in front of me. Bartholomew opened the briefcase using a finger-print scanner, something he only used for top-secret information, or highly dangerous weapons. It made me wonder if I really wanted to see what was in there, but as the lid raised, all I found was a sleek, silver cylinder, maybe six inches in length.

"That's it?" The words came out before I could stop them. I couldn't help it. After all the tense build-up, I had expected much more than just a stick.

"Don't judge," Constantine said.

"I need you to grab it with your right hand so I can program your finger print to it." Bartholomew told me with a smile.

I grabbed the little cylinder and I almost dropped it. It was heavy, so much heavier than I thought it would've been, and it felt solid. Before I had a chance to say anything, Bartholomew turned the container a few times in my hand before he pressed my thumb on top of a symbol that looked like an R.

"Hold still for thirty seconds now," Bartholomew said, his tone more professional than I'd ever heard it. After the time passed, he said, "Good. Now release it." I did as Bartholomew told me. "Perfect. When I tell you to, press the symbol again." I looked at the little stick and nodded back to Bartholomew.

"I would recommend doing it in the middle of the plane and away from your face," Constantine suggested as he moved as far away from me as possible. Bartholomew did the same.

A gnawing worry swam through my stomach. Maybe this was a bomb and they'd just made me arm it. No, they wouldn't blow me up, and Constantine definitely wouldn't let me blow his plane up. I stood up and walked to the middle of the plane, making sure I was as far away from the boys as possible. Then, I took a deep breath and pressed the R.

"Oh God!" I screamed, almost dropping the stupid stick. The six-inch cylinder had expanded and morphed to a four-foot-tall scythe. "Holy crap! You've got to be kidding me." My words were far from elegant, but I wasn't too worried about that right now.

"Isis, meet the weapon of the Reapers," Constantine told me from the window.

"No wonder the rumors are going to start," I told him as I stared at the sharpest farming tool I had ever seen in my life. "Why do I have this? Am I becoming a Reaper?" Panic filled my voice. I might not be pure, but I was pretty innocent. The last thing I wanted was to get killed by Death if I turned bad.

"Girl, please. Didn't I just tell you Death wasn't going to make any more Reapers?" Constantine gave me an evil glare, his tone high-pitched and full of irritation. It amazed me how fast his moods could change. It always had.

"You did, but why do I have this?" Maybe I wasn't becoming a super soldier, but I still had this incredibly scary weapon.

"The scythe is the fastest way to send a vampire to their final death," Constantine said in a matter-of-fact tone. "You're going to be facing them and we aren't taking any chances."

"I thought we were going to a peace treaty," I said, hoping he remembered that part.

"We are, but remember, they hate us as much as we hate them," Constantine said. "Don't let the weapon out of your sight. To retract, hold the symbol again the same way. Got it?"

"Got it."

"Good. Now you need to learn how to use it." Constantine barely finished talking when Bob stepped out from the back. He wore what looked like a fencing uniform, padding and all. "Bob is going to be your assistant. We don't have a lot of time, so pay attention."

The sound of his voice told me I was in more trouble than I knew.

Chapter Five

By the time we landed in Kansas, my arms were burning. It was like being in color-guard tossing a flag around. I did one year of winter-guard in high school, so the movements were not totally foreign to me. The muscle memory came quickly, but the actual muscles did not. I needed to get used to swinging a steel pipe around with a giant blade on one end—not the most natural movement in the world. I was also wondering if I would ever be able to use it. I knew vampires had lost their souls, but as far as I knew, they still looked human. How was I going to know who to chop to pieces?

I didn't have a lot of time to ponder my dilemma. The plane made its way to the secure hangar away from the commercial airport. It was a little secluded and unless you knew where you were going, most people would likely miss it. I retracted my new toy and tucked it inside my cargo pants, thankful I'd chosen to wear my black combat gear for this mission. Although, after Constantine's lecture, I wished I had more weapons.

Kansas was a lot cooler than Texas, so I was glad I thought to pack a sweater. The minute we stepped off the plane, a beautiful blonde waved us toward the black SUV she stood beside.

Constantine strolled over to her and shouted, "Katrina, my girl. What are you doing here?"

"Constantine, my man. I'm your transportation today," Katrina replied with a grin.

"Oh wow. What did you do to get put on the shit list?" Constantine asked Katrina as he climbed on the hood of the SUV, putting him eye level with her. "I knew War was mad at you, but he must be furious to give you a private's duties." He shook his head.

"The usual, I guess. War is always mad at me. This one's a long story," Katrina replied. "At least he didn't kill me off and send me to China." Katrina flashed a weak smile.

"I can't wait to hear that story." Constantine faced the rest of us. "Let's make this quick. Katrina meet the team: Bob, Bartholomew, and Isis."

"Nice meeting all of you." Katrina moved in front of each of us and shook our hands. "How does it feel to be Death's Intern, Isis?" Katrina asked me directly.

Up close, Katrina was even more beautiful. We were about the same height, but total opposites. Katrina had long, curly blonde hair that looked like gold strands in the sun. Her bright-green eyes sparkled when she smiled, and she wore a military uniform. I wondered how many people underestimated her due to her beauty. I was staring at her when I realized I hadn't answered her question.

"Oh, I'm sorry," I managed to mumble. "How did you know I was the Intern?" Normally, most people believed Bob was the Intern since he was the most responsible out of the bunch.

"War gave me a copy of your files," she told me with a smile.

"War has copies of our records? Why?" I didn't like the sound of that.

"He has a record on all the Interns, calls it precaution," Katrina told me.

"Oh wow, you are a Colonel. Congratulations." My cheeks heated with embarrassment. Maybe I should salute her? I wasn't sure.

"For now, until War decides my punishment and I get downgraded to another army to start over," Katrina told us. My eyebrows quirked. What had she just said? I looked at Bartholomew and Bob, and both of their faces matched my own. I was glad I wasn't the only one who was clueless.

"Sorry, Colonel, I think you lost us," I told her, trying to be as respectful as possible.

"Please call me Katrina," she replied, grabbing one of our bags and loading it into the back of the SUV. I followed suit, and soon, she turned to me. "I assume you don't know the requirements of War's Intern?" she asked.

I shook my head.

After the SUV was packed, we all hopped inside. "War only has one Intern at any given time," Katrina said once we were all inside. "We serve for one-hundred years, in many different counties and military branches. We don't age, so you can imagine how bizarre that would be to humans. Every so often, or when we screw-up, we move to a different location with a new identity to start over." Katrina pulled out of the airport and onto the highway.

"How do you blend in?" Bartholomew asked. "No offense, but I'm pretty sure you would stick out in the Chinese army."

Bartholomew had a point. It didn't make any sense.

"You can say we stole that trick from Death," Katrina told us. "Our appearances change depending on what ID we carry at that time. Unlike Death, everyone sees the same person until we decide to change it," Katrina explained.

"Are you not blonde?" I asked her. Maybe she really didn't look like Miss America.

"The camouflage doesn't work with the other horsemen or their people." Katrina pointed at her body as she spoke. "You are seeing the real me. I just don't age."

Bob, Bartholomew, and I all nodded, but inside, I was a bit jealous that Katrina was frozen in time looking like the goddess Venus.

"Great." Katrina glanced at the digital clock on the dashboard. "The elves requested a new location, so if we are going to make it, we need to hurry."

"Where are we going, Katrina?" Constantine asked.

"We are going to our more secluded location, the International Negotiation Center," Katrina told Constantine.

"How bad is it?" Constantine asked

"It's a delicate situation." Katrina spoke so softly I almost didn't hear her.

"What is going on?" That was the first time Bob said anything since leaving the plane.

"Sergeant Johnson, it is you," Katrina said to Bob, who in turn got very quiet and almost pale. I had no idea Bob's last name was Johnson. Finally, after a year of knowing him, I learned Bob's last name.

"Have we met?" Bob asked in a shy tone.

"A long time ago, in Saudi," Katrina told him. "Granted, I was a boy then, so I doubt you would remember me. Private Green." A sad smile covered her lips.

"Private Green? No way." Bob shook his head. "Private Green is dead." Bob's fingers started shaking, as if he was remembering a terrible time.

"Yeah, that was definitely one of my most dramatic deaths." Katrina didn't look back when she spoke. "Thank you, though. You were one of the few nice people in the unit. I really appreciated it. I'm sorry you had to see me die." Katrina's voice was filled with sincerity, but that didn't help poor Bob. He'd turned as white as a ghost. The whole situation had left a thick tension coating the air in the SUV.

"Can you tell us what to expect when we meet the vampires and elves?" Bartholomew cut in, changing the topic. He was amazing for doing that, and I made a note to make sure I told him that someday.

"Oh, yes, I'm sorry," Katrina replied, bringing herself back to the present. "The heir to the elves, Princess Genevieve, is missing. The elf king thinks the vampires have her. The vampires, on the other hand, are convinced the elves are hiding the princess against her wishes," Katrina told us, not taking her eyes off the road.

"Why do the vampires care about this princess?" I asked Katrina. I finally understood why War didn't want to be involved. This sounded like a supernatural Jerry Springer Show.

"War mentioned something about star-crossed lovers. Please tell me this princess is not dating a vampire." Constantine was the one to put the pieces together.

"Not just any vampire. She is engaged to the heir of the North American kingdom," Katrina explained.

"Oh. This is going to be messy," Constantine told us.

I glanced out the window to the flat Kansas land. Out of the corner of my eye, a tree moved. I shifted in my seat to get a better look. I must have imagined it, right? No, it moved again. "Did anybody see that? The trees are moving!" I pointed out the window.

"Yeah, that has been happening all week," Katrina confirmed from the front. "The elf king has been calling all the sleeping elves back up in preparation for the coming war. If this keeps up, it won't be long before humans start noticing."

Katrina was right. If I noticed the trees, the humans would, too. I was, after all, mostly human.

"Not to scare anybody, but we are being followed," Bob piped in. He still looked a little pale from his earlier conversation.

We all looked behind us, and sure enough, two black SUVs were closing in on us. I wasn't sure why I hadn't just taken Bob's word in the first place. He was usually right. Although, I wished he would've noticed before we turned on a deserted dirt road in the middle of nowhere.

"Is there any way they might be going to the treaty with us?" I asked, stretching the words out.

"I doubt it," Bob answered. "They just appeared from one of those odd trails, which probably means they were waiting for us." I really hated his uncanny way of making sense when I really just wanted him to say anything else to make me feel better.

"There is nothing to worry about. This vehicle is bullet proof," Katrina told us in a calm voice.

"What about your tires?" Bob asked Katrina. Last May, Pestilence's disgruntled accountant blew up two of our tires, leaving us stranded on the road. Bob was now paranoid about tires.

"Probably not," Katrina replied, looking at her rearview mirror.

"I recommend you pick up the pace, Katrina." Constantine peered behind him as well.

"This is an SUV, not an Indy car. It only goes so fast," Katrina told him as she tried to accelerate.

The SUV picked up speed, but so had the two behind us. Within a few minutes, they'd pulled next to us. Bob and I watched as the two SUVs boxed us in. There was no way Katrina could get away. We were trapped.

"Slam into one of them," Constantine yelled, but it was too late. By the time Katrina attempted any evasive maneuvers, the enemies had pulled guns on us.

"Duck!" I screamed as I pulled Bartholomew down. My brain knew the vehicle was bullet proof, but my reflexes took over.

Katrina tried to move away, but it was no use. They opened fire on us. Bob cursed under his breath when they shot holes in all four of our tires. Katrina hit the brakes and the two vehicles sped past us.

"You wouldn't happen to carry four spare tires with you?" Bob said it as a joke, but I knew he was serious. After the last episode, he had equipped every vehicle in the house with at least two spares. The ones that could handle the extra weight had four.

"I wish," Katrina told Bob as she pulled over and stopped the vehicle.

"Where is Reggie when you need him?" I asked Bartholomew. Reggie was the roadside king to the supernatural community in Texarkana. Everyone used him.

"We are over twenty miles away. We're not going to make it on foot. We need wheels soon," Katrina told us, and she almost yelled with excited nervousness. She let out a deep sigh as she stepped from the SUV, pulling her phone from her pocket.

"Any ideas?" I asked Constantine, hoping he had a way to fix it.

"I'm blaming the vampires. They're probably trying to stop us from coming," Constantine snapped.

Katrina opened the driver's door and leaned in. "Hey, guys, I found us a way out of this mess. That farmer is going to give us a ride in the back of his truck." Katrina was pointing at a skinny man with a beat-up F-150.

This trip was getting stranger by the minute. We were going to jump in the back of a truck with a total stranger. Nobody else seemed concerned, so I shrugged and followed the team.

"I'm going to have the SUV fixed and dropped off at the center, but we need to get there now." Katrina left no room for argument. We grabbed our gear from the SUV and headed towards the back of the truck.

"Wow. Constantine, she sounds just like you," I whispered to him.

"Where do you think she learned it?" Constantine replied, a cockiness shining from his stance, his eyes, and even his voice. "I freelance for War as his guardian when he gets new Interns."

"I can see you working with War," I told Constantine. "I'm surprised you didn't stay." Honestly, Constantine would make a great wing-man for War. They were both nuts.

"Never. War has an obsession with uniforms," Constantine told me, his whole face scrunching up in a disgusted look. "You can't go around covering this beautiful fur with clothes." Constantine groomed his coat for extra emphasis after he found a comfortable position in the truck. "Now I'm planning to take advantage of these strange accommodations. I recommend you do the same. Who knows what we are going to be doing next?

I was afraid Constantine was right. This little adventure wasn't starting that well. I leaned back against the side of the truck and watched the tumble-weeds roll by. That could only happen in Kansas.

Chapter Six

The twenty miles in the back of the truck seemed to take forever. By the time we stopped and hopped off, it felt like we'd been riding a horse for half the day. My butt had gone numb and every part of my body ached. That dirt road had been rough.

I had no idea what Katrina told the old man who gave us a ride, but he was mumbling something about crazy soldiers when he drove off. We all waved, but he didn't even turn around. I was sure the old man wasn't planning to take that road ever again.

"Are we in the right place?" Bartholomew asked from behind me.

"This is the International Negotiation Center," Katrina answered.

"This place is a dump," Constantine said.

I turned around then, and sure enough, I faced a beaten-down, older-than-dirt house. It reminded me of a house in an old western, from the porch housing two wooden rocking chairs to the wraparound wooden fence that created a barrier around the entire place. And Constantine had been right, it looked like a dump—maybe even worse. It kind of looked like it might go up in flames at any moment.

"No offense, Katrina, but this place doesn't look like a negotiation center?" My words had been a statement, but they sounded more like a question.

"Don't judge a book by its cover," Katrina told me. It was hard not to when this cover looked so beaten down and empty. "This state is under the jurisdiction of War. All supernatural treaties take place here. No one dares to violate the sanctity of this location." Katrina puffed her chest out when she finished her statement.

"Well, that at least explains why Fort Riley is in the middle of the country." Bartholomew stepped closer to me. "I always wondered if the US might have been afraid Canada would invade us one day." Bartholomew shot me a huge grin.

I couldn't help it; I had to laugh. That was a very valid point. Of all the military locations in the US, the ones in the middle of the country made no sense. I understood the ones that were training grounds, or even the prison, but Fort Riley was neither one of those things. If anything, it was the home of one of our most decorated Divisions. I guess if you were a Horsemen, you could claim an entire state as your territory and make people come to you for guidance. I'm surprised Pestilence didn't think of it first.

"Great. Why are we standing outside?" I asked. Truth be told, I was growing tired of staring at the old, dilapidated house. For that matter, just staring at this house made me wonder why anyone would want to stop us from having a meeting here, which made me wonder exactly what our mysterious shooter's motivation was.

"We are supposed to wait for the witch delegation." Katrina answered. Her gaze darted back and forth as she searched the place. In fact, it made her look a little worried. Maybe she didn't like being so exposed.

"Leave it to the witches to always be late," Constantine hissed. Witches were probably his least favorite paranormal creature.

"They should be here by now. We sent them very specific coordinates," Katrina told him.

"I thought you said the elves changed the location? Maybe they went to the first one," I said, trying to give the witches the benefit of the doubt. Not all my experiences had been bad with them, although there had been a few.

"Impossible. We confirmed they received the new info," Katrina explained as she walked over to the house and checked the front door.

I hung back and grabbed Bob's arm to pull him aside. "Bob, are you okay?" I'd been wanting to ask since he'd gone so pale remembering Katrina from the war, but I hadn't wanted to ask in front of everyone and embarrass him.

"I'm fine, just bad memories," Bob told me as he walked away from the group.

"Good. There they are." Katrina pointed to the East.

Either Katrina had hawk eyes, or magical powers, because there was no way she could have spotted those vehicles. I had to strain to see them, and I noticed Bob was struggling to see as well.

"How fast are they going?" Bartholomew asked the group. "I have never seen any vehicle gain that much distance that quickly." Bartholomew was right. In less than three minutes, they were almost on top of us.

"Sometimes, it is safer not to ask," Katrina told him.

The rest of us joined Katrina on the porch to avoid becoming road-kill by a group of speed-racer witches. Within a few minutes, the convoy had stopped in front of us. I was impressed when I noticed three black, shiny limos in front of us. At least they knew how to ride in style. Who needed a broom when you could ride a Mercedes Benz limo?

"You have to admit," I said to Constantine, "they know how to make an entrance."

"At least this group has taste." Constantine's cold tone told me he still wasn't happy.

The limos had created a cloud of dust, so we all covered our faces to avoid inhaling it. The doors to the limos opened, and women stepped out of the cars, their loud voices attacking us all at once. In the sea of different tones, one in particular caught my ear. It sounded rather familiar.

"Oh no. She's here. Why me?" Constantine said.

"Who is here?" Bartholomew asked him.

I didn't wait to hear his reply. I was sure I knew one of the voices. I ran around the limos at full sprint.

"Isis, get back here! What are you doing?" Constantine shouted behind me.

I couldn't reply because I had already started running around the limos where the group of witches had congregated. There were about fifteen of them, and all wore red capes. I must've startled them because as I stopped before them, they all turned as a unit, their wands at the ready.

Definitely not my best first impression.

"Don't come any closer," a woman said. At least I thought it had been a woman, but I couldn't see her face under her hood.

"Who are you and why are you here?" a man asked me. Not a single one of them had lowered their wands yet.

I swallowed hard.

"Easy everyone. She's with me," Katrina shouted as she jogged up behind me. "Isis is Death's Intern and was invited by War to attend."

"Isis?" There it was again. That was the voice I'd been searching for when I'd run around the limo. As I examined the group, a tall figure moved from the back of the crowd. Her robe was different, a rich, deep red instead of a bright color. When she lowered her hood, Godmother's face stared back at me.

"Godmother." It wasn't a question. She might look different with her vibrant, red hair blowing in the wind and her younger features. She might be a bit taller, a little more powerful, and her warm, brown eyes might be filled with shock—perhaps anger—but I had recognized her voice as soon as I'd heard it.

"What in all the stars are you doing here?" My godmother stepped closer to me and her entire coven froze in their place.

"Isis, how do you know her?" Constantine asked me. He stood on top of the limo now, looking down at everyone.

"Constantine, meet my godmother," I said without taking my eyes off her. My godmother stood five feet away from me, looking at me like a wild animal.

"What?" Constantine hissed. "You are kidding. Your godmother is the high priestess of the order of witches? Oh, this day really sucks." Constantine shook his head violently.

"High priestess? What are you talking about?" I glared at my godmother. "You are a witch?" I yelled at her.

"Please tell me you don't work for Death and this bag of fleas?" Godmother asked, looking from me to Constantine and finally back at me again.

"Don't change the topic. I recently took this job, but I'm sure you have been a witch my whole life," I told my godmother. I couldn't believe this was happening to me.

"Everything I do is to keep you safe. You shouldn't be here, and you shouldn't be working for Death. Where is she?" Godmother turned her full anger on Constantine. "Where is Death, you diabolical cat?" She made to charge forward, and I grabbed her around the waist to hold her back.

Constantine's fur stood up on all ends and he hissed like a wild cat. His claws were out, and I had a feeling he was about to pounce right on my godmother.

"Virginia Black, I will rip you to pieces if you dare attack Death." Constantine snarled at my godmother. Both of them looked like they were ready for war, with each other.

"Enough, you two!" I shouted at them. The situation had escalated, and the witches had taken out their wands. Bob and Katrina had rifles out, too, ready to unload. This was getting ugly. "Easy, everyone. We are all on the same side.

Put your weapons down," I told the crowd as calmly as I could.

I wasn't sure if anyone had listened to me, and the tension lasted a few more minutes before my godmother waved a hand at her group. Their wands went down, and Katrina and Bob followed suit, dropping their own weapons. Bartholomew let out a deep breath.

"I don't think I like family reunions," Bartholomew told me.

"Me, either," Katrina agreed. "Okay, so, just a quick recap, everyone. We have business to attend to, remember?" Katrina told the group as she glanced at her watch.

"She is right. We need to get going," my godmother told her people. "When this is over, Isis, you are coming home with me." She gave me a stern look—the one that meant there'd be no arguing with her.

"No, she is not!" Constantine yelled back. "She has a job to do and responsibilities."

I guessed Constantine had no problem arguing against her look.

"You tricked her into this and I'm taking her back where she is safe!" my godmother shouted at Constantine.

"Enough!" I shouted at them both. "Would the two of you stop talking like I'm not standing right here? In case you forgot, I'm an adult and will make my own decisions. Got it?" I turned around and left them standing there. "Katrina, let's go." I walked over to Katrina and took her arm.

"You are not going in there," my godmother said from behind me.

"I'm not a child. I have been doing this job for over a year and guess what? I'm perfectly capable of handling myself." I stopped and looked at her. "You have a job to do. I recommend you do it so we can all get out of here." If she couldn't trust me with her secrets, she didn't have the right to boss me around.

"Oh yeah, that's her daughter alright," one of the witches said.

I had no idea who my godmother was anymore. The woman I grew up with was a little gypsy hippie. She was carefree and not associated with any organized group. Could she really be a witch and the head of the Order? Granted, I always wondered why she never looked like she aged, and why we always had to move every six months. What else had I missed?

"Are you okay?" Katrina asked in a whisper.

"I'm not sure," I answered honestly.

"That's fair. Keep your head up. You are doing great." She offered a kind smile, and I returned the gesture. She was right. I could keep my head up and fake confidence. It worked well for me.

Katrina turned to the crowd once everyone had joined her on the porch. "The rules are simple. Each delegation has two reps downstairs already. High priestess, you are allowed to take your second in command with you." She pointed to the door after she finished, and my godmother and a really tall witch passed us. I refused to meet my godmother's stare.

"Isis and I will be representing the Horsemen," Katrina told the remainder of the group. "I recommend you all make yourselves comfortable. This could take a while." Katrina turned and headed inside.

"You got this, Isis." Bob patted me on the back. It was nice, really. He never cared who I was or what I did. He just believed in me.

I flashed a smile right before I headed inside our little house of horrors. This day kept getting weirder and weirder, and I was getting a pounding headache. Neither of those signs boded well.

Chapter Seven

Katrina was right. The inside of the house was gorgeous. It was one large room with rustic furniture scattered around the place in a very artistic fashion. A sizeable fireplace was located on the far wall, with the biggest flat screen TV I had ever seen sitting on the mantel. The place looked like it should be inside a ski lodge magazine. Katrina locked the door behind us and made her way to a door on the far right. My godmother and her sidekick followed behind her, staying quiet. I brought up the rear, falling behind as I glanced around the room.

I was expecting another impressive room behind the closed door. Instead, a large staircase was the only thing we found. Katrina let the witches go first. I closed the door behind me and followed a few paces back. The entire place was white, and almost had that sterile hospital smell. Katrina was a few paces ahead of me. I could feel the tension pulsating from her, like she was ready for action. We descended at least thirty feet before reaching another large room. This one was at least thirty-by-thirty feet wide with an arched ceiling.

I felt like Dorothy, and I was sure we were not in Kansas anymore. The entire place was white and radiated with a soft glow. There was a stage with a small altar in the middle. Four men in suits were already in the room, two on one side of the altar and two on the other. Neither of them looked like supernatural beings. Instead, they screamed 'over-paid lawyers.'

My godmother walked directly towards the altar and climbed the three steps to the top. The four men climbed the other side to face each other, leaving my godmother in the middle. Katrina and I stayed near the door, away from the group. For some strange reason, my godmother's number two stayed with us.

"This was not what I was expecting for vampires and elves," I whispered to Katrina.

"Their energy is too intense for the old ones to be in the same room," my godmother's sidekick answered me. He had a deep voice that sounded like Barry White. "They each send their most trusted emissaries." He waited while I processed that information. "For our high priestess's safety and yours, I recommend not letting anyone in this room know you two are related." Before I could reply, the mysterious Barry White crossed the room to stand against the opposite wall.

"He is right, you know," Katrina told me.

"I guess, but it doesn't make it any easier to accept the fact that she lied." My voice cracked, and I hated that it had because it showed the hurt I'd tried to bury inside.

"Tell me, what would you have done if she told you two years ago that she was a witch?" Katrina asked me as she looked at the proceedings.

I took a deep breath before answering. Two years ago, I had an ordinary life with no knowledge of the supernatural world. As I thought about that, I realized I would have reacted very differently, so I said, "I probably would've thought she lost her mind and made her take meds."

"Exactly," Katrina said in a soft voice. "The truth can be a very dangerous weapon. Sometimes, we have to ask ourselves if it's necessary." She stared hard at the altar in front of her. "It took me over twenty years to learn that lesson. Just because it's true doesn't mean it needs to be shared. You will find that out as an Intern."

"Twenty years?" How old are you?" I kept my voice as low as possible to ensure nobody overheard me.

"Really, that's all you got out of my whole speech?" Katrina asked me in a teasing manner.

My cheeks heated. "Sorry," I said. I felt terrible because she was right. I did have a tendency to pick the most random details out of a conversation and focus on them. Even while those thoughts went through my mind, I was still trying to do the math. What was wrong with me?

"I was born during World War II to a scared Jewish couple," Katrina answered with a smile. "My parents were the only ones in their family to escape Hitler." Her smile turned to a chuckle. "And I will be turning seventy next year."

Why was I stressing about turning twenty-seven when I stood there with someone who looked so calm and focused at almost seventy? She had really put my life into perspective. The light on the altar caught my eye then, intensifying so much it made the two men closest to it glow. I must have missed something when I was so lost in my thoughts.

"What's wrong with them?" I asked Katrina.

"They are channeling their bosses," Katrina told me.

"Channeling? Like they are being processed by them?" I did not like the sound of that.

"That's a more accurate description," Katrina admitted. "The one on the right is representing the vampire emperor, while the one of the left is here for the elf king." Katrina pointed toward them with her chin.

"What are those men?" I asked Katrina.

"What do you think they are?" I hated when people answered a question with a question, but I guess Katrina wanted to see how much I knew, and that wasn't much.

"I was thinking lawyers, but I'm not so sure now," I answered.

"Correct on the duty," Katrina confirmed with a smirk. "They are a special type of lawyer. We call them mediums.

They have the ability to allow others to communicate through them."

"Can they talk to a ghost?" I would love to know I wasn't the only person that could communicate with the souls of the departed. I had a desire to open my third eye and see what they really looked like.

"Don't even think about it," Katrina told me, snapping me back to reality.

"What? I didn't do anything," I told her in my most innocent tone.

"It never fails. I tell Death's Intern that a person is a medium and you all go checking in with your third eye." Katrina gave me a knowing look. "Then you all scream like banshees and all hell breaks loose. Whatever they are, it is their truth. I recommend you respect it." The last part was more of an order than a request.

I never thought of using my third eye as an invasion of privacy, but I guessed in a way it was. Her scolding had put me right in my place, and I hated to admit it, but it embarrassed me to know I had unintentionally violated people's privacy. I decided to focus on the altar and avoid causing a supernatural incident.

The mediums were all looking at the ceiling. I followed their gaze when curiosity got the best of me, but the ceiling looked the same shiny white color as it had when we came in.

As I was focused on that, the elf representative snapped back to reality. "I demand my daughter back," the lawyer yelled in a strong voice that did not match the elegant suited man on the altar.

"That's the voice of the elf king," Katrina told me. "I'm impressed. They must have hired the best," she added.

I had no idea what that meant, so I gave her a blank stare.

Katrina touched my shoulder. "Only powerful mediums can transmit the voice of their clients," she clarified.

"Stop with the lies! We know you are hiding her," the other lawyer shouted in a rough, mature voice. "She is betrothed to my heir. They belong together!" the vampire medium exclaimed.

"Oh, please. My daughter would never stoop that low," the elf king snapped. "Your devil-son took advantage of her kindness and tricked her," the king finished.

I had met the devil and I was sure Jake would not enjoy his name being used in this conversation.

"Do not flatter yourself. We do not need parlor tricks for people to fall in love." The emperor gave the elf a mocking grin. "I can't say the same for some." I guessed that was an insult since the elf medium was turning red.

If I was expecting an orderly negotiation like the ones on TV, I was hopelessly mistaken. The screaming and name-calling went on for over two hours, with each side blaming the other for hiding the poor girl. Based on their description of the princess, she was either a mindless-puppet or some version of Mother Teresa. Either way, the bottom line was simple: the girl was missing. My legs were starting to cramp, and no amount of stretching made it better. I felt sorry for my godmother, who every five minutes had to hold one side or the other back from strangling the other.

"If my daughter is not returned, we will destroy every vampire city until we find her," the elf king told the vampire.

"Please tell me that vampires live in their own little cities away from humans," I mumbled.

"I wish," she replied, rubbing her forehead. "Unfortunately, they need humans for food supply, so the bigger the city, the better." She met my eyes with a serious look.

"Oh God. We are in trouble," I told her.

Katrina just nodded in agreement.

"Unless you want your precious rainforest burned to the ground, you will return her to us first," the emperor responded. "This is all a trick to play the innocent, concerned parent. We know you have no issues locking your kind away for centuries if they don't comply with your wishes."

The emperor sure was throwing some crazy accusations around.

My godmother pressed a palm against each of their chests to hold them back. If she hadn't been there, they would have plowed into one another. While they were occupied, I crossed the room. Katrina tried to reach for me, but I sidled away before she could grab me.

Before I knew it, I stood at the altar with five pairs of eyes staring me down. "Excuse me, everyone."

"Isis, this is not a good time." My godmother glared at me. That look was reserved for when I was in trouble, but I didn't care. I ignored her warning.

"You are here to observe, not talk, Reaper," the emperor told me. Did I radiate Death or something? How did he know who I worked for?

"Right." That was the rule, and I knew I was only there to watch, not talk. Still, I asked, "I just have one question and then I'll leave you alone. Has anyone looked for the princess?"

Silence encompassed the room. The elf side of the room shrugged and glanced at each other, questions in their eyes. The vampire side were doing much the same.

"There is no reason to look for her because we know they have her," the elf king replied first.

"They have her and are hiding her from us," the emperor shouted.

"I got that part," I told them, raising my hands up to calm both sides down. "You are both blaming each other. Got it. But has anyone actually gone out looking for her?" Silence again, from both sides. "Okay, when was the last time either one of you saw the princess?" I held my breath, afraid to find out how long this girl had been missing.

"Three days," the elf king replied with a sad tone.

"Same here," the emperor whispered.

"I'm guessing that is not normal, right?" I was hoping to keep the conversation somewhat casual and calm.

"Never," the elf king told me. "I knew there was something wrong when I didn't see her for dinner. That is our tradition. My daughter and I always have Friday night dinner together." The elf King's voice boomed through the room, his voice so loud it had started to crack.

"Did she have any enemies? Any altercations that happened lately?" I asked the king.

"Stop stalling already. They have her," the king snapped at me. "I didn't think you were on their side."

"We would rather burn than side with a Reaper," the emperor shouted at me with hate-filled eyes.

"I don't have a side," I said, looking at both of them. "I'm looking at all possible options. I know you both blame each other. But what if the princess is actually missing? Nobody has been looking for her, right?" Silence followed my words again.

"What are you trying to say, Reaper?" This voice was different, and when I turned to find who it belonged to, it was the second lawyer standing on the vampire side. He sounded younger than the emperor, but stronger in a sense, too.

"I understand you are all convinced of the others' guilt, but would it hurt to search for the princess before going to war." There. I said it, and I thought it came out sounding fairly reasonable, too.

Both parties turned towards each other for silent conferences. I avoided my godmother's glare and turned to Katrina instead. She had a huge smile on her face and gave me a thumbs up. At least someone in this room didn't think I was totally useless.

"Who would you recommend I send to look for my daughter?" the elf king asked.

I met his hard stare with one of my own. "I don't know. Send someone who knows her."

"No!" the emperor screamed, and every pair of eyes turned towards him. "It needs to be someone neutral or we will never know if they find her. Those tricky elves could just lie to all of us." He glanced at the elves with an evil glower.

I had no idea elves could lie. Good to know.

"I agree," the elf king concurred.

My mouth dropped open. Had he just agreed with the vampire? Miracles did happen, after all.

"We do need a neutral party," he continued, his eyes meeting mine. "You."

"Excuse me?" I was pretty sure I hadn't heard him right. "What about me?"

"You will search for my daughter," the king told me.

"Not her," the emperor answered. At least someone here had a bit of sense. I could get behind the vampires.

"Do you question that Death's Reaper won't keep her word?" The elf king angled his head, a smirk on his face. He was definitely taunting the vampire.

"Would you dare declare war by betraying us, Reaper?" the emperor asked me.

War? What was he talking about? I just wanted the poor princess found.

"She will do it," Katrina answered for me. I didn't know when, but she had climbed the steps of the altar and was now facing the group. "On behalf of War and Death, we give you our word that we will search for the princess and find her," she told both parties, raising her chin. "You both must agree to grant us passage to your territories to investigate." With those last words, she smiled. I wasn't sure why. I didn't see anything to smile about.

"Fine, but you have three days," the elf king said.

"Yes, three days. If she is not found and returned, the world will pay," the emperor told the group.

"Then this is a binding agreement," my godmother said. "A peace treaty is in effect for three days to allow the Interns to search for the princess. A time and location will be sent out for the next session." Without another word, all groups left the altar and disappeared through doors on opposite sides of the room. Funnily enough, I hadn't even known there had been doors there.

"Let's go." Katrina grabbed me by the arm and dragged me out of the room and then up the stairs. I shuffled along, lost in my own thoughts because I really had no clue what had just happened.

Chapter Eight

Darkness had started to creep in when we went outside again. I wondered if it was because we were up north, or maybe it was because it was almost winter. After our SUV was returned, the boys decided to lounge in the rocking chairs on the porch. I had no idea how, but they all had drinks with little umbrellas in them. It made me a little jealous.

"What are you guys drinking?" I asked.

"Pina-coladas," Constantine told me as he licked his large bowl with three paper umbrellas stuck to pineapples.

"Seriously? From where?" My life was definitely not fair. I was stuck in a basement with life-sucking lawyers and the boys were chilling in the sun, drinking tropical drinks.

"They have awesome roadside assistance," Bob told me, looking more relaxed than he had all day. "We need to tell Reggie he needs to upgrade." If Bob had found someone better with roadside assistance, then they were the real deal.

"Isis, it was awesome!" Bartholomew jumped in. "They brought us BBQ for lunch, drinks, and the SUV." He held up his half-empty glass as he spoke.

"Please tell me they didn't give you one as well." I was not impressed if they were giving alcohol to a minor, even a genius one.

"They made mine a virgin drink," Bartholomew said with a huge smile. "We saved you a huge plate of twice baked potatoes, baked beans, and corn on the cob." Bartholomew was once again my hero, and just the sound of the words had my stomach growling.

"It's official. I'm jealous," I told the boys as I sat down on the steps of the house. "Your afternoon was much better than mine."

"How did it go?" Constantine asked me. "We weren't expecting you for at least another three hours."

"Isis interrupted the negotiations and agreed to search for the princess," my godmother said as she appeared in the doorway.

When she said it that way, it sounded a lot worse.

"Wow, is that allowed?" Bartholomew asked me, his voice higher pitched than normal.

"Unprecedented, but not illegal," Constantine answered. "Did they accept it?" Constantine addressed the question to my godmother, but I refused to look in her direction.

"Unfortunately." My godmother took a deep breath before continuing. "Isis, we need to talk." Godmother came down the steps and stood in front of me.

I wanted to look away, but I knew how childish that was, so instead I faced her. "Not right now, Godmother." The last thing I needed was a lecture.

"No, right now is not the time." Godmother stepped closer to me. "You need to focus on this task, for your sake and the rest of humanity." Godmother stared at me when she finished—no pressure at all.

"Gee, thanks," I said, not able to think of anything else.

"Isis, I love you and I'm always proud of you," Godmother whispered as she came even closer. She lifted my chin and smiled at me. "You will figure this out. You always do. And when you are ready, we will talk."

Godmother held my face with both hands and said a silent prayer over me. I was familiar with the ritual because she had done it often while I was growing up. I always thought she was praying to God or Jesus. Now that I knew what I knew, though, I had no idea who she prayed to.

When she finished her prayer, she kissed my forehead. "I love you, sweetie. Be careful." Then she walked away.

Any other time, I would have rushed forward and hugged her before she left. Today I just watched her climb in her limo and leave. Her entourage was already waiting for her, but they only climbed in the limo after she did. It reminded me of a group of synchronized swimmers.

"Not sure which one is scarier: the fact that your godmother is the head of the order, or that you are Death's Intern," Katrina told me as she sat next to me. "That is one impressive resume. I feel sorry for the fool who messes with you." She chuckled.

"If that is the case, why am I not jumping for joy?" I asked her.

"Katrina is right. That is one impressive mix," a male voice said from behind us, making all of us jump to our feet.

"War, hasn't anyone taught you how to knock?" Constantine yelled at the huge man behind us.

War commanded authority just by his size. He was at least six feet six inches, maybe two hundred and fifty pounds of solid muscle. He had military fatigues on with a name tab that read "Rock," and four stars on his chest. It made sense. Being responsible for every war in the world, he should be the highest-ranking military officer, and I had a feeling he held the same rank—or higher—in every army in the world. Either way, War might be handsome, but he looked familiar, and it was driving me nuts not being able to place where I'd met him.

"It is my house, so why should I knock?" War answered as he leaned against the doorframe.

Bob had moved as far away from War as possible while still staying on the porch. Katrina stood behind me and stared at the ground as if it had turned into the most interesting thing she'd ever found. And good old

Constantine looked at the General like he'd seen better. Much better.

"Yeah, yeah. Minor technicalities," Constantine said. "I'm assuming you heard the whole conversation and we don't have to fill you in." He raised his eyebrows.

"Indeed," War answered, showing his perfect, white teeth. He turned his intense, come-hither stare in my direction. "How long do you have to find the princess?"

Another sense of knowing went through me, but I still couldn't place it. Where had I met him before?

"Three days, sir." I wasn't sure how to address him, so 'sir' was always safe for any officer.

"Not bad at all," War said with a nod. "At least you didn't screw this session up, Katrina." He looked over my shoulder at her.

"Yes, sir," Katrina replied. She was standing at parade rest, a typical military stance, but she still wasn't looking at him.

I had no idea what Katrina had done, but War was not happy with her. He turned around to scan the rest of the group. Katrina never relaxed from her position.

I moved closer to her, acting as casual as possible. "Is he always this intense?" I whispered.

"He is in a good mood now. You haven't seen intense," Katrina told me, following War with only her eyes.

"Sergeant Johnson, what a surprise," War addressed Bob.

Bob's face paled and he grabbed the porch rail so tightly his fingers turned white. I hoped he wouldn't pass out.

"Good evening, sir," Bob said, his voice shakier than I'd ever heard it before.

"I was wondering where you had been hiding all this time," War told Bob as he inched closer. Constantine blocked his path and grew his size, making it harder on War. "I had great plans for you, my boy," War told him with a grin, giving up on getting any closer.

"In that case, it is a blessing Bob found us," Constantine spat. "Your plans have a way of getting lots of soldiers killed, or worse, dismembered." Constantine gave War a fixed stare.

"Look who's talking, buddy." War laughed. "All your plans end in Death and explosions."

I pressed my lips together. War was right about Constantine, so no sense in arguing.

"Well, that's my job. I do work for Death, after all," Constantine said, showing his sharp teeth. Did he have a different set of rules than I did? He was being awfully forward.

War shrugged. "Fine, but we are losing time. I wanted to give a bit of advice." War directed his attention to me. "Start with the vampire territory to maximize the night. Katrina should be able to guide you."

"Where exactly is the vampire territory?" I asked. Surely, Google Earth wouldn't be able to help me with this one.

"New York City, my dear child. Where else?" War said, his voice way too chipper for the conversation we were having.

"Of course. Where else?" My voice dripped with sarcasm, and I shot him a huge grin, just like he'd been doing to everyone. I could play this game with him. No problem.

"Oh, my dear, you should have stayed in the Army. You would have been great," War told me with a longing look that made my skin crawl.

"Keep your hands away from my Intern, you thief," Constantine hissed at War. "What is it with people trying to steal you away today?" Constantine directed his last statement to me.

"What can I say? I am in high demand," I told him, planting my hands on my hips and jutting out my chest.

"Yes, you are," War said. The look he gave me could melt butter, which made me very uncomfortable. "You still have time to come back," he added, his tone more than serious.

"Back off, Guerra, or I'll rip your eyes out." Constantine's fur stood on all end.

"Fine, but the offer stands." War directed his words at me, but his gaze stayed locked on Constantine.

"Whatever," Constantine told him. "How about we focus on the real issue? I guess it is a good thing we brought the jet. Looks like you are going to need it."

"Aren't you guys coming?" I asked him in a hesitant voice.

"It depends who the delegations agreed to have investigating," War answered.

"Just Isis and me," Katrina answered, still at parade rest.

"Why does that matter?" I asked. My chest fluttered. I didn't like this at all. I needed my team with me.

"If you have anybody else with you, it could be seen as treason." Constantine paused. "By either side," he said in a soft voice.

"That is crazy," I told him.

"I never claimed supernatural negotiations made sense," Constantine told me. "I recommended you two get going. Take the SUV." Just like that, he was back to giving orders. He really should've worked with War.

"How are you guys getting back?" I didn't want to leave them stranded in the middle of Kansas.

"We are good," Constantine said with a little too much happiness in his tone. "I'm sure War will give us a lift back as soon as he's done trying to steal our team." He narrowed his eyes in War's direction.

"Come on, old man. Have a little faith in me." War leaned down and tried to pet Constantine.

Constantine jumped away and extended his claws.

War shrugged and stepped away. "Fine. I won't do that again."

"Hey, Isis, take this. You are going to need it." Bartholomew stepped around War and headed toward me, pulling a heavy-duty, industrial quality phone from his pocket. He handed it to me.

I took it and examined it. "Do you always carry extra phones with you?"

"Only when we leave Reapers," Bartholomew told me. "I'll take your old phone. This new one is secure, and nobody will be able to trace it besides me." I handed Bartholomew my old phone, more than impressed with his forward thinking. "Your credit card, please." He held his hand out.

"What? Why?"

"Well, let's see," Bartholomew started. "What's the point of giving you an untraceable phone when people can just monitor your card transactions?" His eyes lit up with humor.

I really had no clue how he thought of those things.

I handed Bartholomew my credit and debit card. He gave me some fancy platinum card that read Reapers. I put that in my wallet and wondered what else we needed to trade.

"I have a couple of buyers in the city," Bartholomew said, back to talking shop. "Give me a call and I will set up a meeting if you need anything. Be careful and stay in touch." Before I could reply to him, he wrapped me up in a huge hug. It warmed my heart. I loved the kid more than he knew.

"Great. Now that all the logistics are taken care of, it is time for all of us to go." Without checking for confirmation, War walked back inside the house.

"Bye, Katrina." Bartholomew waved at her. "See you at home and be careful," he said to me as he gave me another hug, then he walked back to the porch.

Constantine and Bob had stepped over to us and were waiting their turn.

"Bartholomew is right, you know. You need to be careful," Bob told me, giving me a squeeze of his own.

"Are you going to be okay?" I asked him quietly.

"I'll be fine," Bob answered and pulled away, but I refused to let him go. "I promise, alright? Come home soon, okay?" He squeezed me back and I let him go.

I knelt down to look Constantine in the eye.

"I'll keep an eye on him," Constantine told me as we both watched Bob and Bartholomew move side-by-side toward the house. "You need to focus on you. Remember, you can't trust vampires or elves, no matter what they say. Keep your scythe on you, and if you feel threatened at any time, chop their heads off."

Motivational speeches from Constantine were always epic.

"Got it," I told him. I waved at the boys as they made their way in the house

Katrina stood at the SUV, so I jogged to catch up. I could tell she was deep in thought, so I didn't say anything as we climbed in the vehicle. It was safer to be quiet, which meant it was going to be a very long night.

Chapter Nine

We drove for about thirty minutes. The only thing Katrina said during the ride was that we were making a short stop by her house. She needed to change and pick up some gear, which was fine by me. I wished I was close enough to home to stop and pick up some stuff myself. I'd only brought an overnight bag, so I had a feeling I'd be using this new credit card a lot over the next three days.

I was afraid the ride was going to be awkward, but I spent most of it trying to figure out how to use the new phone. Like everything Bartholomew gave me, this one was fingerprint activated.

If all the things that happened in those Mission Impossible movies were possible, then breaking into our house, or any of our equipment for that matter, couldn't be that difficult. People just needed my fingers, which would be easy enough to cut off. However, Bartholomew was a genius hacker, so I had a feeling he thought of everything that could happen ahead of time. At least I hoped he had because I'd grown kind of fond of my fingers.

If I thought Texarkana was small, Junction City was tiny. The city had less than twenty-five-thousand citizens and sat just on the other side of Fort Riley. I couldn't see much of the town, but the parts I could see looked really pleasant. I wondered how many soldiers retired in this town after they finished their military service.

I was deep in thought when Katrina turned off the main street to a desolate area on the far side of town. She pulled up to a three-story apartment building with a manicured lawn and cute little porches. From the outside, I figured the building had at least six apartments.

"Welcome to my home," Katrina told me as she parked the SUV.

"Which one is yours?" I asked her, trying to find something safe to talk about.

"The whole building," Katrina told me as she got out.

I grabbed my bag from the SUV and hopped out, following behind her. "What do you mean by the whole building?" My gaze went over the apartment building.

Katrina stopped for a second and shrugged her shoulder. "I spend a lot of time in this part of the country, so it was easier to buy the building than to try to find housing every time I come back." She spoke like it was the most normal thing in the world. "For the record, the military shows that I'm renting the place. The soldiers that lived here are my elite force. I trained them myself. A tougher version of the Green Berets."

My mouth dropped at Katrina's statement. That was unheard of.

I knew a little about the Army's deadliest soldiers, and not just the ghost stories I'd been told as a soldier. The Special Forces and the Green Berets were almost legends in the Army. Their training was brutal, and their missions were classified. To imagine a group of soldiers deadlier than either of those two...well, it gave me goosebumps. I had a new appreciation for the pretty blonde in front of me. If she was capable of training killing machines, I was pretty sure she could snap me in two. Why did War need me in this mess? He had G.I. Jane and the G.I. Joes here, so surely, I couldn't add anything better to the mix.

"Isis, are you coming?" Katrina asked me from the entrance to the apartment.

I'd been so lost in my thoughts I had stopped walking and she had kept moving forward. Did I really want to go in there? What if Katrina was mad that War was being nice to me instead of her? Would she try to kill me? I took a deep breath to calm myself and slowly started walking again. I really missed Bob.

"Good evening, ma'am," a tall soldier said from behind the door. I almost screamed. I didn't see him and had no idea where he had come from.

"Hi," I tried to say, but it came out more like a squeak.

"Could I take your bag?" a second shadow ghost asked me from my right side. Where were these guys coming from? They weren't soldiers; they were crazy ninjas.

"Thanks, I got it. It's really light," I told the second ninja, trying to keep my cool. There was no way I was giving them my bag. If all hell broke loose, I needed weapons to shoot these fools because hand-to-hand combat was out of the question.

"Isis, meet Jones and Smith." Katrina pointed at the ninjas, but I had no idea which was which. "They are in charge of security." She beamed like a proud mom.

"You are both doing a great job," I muttered before I took off behind Katrina.

"I'm leaving in twenty and won't be back for seventy-two hours. Make sure to cover for me," Katrina told her ninjas.

"Yes, General," they both replied in unison, then they disappeared, probably back to their posts.

They were so creepy it sent shivers down my spine. Funny, since I worked for Death and all that.

"I thought you were a colonel?" I asked Katrina. I had sworn her uniform had an eagle.

"I have been all ranks in every branch of the military and every part of the country," Katrina answered as she headed up the stairs. "My troops are the only humans who know my true identity and my real missions. When I recruited them, I was a General at the time, so the title stuck. Now they travel with me to every post and assignment." When she finished, we stood in front of a door on the third floor. She made a sweeping gesture as she opened it and said, "Welcome to my home."

I went inside the most luxurious apartment I'd ever seen before—if the word apartment could be used to describe the place. It ran the whole length of the building. Beautiful Persian rugs were strategically placed around the hardwood floor. At the far end of the living area, there was a granite fireplace. Antique furniture was placed on the left side of the room, while on the right she had ultra-modern leather couches with a large-screen TV and an office area. Over the fireplace, she had a Picasso. I wasn't sure what to do or where to look, so I kind of just looked everywhere all at once.

"Is that an original?" I tried to sound normal, but my voice came out high-pitched with excitement.

"Yes. He gave it to me as a gift for my birthday." Did she mean Picasso gave it to her for her birthday? No, she couldn't mean that. Could she? That thing was probably worth a small fortune. I was not used to being around so much luxury or wealth. I was a little self-conscious and afraid of breaking something.

I had no idea what to say, but I finally settled on, "Impressive." I figured she was waiting for me to say something.

"Isis, stop walking around all self-conscious. It's a house, not a museum," Katrina told me. "The kitchen is down the hall on the left. Go grab yourself some food. You never eat anything, and we have a long night ahead of us. I need to change and take care of some business before we go." Katrina headed towards a hallway which I assumed led to her room.

I made my way around the antique furniture and priceless Asian art until I entered a modern, but rather normal-looking, kitchen. My shoulders relaxed and my heart rate slowed down. I could handle stainless steel appliances. I walked over to the cabinets and was relieved to find that her dishes were not pure crystal or fancy china. On her counter, Katrina had a cookbook on a stand. I loved the idea and made a mental note to get one for Bob. The cookbook was titled: The Vegan Life.

Well, that is a surprise, I thought.

"I'm a child of the Great Depression," Katrina said from the doorway. I didn't hear her come in, so the sound of her voice made me jump at least two feet off the ground. She just smiled at me. "My parents didn't have a lot of money, so we grew up eating a lot of vegetables that we grew ourselves. The habit stuck with me. No worries, though. We can pick you up some meat on our way to the airport." Katrina winked at me.

"I actually don't eat meat. So, anything you have in the fridge is probably fine," I replied, leaning against the counter.

"You are definitely not a typical Death's Intern," Katrina told me as she studied me more carefully.

"I hear that a lot," I said as I stood straight and turned to open her fridge.

"It's not a bad thing, trust me," Katrina replied as she turned around. "I was going to tell you to try the eggplant lasagna. It is to die for." After those words, she waltzed out of the room again.

Eggplant lasagna sounded nasty. Last time I checked, Vegans didn't eat anything animal based, which included dairy. What kind of cheese-like product did she use in a lasagna? I was really afraid to try it, but I was also really hungry.

Katrina's fridge was just as impressive as her house. The inside was super organized, and each item was labeled with a date. I found the lasagna, as well as some Thai noodles, honey glazed carrots, some sort of Rice Krispy treats, and chopped cantaloupe, which I had no idea was in season. My stomach grumbled and my mouth watered at the sight of all the food. Before I could stop myself, I pulled everything out. It was better to try it all and find something I liked than to try one thing and hate it, right?

Ten minutes later, I was still eating. Everything was amazing and I felt like I was at the best all you can eat buffet. I wasn't crazy about the eggplant lasagna, but it wasn't as bad as I had imagined. On the other hand, the Thai noodles were amazing. They were covered with spicy peanut sauce and had chopped veggies mixed in—a fabulous combination of noodles and veggies. The carrots were tender, and the cantaloupe was sweet and delicious. On top of that, Katrina had some frozen treat that tasted just like ice cream made out of almond milk.

I was lost in food bliss when my phone rang. The new ring tone scared me to death. I was putting that on silence ASAP.

"Hello," I said.

"Isis, where are you? Why haven't you called me back?" It was Abuelita on the line. I guessed Bartholomew had at least managed to forward the calls from my old phone to this one.

Abuelita was my pseudo grandma in Texas. She was in her sixties, a beautiful woman about five eleven with amazing silver hair. Abuelita had always reminded me of my godmother. Now that I thought about it, of course she did. She was also a witch. Why hadn't I ever thought about how similar their mannerisms were?

"Isis, are you listening to me?" Abuelita snapped, her persistence shining through the phone line.

"Sorry, Abuelita. I was trying to chew and swallow." That was technically true. I sucked at lying, especially to those who knew me. "What's going on?"

"Where are you?" Abuelita asked, a worried lilt in her tone.

"In Kansas, on a mission," I said and left it at that. I didn't know how much I could tell people.

"Kansas? Isis, you better hurry home. Not even Dorothy wanted to stay there," Abuelita said, her voice completely serious.

I couldn't help it. I laughed. "Working on it. But what is going on? I'm sure you're not calling just to check on me." I stuck a forkful of Thai noodles in my mouth, figuring I could chew while I waited for Abuelita to respond.

"Please tell me it was not your idea to sponsor the Halloween parade." I coughed and sputtered, spitting noodles onto the counter. Maybe it hadn't been the best idea to take a bite...

"What parade? Explain," I demanded. In our area, most churches were against Halloween. I was sure the Main Street group downtown was not promoting this event.

"We are having our first annual Halloween parade. According to the flyer, the main sponsor is Reapers Incorporated," Abuelita said, the words flowing out in one long breath. "Isis, the local churches are planning to boycott the event and your business. Of course, they still haven't figured out how to boycott you. Probably because nobody in the community has a clue what you guys do for business. But the parade boycott is on."

I couldn't tell if Abuelita was mad or excited about this.

"Not my idea, Abuelita. I'll ask Constantine when I get back. What do you recommend we do until then?" I was hoping for some solid advice because I had no clue what to do with any of this information.

"Honey, I have no idea, but we have a stand for the night and business will be booming." So, Abuelita was excited. She was the ultimate capitalist. "Whatever you do, be careful. I heard a few wizards have moved into town looking for sanctuary. They are planning to have a float, too."

She is just full of good news tonight, I thought.

"I'm assuming the word is out on the Texarkana Haven?" It was more a question than a statement.

"Oh, honey, this is great news." Abuelita's voice filled with excitement. "We haven't had a Haven in North America for over thirty years, and now there is one in Texas? This is huge. You know, everything is bigger in Texas. This parade is going to be wild. Okay, honey, finish your mission and hurry home."

"Will do, Abuelita. Love you," I told her and killed the call.

"You don't look happy at all," Katrina said from the door.

"Drama at home. Nothing I can fix from here," I told her as I shoveled more food in my mouth.

"Focus on the things you can control. Everything else can wait," Katrina said as she made her way into the kitchen. I agreed that wisdom came with age, mostly because Katrina was full of it. "Whenever you are ready, we can go."

I was enjoying the food too much, but I realized I was procrastinating. Who could blame me? In a few hours, we were going to be in New York City facing a bunch of killer vampires. I was not a happy camper.

Chapter Ten

Katrina left the company SUV in the parking lot and we took her personal vehicle. I didn't know what difference it made since her SUV was almost an exact replica of the company one, but I figured it was better not to ask. Sometimes, knowing a person's motive was more traumatizing than the actual act. I learned I could forgive somebody's actions as long as they had good intentions.

We drove in silence, but when we hit the highway, my thoughts took over and my curiosity kicked in. "Katrina, why is the elf king so against his daughter dating or marrying this vampire heir?" I asked her, hoping she wouldn't be as critical as Constantine.

"How much do you know about elves?" Katrina asked me without taking her eyes off the road. She sure had a way of answering my questions with questions of her own. I hoped she wasn't planning to do that every time.

"Absolutely nothing useful," I admitted. "Unless you count the stuff you see on TV."

My job was to deal with the dead and they were mostly all humans, so I wasn't that concerned about the supernatural beings that were living.

"That's probably a good thing," Katrina told me. "It means you haven't dealt with them." Katrina took a long pause and I was afraid that was all she was going to tell me. Then, she spoke again. "Elves are purely magical, beautiful beings that are very old. Their very essence has an effect on the natural world. Unfortunately, most are proud and arrogant. They don't believe in their kind mixing with any others. They want to keep their essence pure." She gave me a quick look as she waited for my reply.

"Oh great. So, basically, we are in the middle of a West Side Story or a really complicated Romeo and Juliet," I told Katrina as I took a deep breath.

"I'm hoping this one has a better ending than Romeo and Juliet." Katrina offered me a sad smile.

I had to do a double take to make sure Katrina was serious. "I didn't expect you to be a romantic."

"Isis, there is only one thing worth fighting for and that is love." Katrina's eyes went back on the road. "Soldiers fight and die for love of country, love of their brothers and sisters in arms, or love for their families. You know that." Katrina said, not really expecting an answer. She knew I would agree with her—every soldier would. She continued, her voice a little softer this time. "I have seen them together. They radiate joy and it is contagious. It's the kind of stuff you only see in movies."

"Are you telling me the vampires only want her back for love?" I wasn't sure if I was buying that.

"Oh, please. Arthur wants her back because he is crazy about her and will die his second death to protect her." Katrina didn't sound amused. "His master, the self-proclaimed emperor of the vampires, needs her for political leverage." Katrina glanced at me, and I must have looked lost because she kept going. "The emperor decided that North America wasn't big enough for him. He wants the whole world under his command. He has started a takeover. If his heir marries the elves' most beloved princess, he is hoping to discourage others from fighting." Katrina rolled her eyes at the end.

"How do the lovebirds feel about all this mess?" I wasn't sure how I would handle all that drama.

"Better than imagined," Katrina answered, almost smiling. "Genevieve is a brilliant strategist and one of her father's greatest Generals. She was working on a way to not be used as a pawn by the vamps and convince her family to agree." Katrina's voice carried a tone of pride in it. "Do you really think she might be missing?" She looked at me when she asked the last part.

"Maybe," I answered honestly. "But it is a possibility that needs to be ruled out. We need to check with people on both sides to make sure they really haven't seen her. Nobody is looking for her and she could be in serious danger."

I stared out my window, reminiscing about the time Bob had been kidnapped. Homeless people in Texarkana had disappeared and not a single person had been looking for them. If we hadn't found them, they'd all be dead. I didn't want this princess to end up the same way.

"You are right," Katrina said and we both fell silent. Silence was really comfortable with Katrina, like we had been friends for a long time.

After several minutes, Katrina cleared her throat. "I was hoping this was part of Genevieve's plan to get everyone to accept their engagement and let them be happy."

"Do you really think she would risk a war to achieve that?" If this princess was so well-liked, I was hoping she loved her people enough not to volunteer them for war.

"No, never," Katrina said in a dry tone. "So, now, I just hope we aren't too late." Katrina shook her head.

"Nobody has contacted either side asking for a ransom, so we might be in luck." Or we might not, but I didn't want to voice my fears that the reason they hadn't asked was because she was dead.

"Our friends are back," Katrina announced as she stared into her rear-view mirror. "It took them long enough."

"Who?" I had no idea what she was talking about. I glanced out the back window, but I couldn't see a thing. I wondered if War's gifts to his Intern included night vision. That would be awesome.

"If I'm correct, and I'm sure I am, our shooters from this afternoon are back." Katrina looked way too cheery for my taste. "Isis, take the wheel."

Before I could ask for explanations, Katrina climbed out of her seat. I snatched the wheel and realized this looked a lot easier in the movies than in real life. When Katrina made her way to the back of the SUV, I jumped in the driver's seat. I tried to glance around but I couldn't see what Katrina was doing.

"Isis, open the sunroof," Katrina said from somewhere in the back. I searched the dark SUV for the button. "It is next to the rear-view mirror," she told me.

"Got it," I told her as I pressed the little button. "What are you planning to do?" I had a horrible feeling I already knew, but I figured confirmation was in order.

"Just planning to return the favor to our welcoming committee." Katrina's voice gave me goosebumps.

I angled myself and glanced in the rear-view mirror to find Katrina pulling the barrel of a 50 Caliber from who knew where.

"For the love of God, do you always carry a 50 Cal in your car?" I blinked hard and looked again, hoping I had been seeing things. Nope, it was still there. Who kept a machine gun in their vehicle?

"Where else would I carry it?" Katrina replied, her voice way too calm. "We have several on the roof of the compound, plus a few rocket launchers." She beamed with pride.

"Do you need help? I can stop the vehicle." Last time I checked, the gun and the tripod weighed over a hundred pounds.

"Not at all. I just need to install the barrel." Katrina wasn't even breathing hard when she spoke.

"Girl, how much do you bench press?" I asked, completely in awe of her.

"On a light day, two-twenty-five, maybe two-fifty." Katrina flashed me another smile before going back to the open sunroof.

"Oh, okay. I guess you got this, then." My eyes went back to the road and I focused on driving and staying in my lane. Super Trooper could handle everything else.

"Isis, I need you to speed up," Katrina told me.

Peering over my shoulder, I saw Katrina carrying a box of ammo up. "How fast?" I wasn't sure what the top speed for a SUV was, but I didn't want to lose Katrina in the process.

"Gun it. I want to see how many are following," Katrina answered as she put on her goggles.

At least she believed in some sort of safety measure. Not much when she was planning to fire a 50 Cal from an SUV. I prayed she had done some big modifications to this vehicle or we were in for a world of hurt.

Looking at the rear-view mirror, all I could see was Katrina's legs and the empty road. This was definitely the craziest thing I had ever done in a moving vehicle—at least in the states. Without thinking too much about the situation, I hit the gas and the SUV roared to life. I was pondering what kind of engine they added to this thing to make it move this fast when Katrina brought the 50 Cal to life. The sound filled the night like thunder.

"Damn it!" Katrina screamed.

I looked at the rearview mirror as Katrina lowered her head inside.

"I hit one, but we got three more on our tail," Katrina said, her voice exasperated. "Isis, underneath your seat you'll find a 9mm. You are going to need it." After those words, she popped up again and started firing.

The vehicles behind us all turned their headlights on. I wondered if they thought Katrina had night vision glasses and they were hoping to blind her. Poor fools. They just made this a lot easier on her. Within seconds, she took another one out. The lights made it a lot easier for me to see, which helped. From the looks, I had a feeling their vehicles were bullet proof, but I was certain they weren't 50 Cal proof.

The two remaining cars swerved again and again, trying to evade Katrina's full onslaught of bullet sprays, but when they started slowing down, a sense of panic drifted through my chest. I glanced ahead of us and found the reason they'd slowed. They hadn't meant to take us out. They had been herding us to a roadblock, and sure enough, a line of vehicles blocked the road ahead of us.

This just kept getting better.

"Katrina!" I yelled, hoping she would hear me.

"What?" Katrina yelled back, as she pulled her head in.

"I'm going to need you to clear the road," I told her as I pointed toward the roadblock. "Hold on, I'm going to give you a clear shot."

Katrina gave me a weird look, probably questioning my skills. I didn't blame her. I did, too. I prayed to God that Bob's training paid off. If it didn't, we were going to become part of the road.

Right before I took my foot off the accelerator, I made a cross sign over my heart. Then, I propelled us forward and turned the vehicle one-hundred-and-eighty degrees. As soon as I had us facing the opposite direction, I shoved it in reverse.

I was lucky. Bob had made me drive hundreds of times like this, so it was easy for me. Sure enough, it worked. Katrina had a clear path to shoot as I drove us forward as fast as possible.

Since Katrina was a sharp shooter, she demolished the line of vehicles with the machine gun. People darted out of the way and dove behind trees on the side of the road to avoid being shot. I headed straight for them, not caring. I figured if this SUV could handle a 50 Cal, it had probably been remodeled to take a large-collision impact and keep on going.

We plowed straight into the pile of cars that was left after Katrina's massacre. Fortunately, nobody decided to jump in front of us. I highly doubted I could have stopped fast enough not to hit them, anyway. We went about a mile before I turned the vehicle around. After Katrina dismantled the 50 Cal, she joined me in the front.

"Isis, you are amazing," Katrina said, giving me a high five.

I couldn't help it. I smiled at her praise. "Here, text Bartholomew and give him a status update." I handed her my phone. Since Bartholomew had programmed everyone's phone numbers for me, I pressed his picture for her. "We need to be in the air as soon as we get there."

"Too easy," Katrina replied as she started typing.

"Any idea who keeps trying to take us out?" I asked as I focused on the road and the rearview mirror. Not the most affective form of driving, but I was paranoid now.

"Those looked more like human mercenaries than supernatural creatures," Katrina answered, not looking away from the phone. "The elves would never hire humans to do their dirty work. It would be stooping too low for them. Plus, according to them, humans are too messy." Katrina rolled her eyes again. I guessed she wasn't too fond of the elves. "I doubt it was the vampires either. One master vampire could tear this vehicle apart with their bare hands, so they wouldn't waste funds on parlor tricks like that." She handed me my phone back.

"Unless they don't want to kill us. What if their goal is to enrage our Horsemen? All they'd have to do is slow us down," I told her, my eyes wide open as the thoughts poured through my mind. "Whoever is doing this seems to want to start a war, right? It would be way easier if we missed our deadline." And, I had no idea which side was doing it, but I wasn't interested in ruling either side out just yet.

"I just want to know how they keep finding us," Katrina said as she looked out the window.

"Would it be possible for your locations to be compromised?" People always tried to bug our locations. We had to do sweeps often to ensure they didn't get away with it.

"I wondered that myself," Katrina told me. "I sent orders to the guys to check each location. Not much we can do now." She made herself comfortable and buckled her seatbelt.

"I guess, but now we need to watch our backs because they might know where we are going," I told Katrina. I wished I knew her secret to staying calm because inside, my heart raced and panic settled in my chest.

"One thing at a time," Katrina told me. "We will cross that bridge when we get there. Airport first."

Katrina had a point. What was the use in stressing over things we couldn't figure out now? There was plenty to stress about without that.

Chapter Eleven

The Manhattan airport in Kansas was deserted when we arrived. I was grateful. I hadn't realized how worried I'd been that our little mercenaries would be here when we showed up.

George and his crew were ready to go when we stepped out of the SUV, which was the blessing of a private jet. They were always ready to go, no matter the time. But after passing a few with loaded rifles, I wondered if they had company. I shrugged it off and kept going.

After Katrina gave the crew instructions, we jumped on the plane and settled in for our flight.

"From the little apple to the big one," Katrina said.

I chuckled in response, and then the jet took off. A few minutes later, a beautiful flight attendant walked over to us.

"Ms. Isis, you have a call." Her voice was smooth like velvet as she pointed to a phone by the wall.

Why was I surprised the jet had phones that worked?

I stood and moved to the phone. When I picked it up, I said, "Hello." And that was all I was able to say before the avalanche of questions bombarded me from the other end.

"Isis, are you guys okay?" Bartholomew asked, concern etched into his tone.

"How did they find you?" Constantine yelled over him.

"What happened?" Bob added, and his voice could barely be heard, as if he stood farther away from the phone.

I felt a little rude having a private conversation in front of Katrina, so I put the phone on speaker mode. Besides, with the amount of questions the boys had, I had a feeling I would need Katrina's help.

"We are fine," I told the rambling trio. "We think somebody bugged us. Bart, could you get that checked?" If anyone could figure out what happened, Bartholomew would be the one.

"On it," Bartholomew said. He sounded distant, so I assumed he had already headed towards his computers.

"Are you going to tell us what happened?" Bob asked, his voice louder and tight with anxiety.

"Nothing major. We were chased and Katrina took care of them." I really did not want to tell Bob about the 50Cal part, or every vehicle in Reapers would have one installed.

"Big Bertha took care of it," Katrina added.

I narrowed my eyes at Katrina and jerked my head to the side once. I had to hold myself back from marching right up to her and choking her. She'd opened a can of worms and had no idea she had even done it.

"You had a 50Cal in your car?" Bob asked, his voice tinged with excitement.

I'd known exactly what would happen. It had started. My fears were coming alive.

"Doesn't everyone?" Katrina answered him.

I shook my head slowly. Normal people did not have automatic weapons for their SUV.

"Big Bertha?" I was finally able to ask when they quieted.

"It was our unit's name for the 50Cal," Bob answered for her. I guessed they really did serve together.

"Bob, don't even think about it," I told him before he could say anything else. "We are not installing a 50Cal on Ladybug." I couldn't have been more serious.

"And stay away from The Camaro with that thing," Constantine said.

I laughed. That would definitely be a sight: a yellow Camaro with a 50Cal on top

"Who's Ladybug and The Camaro?" Katrina whispered at me.

I put the phone on mute before talking. "Ladybug is my Mini Cooper and The Camaro, formerly known as Bumblebee, belongs to Constantine." I told her. Not sure why I bothered with mute since the boys were having their own heated conversation on the other side about the merits of automatic weapons in vehicles. I was afraid to find out who would win.

"I definitely feel a lot better about naming my guns now," Katrina told me with a smile as she leaned back in her leather seat.

I grinned back at her, then took the phone off mute. "Okay, guys, you can continue this discussion at a later time," I told the boys, which was my way of getting them back on track. "We are headed to New York to meet a bunch of vamps and I don't think I'm dressed appropriately."

"Isis, my guy is in the upper East Side near Central Park. I'll program his directions on your phone under dealer," Bartholomew told me. "I'll give him a heads up you'll be coming. Just tell him Big Papa sent you." I could almost see Bartholomew's chest puffing out at that statement.

"Big Papa? Are you serious?" I lost it; I couldn't help myself. I laughed so hard and for so long that my side hurt when I regained control. "Bart, who are you? Biggie-Smalls?" It was hard not to think of the dead rapper every time people used that phrase.

"You can't hate the player, just blame it on the game," Bartholomew replied.

"OK, my wanna-be-thug," I told him. "You are good, but I'm not calling you that." No way would I call my twelve-year-old brother Big Papa.

"Please don't," Bartholomew said. "We don't want people knowing my true identity." Katrina choked at that statement, and I had to bite my tongue not to laugh. Bartholomew had been watching too many Tom Cruise movies.

"We won't tell a soul, my little spy," Katrina jumped in. "We do need some wheels, though."

How had I not thought of that? I was glad to have Katrina with me, especially in that moment. It would have slowed us down not to have a car lined up.

"Taken care of it," Bartholomew replied, sounding far away again. "A car is already waiting for you at the hangar."

I pressed my lips together and nodded, completely impressed. I guessed the boys had been busy.

"My guy made sure it was clean and free of tracking devices, so you are good," Constantine added.

"I got the plates for the group that chased us," Katrina told the boys.

I was impressed. That was something I hadn't thought about, and I had no clue how she remembered that after everything that had happened.

"I doubt it would do us any good," Bob came back on the line, this time a little less giddy. "Bartholomew ran the ones from the first incident and he just found an overseas shell company. He is still working to track it down. Might take a while." Bob didn't sound too confident about it.

"Hey, I can do it," Bartholomew said, clearly offended based on his high-pitched tone. "Whoever hired them is really good at covering their trail. But I got this."

That was not good news. If our resident boy-genius was having trouble, it meant whoever was trying to slow us down was really good.

"Bart, just keep trying," I told him. "I'll send you guys a text when we land."

"Don't bother," Constantine replied. "Focus on getting some answers soon. George will keep us posted on arrivals. You are losing an hour crossing the time zones.

We can't afford for you to lose any more time." Constantine was right. I'd forgotten all about time zones.

"Got it," I got out right before the call went dead. Constantine had surely disconnected it. He was notorious for ending calls that way. The crazy cat loved hanging up on people.

"Want to play?" Katrina asked me after I hung up the phone. She pulled a deck of cards from her jacket pocket.

"Do you always carry those with you?" I asked with a smile.

"I'm sure cards are standard issue to every soldier," she said.

I was pretty sure she was right. Come to think of it, I used to play cards all the time. Although, since I had left the army, I hadn't played once.

"Besides, it's a great way to pass the time without worrying about what's ahead," she added.

Katrina was right. Not to mention, a distraction might help me relax.

"Sure, why not. We've got a few hours before we land," I told Katrina as she cut the cards.

As I relaxed, I realized how grateful I was for having Constantine's private plane. Our fabulous flight attendant brought us drinks during the flight, and a meal, but I was still full so I skipped it. Katrina, on the other hand, got some vegan pasta and she looked like she was in heaven. Constantine thought of everything for his plane and it was the smoothest flight I'd ever had. The best part was we didn't have a connecting flight, so when we landed, we went straight to La Guardia.

"Ladies, your car is right outside," the flight attendant told us. We will be ready to depart as soon as you arrive.

"Thank you, ma'am," I told her.

She flashed me the biggest smile I had ever seen, and on our way down the stairs, she handed us our bags. The hangar was immaculate, and just like the flight attendant had told us, a black Lexus waited for us right outside the plane. Katrina and I stepped towards the vehicle.

"I'm pretty sure this one doesn't come with a 50Cal," I told Katrina with a smirk.

"Probably not, but I still got a few tricks with me." The gleam in Katrina's eye scared me more than I wanted to admit.

"Do you mind if I drive?" I asked her before heading to the driver's side of the vehicle. In theory, she was older than me by at least fifty years. I was all about respecting my elders.

"Isis, you are a beast behind the wheel. You can have it," Katrina replied, and I could've sworn I heard a sense of pride in her voice.

I just smiled. My peeps were so weird.

We got in the luxurious Lexus. I programmed Bartholomew's instructions into the vehicle's GPS and headed out of the hangar. I was pretty sure a Lexus would blend in better in NYC than a truck, but did Constantine have to pick the top of the line? That cat had enough money to burn a wet mule, as my godmother use to say.

A comfortable silence settled between us as we drove. Katrina checked each one of her weapons in her backpack, while I stayed lost in my thoughts. An awful feeling had settled in my stomach about this trip, and about being back in the city. I hadn't been there since I accidently pushed Death's old Intern Teck from a fire escape, which was the main reason I had become the new Intern. I know it was an accident, but the memory still haunts me. And after it happened, I had fled the city and hadn't looked back once. I couldn't shake the butterflies from my stomach that something bad was going to happen. I knew there was no rational explanation why I felt this way, but I couldn't shake the feeling of uneasiness.

"Isis, I just need to warn you," Katrina told me as she put her last gun away in her backpack. "Whatever happens, do not look into the eyes of any of the vampires."

I raised my eyebrows as I peered over at her. "Okay, why?"

"I don't know what it is, but every time one of Death's Interns makes eye contact with a vampire, they go berserk." Katrina's serious tone scared me. "They flip out and go on a rampage. Most of them end up dead."

My eyes found the road again. I had no words, so I pressed my lips together and swallowed the information she'd given me. I wanted to stare at her, but since I was the driver, I couldn't.

If only she would have told me that story before we landed. Better yet, before we went to the meeting in the first place. Maybe then I wouldn't have opened my big mouth and gotten myself into this mess.

"Arrive at your destination," the GPS chimed in before I found the courage to ask any more questions.

"Is she serious?" Katrina asked me.

When I glanced at Katrina, she looked about as confused as I was. Never in a million years did I think I'd be sitting outside a high-end children's clothing store.

"This is weird, but if Bart says this is the place, then this is it." If I was wrong about what I just said, I might kill Bartholomew because I definitely didn't fit in kid's clothing.

I parallel parked in a spot right in front of the store. I had to thank Bob for my parking training. For the most part, I could never parallel park until he made it his personal mission to show me. We practiced it until he was convinced I could do it with my eyes closed.

Before I chickened out, I climbed out of the Lexus and headed towards the little shop. Katrina followed me quietly.

"Good evening, how can I help you?" an older lady with white hair and a bright-pink dress asked me as we walked in.

"Good evening," I replied in my most professional voice. "Big Papa sent us for a pick-up." I felt so foolish saying that, but I made sure not to show it—even if I had no idea how I did that.

"We have been expecting you," the older lady said with a smile. "Please, follow me." She led us towards the back of the store to an area labeled 'dressing rooms.'

The store was very uptown chic and I could tell everything in there was expensive. We followed the older lady down the hall. I glanced at her feet, noticing she was wearing a pair of four-inch stilettos. I pointed out the shoes to Katrina who arched an eyebrow at me. I smiled back. Maybe things in this little shop were not as they seemed.

We walked to one dressing room with a large curtain in the front and a six-foot-tall mirror on the back wall. The old lady motioned for us to get inside, so we scooted forward. The curtain closed behind us. When everything was securely in place, she walked to the mirror and placed her hand in the center of it. I gasped as the mirror opened down the middle.

I met Katrina's eyes when the older lady walked into the room and motioned for us to follow her again. She just shrugged at me, and we both followed the stylish, creepy, old lady into who knew where. I was going to have to talk to Bartholomew about his dealer selection. Maybe he could use someone who didn't remind me of a villain in a horror movie.

And then we walked into the best arms room I had ever seen. The place was lined wall-to-wall with every kind of weapon imaginable. I forgot all about the talk I was planning with Bartholomew as I looked over at Katrina. She wasn't looking at me, instead her eyes were glued to the weapons as if she had just died and gone to heaven. Trust me, I knew that look. I had seen it a few times.

"Oh my God. I need to talk to Bartholomew," Katrina told me. "I will call him whatever he wants if he hooks me up with his dealer's info. This is amazing."

Well, it was official. Bartholomew had a new fan.

"Hi, ladies. Welcome." A man about my size came up to us. He was handsome, with a chocolate complexion that looked almost Spanish, but his name tag read Welch, which couldn't have been Spanish at all. Perhaps his mother was Spanish and his father Dutch? Either way, it didn't matter. He had a fantastic smile. "Big Papa called in your order. I believe we have everything you need, if you'll just follow me, please."

I had no idea what Bartholomew had ordered for us, so we followed Welch to the back of the room. I had to drag Katrina away. She was definitely suffering from what I liked to call "shiny object syndrome." Every time she saw a new gun, she got distracted. I could imagine Constantine behaving much the same, only not quite as bad.

Welch had two dressing rooms ready for us. I hesitated, but only for a moment. If Bartholomew trusted him, then he was probably the best in this area, so I went in my dressing room and inspected my new gear. Bartholomew had ordered me a pair of black-leather pants, a very stylish black tank top, a black trench coat, and a pair of black boots. The size was perfect, and as I inspected myself in the mirror, I realized I finally had muscles on me and didn't look skinny as hell.

I also had to admit that these clothes would fit in better in the city than my cargo pants.

In less than ten minutes, I was dressed and ready for battle. I stepped outside the dressing room and over to a long mirror on the store floor. Under the brighter lights, I looked more than intimidating. I looked intimidating, and I kind of liked it.

"Perfect fit," Welch said from beside me, looking me up and down, although I couldn't tell if he was checking me out or his work.

"Thank you. Nice job picking them out," I told him with a smile.

"Your clothes are made of the same material as your work gear, anti-spells and all that other fun stuff," Welch told me. "The trench coat will protect you from bullets, and the boots are silver-toe to give you an extra edge." Oh yeah, now I was really impressed. "Big Papa said you needed another one of these." He opened a case to show me a silver machete.

"Is that actual silver?" I wanted to make sure I didn't lose that thing.

"Of course," Welch replied, puffing out his chest. "You have a slot for it inside your coat." Welch pointed inside my trench to a pocket I hadn't realized was there.

"Fashionable and practical. Not bad," I told him.

"We aim to please," Welch said as he cranked his smile up to breathtaking. My cheeks heated, and I knew I was blushing, but it couldn't be helped.

I turned around, if only to break eye contact with Welch, before I embarrassed myself even more. "Katrina, are you ready?"

Fortunately, Katrina walked out looking like the badass version of Combat Barbie. She sported the same black-leather outfit as I had on, but I was pretty sure she wore it better than me.

"I'm ready to rumble," Katrina said with a grin.

"Sounds great," I told Katrina, then turned around to face Welch. "Where do we pay?" I didn't see a cash register anywhere.

"It's all taken care of," Welch said in a soft voice. "Come back soon." He gave me a wink that sent goosebumps running down my spine. I was always a little awkward around attractive men.

Before I could reply, he walked away. I hadn't noticed, but two more customers had walked in, so he had gone to help them.

Katrina was still posing in front of the mirror, as if she couldn't get enough of her new look.

I chuckled under my breath and shook my head. "Time for us to go. We have a long night ahead of us." Then we left the store.

Chapter Twelve

New York was truly the city that never slept. It was past midnight on a Monday night, or was it Tuesday morning? Either way, the streets were still filled with cars. I hadn't been in the city in months, so I took my time driving down. New York City had a rhythm like nowhere else. The rush of the people and the flow of the cars was like watching blood pumping through the body. It was almost hypnotic. I was so lost in the drive that I was startled when the GPS made me turn down a residential street in the West Village.

"Katrina, where exactly are we going?" I asked her as I looked around, taking in the street packed with a large group of people just standing around. It was really odd for this time of night.

"The building at the end of the street," Katrina said as she pointed to a townhouse on the right-hand side. "The club is in the basement."

I gave Katrina a wide-eyed look, then turned that same look to the building. "They have a vampire club in the middle of a residential area?" Was she serious?

"Easy way to hide," Katrina told me. "This place is by invitation only. Not many people can find it."

"Katrina, if the only ones who can come here are the ones who know where to find it, who are all these people just standing around?" I pointed at the crowd for extra emphasis.

"What people?" Katrina asked me as she scanned the area. Not a good sign.

"You don't see anyone?" My heart sank. How had I not noticed the people standing there weren't alive?

"None," Katrina answered, still looking around. "How many are you seeing?" She met my eyes, and hers were soft with sympathy.

"At least twenty," I told her as I pulled in a spot to parallel-park, trying to avoid the two souls standing in the empty space. I waved at them and they moved, apologizing as they went.

"Isis, should I be worried?" Katrina had pulled one of her guns from her ankle strap. "I can't fight an enemy I can't see," she said, even though she looked more than ready to try.

"Only if you are afraid of the dead. Other than that, we are perfectly safe," I told her, and I was sure we were safe from the dead. I just wasn't sure about anything else on this street. I swallowed hard and turned the car off. "Are you ready?"

"That is so creepy that you can see the dead," Katrina said. She strapped her gun and we stepped out of the car.

It was a little overwhelming to have that many souls in one place. It was also more than disturbing that none of them were moving. As we stepped through the souls, we made our way towards the stairs leading to the lower level. Before I made it, two ghosts rushed me, their cold fingers digging into my shoulders.

"Please, don't go," a beautiful lady, maybe in her thirties, with a fabulous Southern accent said.

Katrina almost jumped out of her skin when she saw her. Ghosts become visible to humans when they are connected to any of Death's Interns. It comes in handy when I'm trying to show my team the situation at hand. It is terrifying when it happens in front of civilians, though. Most of the time, they all panic.

"It's not safe for you," a teenage girl with freckles and a skater outfit told me from the other side.

I needed to do something quickly because the other ghosts had noticed us and had already started heading our way. The last thing I needed was a scene in the middle of the street, so I reached out and took one hand from each of them in my own. Ghosts had no body temperature, so if I thought their hands had been cold through the clothing covering my shoulder, they were freezing now. I gave them my warmth, hoping some of my confidence drifted to them as well.

"It's okay. They are expecting us," I told them both. "Our business is brief. As soon as I'm done, I'll be back to get you guys home. Deal?"

The women only gripped me tighter, and I could feel through their grip they didn't want to let me go forward.

"Isis, we need to go," Katrina told me as she headed down the stairs.

"Please, let me go," I begged the ghosts. "I can't let my friend go alone." The last part did it and the souls released me.

"Be careful," my little skater friend told me.

I nodded and smiled before I rushed down the stairs behind Katrina, that way the ghosts didn't have a chance to change their mind and charge me again. Katrina was already knocking on the door when I reached her.

"Remember, don't look them in the eye," Katrina told me one last time as the door opened.

We stepped inside, and I did my best to avoid eye contact. It was really hard to assess the situation when you were looking at the floor. I wondered if the guy who opened the door was the bouncer. I gave him a side glance and realized he was over six feet tall and at least three-hundred pounds. That dude could bench press me for breakfast.

"We are here to see Arthur," Katrina told the giant in front of us.

"No weapons allowed," said the giant. "That means I will need to search you if you want to see Arthur." Giant inched closer to us.

"I don't think so," Katrina told him.

"You will let me search you, little lady," the giant said, almost purring.

"Not happening and you can stop with your Jedi mind tricks. That shit doesn't work on us," Katrina told the giant as she put her hands on her hips.

Panic settled in my chest. I had no idea what was happening.

"Oh, really," the giant replied in a condescending tone. "How about I start with your friend?" Before I realized what happened, he stood next to me and had grabbed my butt.

It wasn't my fault; I reacted without thinking. I slapped the giant's hands away from me and pushed him aside. Unfortunately, when I did that, it put my eyes staring right into his. In less than a second, my third eye flew open and I was face to face with a monster.

"Holy crap!" I screamed.

"Demon!" the giant screamed at me and opened his jaws.

I wasn't sure what he was. Hollywood claimed vampires were bat-like. I had never been afraid of bats before, but this thing was a cross between a bat, a snake, and probably a shark. It had rows upon rows of teeth, huge eyes, and claws for hands. I had taken a few steps back and realized the entire room was full of similar beasts. They radiated death and moved like streaks of light. I wasn't sure what came over me, but I grabbed the scythe with my right hand and activated it. The beast hissed at me and lunged. There was no place to run. The thing was between me and the door and I was sure his friends were heading my way.

He moved faster than anything I imagined, but I could still follow him. I wasn't sure how, but I could anticipate his moves. His claws extended as he tried to scratch my face off. I turned into him and elbowed him in the chest. That caught him off guard, giving me enough time to spin around and cut him down the middle with the scythe. I was expecting blood to gush at me, screams, or even curses. What I didn't expect was the beast to explode into a shower of ashes from the cut. I was spinning the scythe like a baton, ready to take on the rest of the monsters.

I turned around just in time to see Katrina kick one of the monsters across the room. Through my third eye, she looked like a mystical warrior. She was covered in a pure, golden light, even more beautiful than she was in real life.

Out of the corner of my eye, I saw three more monsters heading her way from behind.

I rushed forward and screamed, "Katrina, down!"

Instead of ducking like a normal person, Katrina dropped down in a full split.

I didn't have enough time to admire how flexible Super-Trooper was. I jumped over her and slashed the head of the monster closest to her. More ashes went flying everywhere as I kicked the second in the groin. It had to have been the silver that brought him down. He looked too strong to be bothered by a simple kick. I spun my scythe around, looking like a deadly version of Bruce Lee. There were too many of them, but we were not going down without a fight.

"Enough!" a male voice shouted from the rear of the club.

The monsters stopped coming. Katrina gracefully got up. She really did make everything look easy. I didn't take my eyes off the beast. They cleared a path and a tall man with jet-black hair walked towards us. He was glowing, something I had never seen in humans. He wasn't dead, but he was something other than alive.

"Master, she killed Caleb and Cain. Let us kill her," one of the monsters said.

I had no clue why they called him 'master.' He was nothing like them.

"If they were dumb enough to challenge a Reaper, then they deserved to die," the man said to the crowd.

"We don't mean any disrespect," Katrina said quickly. "We are here investigating Genevieve's disappearance," she told the crowd.

"The emperor really did make a deal with a Reaper?" the same monster asked the man. I could feel all the creatures looking at me. In that moment, I understood Constantine's warnings. This group would tear me apart.

"Yes, he did," the man replied. "I knew she was beautiful, but I had my doubts she was deadly enough to handle the challenge. I guess I was wrong." He gave me a wicked smiled as his eyes roamed over my body. He had the same predator demeanor as the monsters. "If we behave, would you promise to do the same, Reaper?"

"I came here in peace," I said in answer. I was surprised how calm my voice sounded because my heart was beating double time. "Your pets attacked me. I will behave if they do the same."

The man gave me a nod and the crowd retreated. I looked around and retracted the scythe. It wasn't much of a peace offering if I kept it out. The man smiled and motioned for us to follow him towards the back. I did not like the idea of entering this twisted den of beasts, but he'd given us his word. Katrina followed him first and I was right behind her. He led us to a table in a corner. I took the seat that let me face the room, which meant my back faced a wall. I was not taking any chances.

"Are you okay?" Katrina whispered.

I just nodded.

"You don't look good," she said.

I had no idea what Katrina saw in my face, but I was too busy scanning the room to focus on that.

"Please don't look at my men like you are planning to kill them by breakfast," the man told me as he took the seat right between Katrina and me.

It took me a minute to realize my third eye was still open. I took a deep breath, closed my real eyes, and focused on closing my third. I always imagined my third eye being in between my two real eyes, maybe up a little on my forehead, and to close it, I had to visualize a curtain shutting, but it wasn't working. Whenever I opened my eyes again and looked anywhere in the room, it popped open again. The strain of trying to close it was giving me a headache. After the fifth time, I decided to do something different. Instead of closing my eyes and shutting the curtain, I kept my real eyes open. I imagined I was draping a veil over my face. It actually worked. I could still see the shapes of the monsters, but now I was able to see the human body they showed to the outside world.

"Oh God, that is so creepy," I said aloud.

"What do you see?" Katrina asked me.

"Our true forms, right?" the man answered.

I nodded in reply. "Why are you different, though?"

"Am I that different?" he asked me.

"Yeah. You look human, while they all look like the monsters right out of a nightmare," I told him.

Katrina shifted in her chair and glanced around the room with a lot more caution.

"I would ask you not to repeat that again, or it will be hunting season on the elves to bleed them dry," he told me. My mouth dropped. "Yes, Reaper. Ginny and I share more than our bed."

I held up my hand, stopping him before he could go any further. "No need for details." This whole experience had already traumatized me so much I feared I'd start having nightmares again. Somehow, I forced myself to take a calming breath and addressed him again. "No offense, sir, but let's get to the point. When was the last time you saw your fiancée?"

"You are serious?" the man asked me, his voice lifted with surprise.

I raised one eyebrow at him. I had no clue what he was thinking.

"Are you actually going to look for Ginny?" he asked.

"Yes. Why else would I be here?" Did I look like I was having fun?

"You are different," he said softly. "We figured you just wanted to find one of our locations and set up a trap to kill us." He gave me a fixed stare.

"And you still agreed to see me?" I asked him in disbelief.

"This place is surrounded," he told me. "If you refused to stop, we were planning to sacrifice every man we had to kill you," he said in a serious tone.

"That is crazy," I told him.

"Very practical," Katrina added. "It would make a huge statement that you are willing to go to war with Death just to get what you want. Are you sure that's wise?"

"Katrina, what would you do for the person you love?" the man answered with a question.

"Arthur, we are not the enemy," Katrina told him as she grabbed his hand. He didn't pull away. "What if Isis is right and Ginny is missing? We are wasting time."

I hadn't considered that Katrina was friends with either one of them. Arthur relaxed and took a deep breath.

"Last time I spoke with her was Friday night," Arthur said as he leaned back in his chair. Then he took a deep breath, and I wondered if he actually needed to breathe or if it was just a nervous habit. "She was going to tell her father she was giving up her claim to the throne, the army, and leaving everything. She was supposed to call me back after she did it. I never heard from her, and I knew something had happened." He looked fragile as he spoke of his fiancée.

"Did she have any enemies?" I was horrible at questioning people, but every show I had seen always asked that one.

"Not a soul—at least none that are alive," Arthur answered. "She is one of the most loved elves in over five-hundred years."

I glanced at Katrina, and she nodded once in agreement.

My mind was having a hard time processing that fact. I wondered if it was because I was still struggling to close my third eye.

"Who was she close to in her house?" I asked Arthur, hoping she had a girlfriend who could help us.

"Her brother, Iason," Arthur answered. "They are twins. That's why I figured she was fine. Iason is not concerned. They have a special bond and can feel if the other is in trouble."

"Makes sense," I told Arthur. I was also wondering what kind of name was Iason. Granted, with a name like Isis, who was I to talk about odd name selection?

"Guess we need to find the prince now," Katrina told me.

"Here." Arthur gave me his card. "Please call me if you find anything. If you think Ginny is actually in trouble, I want to help." He looked crushed, and it made my heart sink.

"Okay, I will." I took his card and put it in my trench coat. "I'm sorry about your friends." I told him as I glanced at the floor, seeing the ashes still lying there.

"Don't be," Arthur told me. "They were planning to rip your head off. I am impressed you managed to stop when I asked you."

"Why?" I asked him.

"I will explain in the car," Katrina told me instead of Arthur. "Thank you, Arthur. We will stay in touch. Isis let's go." Katrina did not wait for my answer. She got up and out of the chair, then pulled me up, too.

I waved at Arthur and followed her out. I didn't want another episode, so I kept my eyes on the floor as I walked. Plus, the strain to keep the thin veil covering my third eye was already too much. If I looked at a single one of the monsters, I knew it wouldn't last, which would put me in even more trouble. And we couldn't have that.

Chapter Thirteen

The moment I stepped outside, my breaths came normally again. It felt like I'd been holding my breath under water for hours and had just broken through the surface. My lungs burned and my head pounded, so I squeezed my eyes shut while I attempted to close my third eye again. I couldn't face a street full of ghosts with it open. Bending over, I grasped my knees and tried to breathe. If I didn't calm down soon, I'd end up having a panic attack, and I didn't want Katrina to see that.

My head spun as I straightened. Inside, I felt despicable. I had never killed anyone before, a fact I'd prided myself on. But tonight, I didn't think twice before turning those vampires to dust. That made me a hypocrite, and that thought tore my heart apart. If either of those vampires had been human, if they hadn't looked like monsters beneath the surface, I knew I wouldn't have been able to hurt them. I hated the reality of that. It made my stomach churn, and I had to swallow down the bile that rose in the back of my throat.

"Isis, are you okay?" Katrina asked, but I hardly heard her. Her voice sounded muffled and distant.

I waved at her, hoping she understood I was okay. With my left hand, I held myself against the wall. Slowly, I started counting backwards from one hundred to clear my thoughts. It took over a minute and a lot of deep breaths before I could close my third eye. The moment it closed, my entire body relaxed. My breathing went back to normal and the pounding in my head stopped. I let my eyes drift open to find Katrina standing less than six inches away from me with her 9mm out. She scanned the area, ensuring our safety. I had to smile. At least I knew if I ever needed back-up, she would do it without asking.

"I'm good now, thank you," I told Katrina.

"Let's get upstairs and away from the building," Katrina whispered, still eyeballing the area. "Their hearing is amazing."

I looked at her and nodded. If they could hear through concrete walls, we were in trouble.

We climbed the few steps and I was glad my legs weren't shaking. The street was still filled with souls—even more than there were when we arrived. I had a feeling it was going to be a long night.

"Katrina, I'm sorry about downstairs," I said before I could stop myself. Truthfully, I needed to apologize to her because I could have easily gotten her killed. "I don't know how it happened, but my third eye opened on its own and those beasts scared the hell out of me."

"Please, don't apologize." Katrina patted my arm. "They were out for blood, literally, and we were on the menu. I was very impressed you managed to stop." Katrina smiled when I angled my head toward her. "Most of the time, when your peers get to that point, they become worse than Kamikaze soldiers. They go straight berserk and kill everything in sight. I'm surprised they never attacked me, honestly."

"Oh, trust me, you have nothing to worry. You stick out in that crowd," I told Katrina. Granted as I looked at her again, I realized she would stick out in a group of super-models.

Do I want to know what you saw?" Katrina asked me in a serious tone.

"That would be a no, at least if you ever want to do business with them again. You would never see them the same way again." I wished I could erase the memories from my head.

"Should we go?" Katrina asked me, pointing towards the car.

"Not yet, I still have my real job to do," I told her, pointing to the souls. I knew she couldn't see them, and that was probably a blessing because they just kept coming. "I need to get ahold of Death."

"Oh wow, how?" Katrina asked me, a little too giddy for my taste.

I pulled out my cell phone and waved it in front of her. Her bottom lip actually stuck out. Was she disappointed? It sure looked like it.

"You're texting Death? That is so boring," Katrina said, rolling her eyes.

"I'm actually texting Constantine since I can't contact Death directly," I told her. Talking while texting wasn't as easy as it looked.

"How long would it take her to get here?" Katrina asked me.

"Not long, I promise," Death answered from behind us.

Katrina jumped at least three feet off the ground. I had to give her credit, she didn't scream. I guessed I should have warned her that when it comes to work, Death answers immediately. Not sure how Constantine got the message to her so quickly, but it worked.

"Good evening, Katrina," Death said, her voice as soft and sweet as I had ever heard her.

"Hi, Death," Katrina replied back, not looking at her.

I was kind of glad Death was a woman for Katrina, too. It really helped when we were having conversations about her.

Greetings were cut short when three souls came over to Death. They were young, maybe pre-teens and they looked like siblings—two girls and one boy, all very thin. Death walked over to them and extended her hands towards them. The tallest of the three stepped closer and wrapped her arms around Death's waist. The other two followed and grabbed her hands.

"I should be grateful they just died from lack of blood and weren't turned," Death told me over her shoulder. "You know what to do, Isis. Let's move quickly." Death didn't wait for my confirmation before she disappeared with the three kids.

"This might take a while. You should wait in the car," I told Katrina, who still stood gaping at the empty space where Death had been standing a moment ago.

"Sounds like a great plan," Katrina said, and I heard the relief in her voice. "Sorry I can't help, but this part gives me the creeps. Good luck." She gave me a soft shoulder tap and hurried to the car.

I couldn't blame her. It was overwhelming watching Death's work.

I inched my way forward towards the lady who had warned me before I went into the vampire club. She still hadn't stopped smiling.

"You came back," she said.

"I told you I would," I replied, but I understood her concern now. It had been close downstairs in that club. There were too many of them for just me to handle, but she didn't need to know that. "Are you ready to go home?" I had no idea how long she had been wandering this street, but I was sure she was ready.

"I can wait a little longer," she told me as she scanned the crowd. "Did you know as part of the treaty with the vamps, Death is not allowed to come within fifty feet of any of their buildings?" I shook my head and she continued. "That's what they tell us when they are draining us. If we refuse to be turned, they leave us by the door of the building to die. They told us it was our punishment for being stupid. Most of us were too lost and confused by the time we died to walk the fifty feet to reach Death. And every night, like clockwork, Death stands at the edge, waiting and crying for us."

I had tears running down my cheeks. Anger boiled inside me. They weren't punishing the dead, they were torturing Death. How could they make her watch her children wandering each and every night, helpless? And she could do nothing to help.

It made me feel a lot better about what I had done to those vampires back there, although a small part of me still felt horrible. The thing was, they weren't human, and the Lord knew they weren't alive. Even with all the facts stacked against them, I wanted to give them the benefit of the doubt. I just couldn't because every time I thought of those monsters, it made me want to run screaming.

"Please don't cry. We are going home now," the soul told me as she wiped away my tears. "Go on. Take them first. I watched over them for decades and it will make me happy to see them set free." She released a contented sigh. "I will wait right here for you."

If I tried to answer her, I'd start crying again, so instead, I just nodded and went to work. Whenever I reached a soul, they extended their hands, which meant I didn't have to work too hard. These souls knew they were dead and were ready to move on. Every time I grabbed their hands, tears of joy filled their eyes. As soon as I grabbed them, they relaxed, like their whole body sighed in relief, and then Death appeared to take them away. We worked fast, but it still took us at least an hour. Every time I thought I was done, more appeared.

"Are you ready?" I asked my new friend. "You are the last one." I smiled at her.

"I would like to stay," she told me.

I took a step back. "Why?" Had she lost her mind?

"As soon as you leave, things will go back to the way they were," she told me. "The vamps granted you amnesty for this night, so Death could cross the threshold because of you. When you are gone, she will go back to standing on the sidelines. I can help now. I know there is hope. Please let me do this. I was useless in life. At least I can make a difference in death." This time she was the one crying.

"I don't know," I said. I didn't know if I could live with her being stuck there.

"Death," the soul said, peering over my shoulder. "Please let me help."

I turned to find Death walking toward us.

"This is normally an Intern's work, Anastasia," Death told her softly. "As long as Isis is okay with you helping her, I will respect your wishes."

Both of them met my eyes, then.

"No pressure, thanks," I told them, shaking my head. "I don't have a problem with it, but what if they catch you?" If the vampires hurt her, or any more people for that matter, I was ready to burn down the building to make them pay.

"I'm already dead. What else can they do?" Anastasia answered, shrugging her shoulders.

She had a point, but I wasn't telling her that.

"In that case, it is settled," Death said with a smile. "Meet me every night at sunset at Saint Patrick's Cathedral. Bring any soul you find. From now on, they will all make it home."

"Thank you." Anastasia leaned in and hugged us both. Then she ran down the street like she was on a mission from God. Maybe she was.

"That was kind of you," Death told me as I watched Anastasia disappear.

"I didn't do anything," I told Death as I turned around.

"Most humans don't like sharing power, especially a territory," Death said as she looked around the city.

"Oh, trust me. It is not going to hurt my ego to have somebody else ushering souls home," I told Death and I meant every word. I needed all the help I could get. Besides, I was pretty sure this was Anastasia's redemption road. Who was I to deprive her of that?

"I'm glad," Death said, and then she turned serious. "Isis, be careful. This is a lot bigger than anything War imagines.

I don't want a war, but I don't want you dead, either. Be careful who you trust. The elves and the vampires only care about their own interests. Don't let them use you." Death didn't sound mad, just concerned.

"I will." It was one thing if Constantine didn't trust them. He didn't trust anybody. If Death said to be careful, I knew I was in trouble.

"You better hurry. You are running out of time," Death told me as she walked forward in the same direction Anastasia had gone. She stopped a few paces away from me and turned. "Isis, thank you."

I had to smile. This time in the city had been better than last time, but not by much. Another man was dead because of me, but this time, it had been in self-defense. I knew I'd thought it before, but I really didn't like New York City very much. On a good note, this horrible trip hadn't been a complete waste of time. Some souls had finally made it home, and that was worth the suffering on my part.

I ran back to the car and jumped in the passenger's side. "Ready?" I asked Katrina.

"That was totally creepy," Katrina said. "One minute you're standing alone, and then you're holding people. By the way, even after all these years, Death still scares the hell out of me," she finished, not making eye contact with me.

"She has that effect on people, but at least you're not working for Pestilence," I told Katrina.

"Oh! You are so right," Katrina replied, and I could tell she was calming down. "Does she still make her Interns call her Mistress?" She smirked.

"Unfortunately," I told her.

Katrina started the car and chuckled. "She is one crazy bitch."

That is putting it mildly, I thought to myself.

"Where to?" I asked her.

Katrina adjusted the mirrors. "Heading to sunny California," Katrina told me.

It couldn't be that sunny. It was the middle of the night.

"We have a date with an elf. George is ready for us," she said. With a smoothness one only acquired from years of practice, Katrina pulled onto the road.

After a few moments of building up the courage, I spoke. "I have to ask, what's up with War? I don't know why, but I feel like I know him." It was a creepy feeling. He looked familiar, but I couldn't place him.

Katrina laughed before speaking. "He is going through his Rock phase."

"What?" I asked. "What does that mean?"

"He is infatuated with the wrestler, The Rock," Katrina told me, doing a perfect imitation of the Rock's famous eye brow raise.

"Oh my God. He does look like The Rock," I told Katrina and it finally clicked. "That is nuts. Does he do that often?" I guessed if Katrina could become any soldier she wanted, it made sense War could become anyone he wanted to.

"Not as often, fortunately," Katrina answered, not taking her eyes off the road. "His favorite look is Sean Connery as James Bond. He goes back to that one often. At least the accent is fun." Katrina shook her head.

We talked all the way back to the plane about the idiosyncrasies of the Horsemen. I didn't realize how much fun it was to have another girl around for a change. Some things didn't need as much explanation with Katrina—unlike with the boys back home—which was something I could get used to.

Chapter Fourteen

Getting spoiled while traveling in style was amazing. Unfortunately, even our luxury plane had to follow the laws of nature, and the flight took over five hours. I had been hoping for a nap, but instead I talked the whole flight with Katrina and our friendly crew.

My body was sticky and gross, and my hair felt chalky, probably from the ashes still in my hair. After hours of sitting there feeling disgusting, I turned to Katrina. "I need a shower. No, I crave a shower."

Katrina just laughed and shook her head.

"I can make that happen," our super helpful flight attendant said.

I raised my eyebrows towards her. What I needed was a real shower with lots of running water, not some strange version that she could create in a plane. Honestly, there was only so much water a plane could hold.

Although her offer moved me more than I could say, I declined and settled for checking in with Bartholomew to get the address for our safe house in Cali.

According to Constantine, we had locations in every state. I had only visited a few of the safe houses since I made sure my trips were not long enough to require overnight accommodations. Fortunately, all our locations were fully loaded with everything you needed, so I was sure we would find Cali appropriate clothes there.

Hopefully there would be time to stop by the house before the meeting.

"The safe house is in Encinitas. Will that leave time to stop by the house?" I asked.

"Absolutely not. We are meeting the twin brother of the princess at La Jolla's beach at sunrise. It's going to be close already."

This had officially turned into the day that wouldn't end.

We ate breakfast on the plane to maximize our time. I had no idea where they had a kitchen, but they had the best oatmeal with fresh fruit I had ever had. We even had fresh-squeezed orange juice.

A white Cadillac was waiting for us at the hangar. Between the luxury plane and the fabulous cars, I imagined Constantine was in heaven. He loved buying stuff, and he usually went all out for things like this.

Katrina jumped in the Caddy and didn't waste any time getting us to the beach. I wondered how she was so familiar with the area. Then I noticed the Marine Corps Air Station, Miramar. Working for War, Katrina probably knew the locations and surroundings of every military base in the world.

I googled the time for sunrise in San Diego. For October twenty ninth, sunrise was at seven a.m., which left us exactly eighteen minutes.

Katrina drove like a madwoman, trying to beat the rush hour traffic of commuters heading to work. It didn't matter the city, traffic was always our worst enemy. I was starting to doubt we would make it until Katrina jerked the wheel and took us down some barren road. The bumps threw my head into the top of the car, but with less than three minutes to spare, we made it. Katrina drove the Caddy straight on the beach, too. No surprise there. She didn't care much for rules.

Katrina stopped the car and draped her arms over the steering wheel as she took a few deep breaths. Then she turned to me. "Ready?"

Was she asking me, or herself? I gave her a nod, and we both climbed out of the car.

We plodded towards the water. I hesitated. The meeting wasn't taking place in the water, was it? I had left my new trench coat on the plane, but I still wore my boots and leather pants. Those leather pants would not handle salt water very well. This could get ugly.

We stopped right at the water's edge just as the sun came up. The sight took my breath away. I'd never seen anything that compared to it, at least until the most gorgeous man emerged from the water. It looked like the scene in James Bond when Daniel Craig came out of the ocean in that skimpy swim suit, except this man-made Craig didn't have a scrap of fabric covering anything.

"Didn't think you would make it," the man told Katrina as he approached us, and his voice was like velvet running down your skin.

I couldn't help it; my eyes were locked on him and they weren't going anywhere anytime soon. I reached my hand up to make sure I wasn't drooling on my chin, and still, I stared at him. He had to be at least six feet four, with strawberry-blond hair, a chiseled jaw line, and more muscles than The Terminator. When he smiled at me, I swore my heart rate tripled, and that was when I noticed his aqua eyes. He was unreal.

"Traffic," Katrina replied, looking unconcerned by the naked man in front of us. "Iason, meet Isis. I'm sure you know who she is already."

"It's a pleasure to finally meet you." Iason gave me another one of those disarming smiles. The guy's looks were a lethal weapon all on their own.

"Hi," I said, and it came out in a squeak.

I was transfixed with the man in front of me, I didn't hear the other man sneaking up behind me. By the time I noticed him, he was handing Iason a towel. I guessed he was Iason's servant, maybe his bodyguard. They spoke in a language I didn't recognize. The prince covered himself with the towel and I felt like I could think again.

I made a mental note to never confront an elf when they have so much flesh showing. The bodyguard stepped behind us again. I peered over my shoulder and followed him with my eyes. I had no clue how he did it, but he blended in with the background like he wasn't even there. It was amazing and worked so much better than the army's fatigues.

"Ms. Isis, why do you believe my sister is actually missing?" Iason asked me as he started walking towards a lounge chair on the beach.

"It's been three days and nobody has heard from her?" The words came out as a question, and I hated myself in that moment. I needed to find my confidence again, but this elf unnerved me.

"We are over half a century old. Time moves differently for us." The prince took his towel off and started drying his legs. I spun around and watched the waves. No way would I fall for that trick again.

He laughed, and it had to be the most melodious sound I had ever heard.

"What?" I asked him as I eyed him from over my shoulder. Maybe he was laughing at my clothes. I was sure they were ruined from the back.

"You learn fast," he said in a gentle tone.

"Happy now? She passed your test." Katrina almost growled. "Turn down the glamour."

"You are doing that on purpose?" I asked in a high-pitched voice. A sigh of relief escaped me. I should have known. Nobody was that damn attractive naturally.

"Just a bit," Iason answered with a mischievous smile. "If I can't trust you to control your animal impulses in casual settings, there is no way you will be able to save my sister."

That was a horrible logic, but I could see his point.

"You do think something happened to her?" I asked him without realizing I'd turned to face him. Iason must have turned down his glamour since I could now face him and form coherent thoughts. He was still hotter than the sun, but at least it was manageable.

"Not at first," he answered, a little somber. "My sister and I are able to communicate telepathically, a rare gift even for our kind. Over the centuries we have develop a security system to make sure each one is okay. I hadn't heard from her, but she also hadn't sent me any alarms. I figured she was with Arthur. It was rather normal for her to be gone with him for days." Iason draped a button-down shirt over his back and began buttoning it.

"What made you change your mind?" I asked him.

"You." He met my eyes.

I looked away, finding Katrina's eyes on the ocean. So much for moral support. And, Iason wasn't saying any more. I guessed he was going to make me drag it out of him. "Please explain."

There. Easy, peasy, I thought.

"Your idea that she could possibly be missing was outrageous," Iason told me, but he wasn't smiling. "Then, when the vampires agreed to allow you to search for her, I knew something was wrong. I tried reaching Genevieve and she didn't answer. That's when I realized my error." Iason ran a hand through his hair as he watched the waves crash against the shore.

"You hadn't contacted her until yesterday!" I shouted without meaning to. This was madness. "What were you thinking?"

"The connection between my sister and I is deeper than you can imagine," Iason said, his tone like velvet. "Not only can we communicate telepathically, we can also feel what the other is experiencing. This was not the first time Genevieve went missing. After walking in on her mind when she was busy with Arthur, it discouraged me to ever do that again. We can also block each other if we need to. I figured she was busy again." Iason's cheeks turned a rosy red, and I almost chuckled at the very human reaction.

Although, I understood. I would probably die if I ever walked in on Bartholomew while he entertained someone. Yuck!

"I understand, but what did you find this time?" Impatience brought out the irritation in my voice, but it wasn't my fault. The sun had gotten much warmer, and my leather pants had sweat pouring down my legs. Iason needed to get to the point and fast.

"Nothing. That's the problem." He started pacing. "I searched for her mind and there was nothing, so I tried to use our bond to make contact. Nothing again. It's like she disappeared from this planet." He stopped and frowned.

"Do you think she is...?" I couldn't finish the sentence.

He knew what I meant, but he didn't answer. Instead, Iason turned away from me.

"He would know if she was dead," Katrina said, now facing us. "Their bond is so strong that if one dies, so does the other." She pressed her lips together and offered Iason a gentle glance. "At least, that is the rumor."

"Oh God. This just keeps getting better," I told them both. "Basically, you both could be in danger. Great."

"Didn't you hear what she said. It's only a rumor," he said, amusement clear from the smirk lighting up his eyes. The thing was, none of this was anywhere near funny.

"Fabulous. I really don't want to test it now," I said. "Let's get to the business at hand. Does your sister have any enemies?" I wasn't sure why I asked. I was sure he was going to say no like everyone else.

"Everyone loves her," Iason said.

Of course, they did. This was getting old.

I took a deep breath. "Got it." After a few more deep breaths, I gained a bit of control back. "Do any of her loving fans act weird to you, possessive maybe?"

His forehead scrunched, and he gave me a blank look—a deer in headlights kind of gaze.

"Isis wants to know if any of Genevieve's friends or followers have been acting strange lately?" Katrina asked

Iason.

Her question was worded a bit different, but it was still the same thing I'd just asked. For some reason, this time, he widened his eyes in understanding. Go figure.

"Maybe, but it's crazy," Iason said, waving one hand in the air. "He is a half-breed. The boy is harmless." I looked at Katrina and then back at Iason.

My gaze went to Katrina, then back to Iason. "What boy?" I asked a little quieter, hoping he would continue talking and not shut down.

"Noah. This boy that follows my sister around like he's her shadow," Iason said. "Genevieve has a tendency to collect strays and befriend all the outcasts." He angled his head up towards the sky. "I guess Noah has been acting more odd than usual lately, following Genevieve everywhere. But he is mostly human. What could he possibly do?"

My lips parted in wonder. Pestilence had described the accountant much the same way. Like the girl was less than culpable because she didn't fit the norm of the place.

A horrible feeling swam in the pit of my stomach. "Do you know where we could find Noah?" The words came out rushed. I really didn't know how much time we might have if he had her.

"I don't, but Aeneas can send it to you." He pointed at his bodyguard. "I'm already late and need to get back before someone misses me. Aeneas can text you the info in about an hour. Please, Reaper, find my sister." Iason moved towards his bodyguard, and they both disappeared.

"He never asked for my number, how is he going to send it me?" I asked Katrina, running a hand through my dirty hair.

"Reapers Incorporated information is public knowledge to include the Intern's number," Katrina told me with a wicked grin. "People might not be able to trace your new phone, but they can find you." Katrina stepped towards the car.

"Nobody has ever called me," I told her as I jogged to catch up.

"Who would be crazy enough to call Death?" Katrina answered.

"Touché." I couldn't argue with her logic. "Now what?" That hadn't been the most helpful meeting, but at least we had a place to start. In an hour, give or take.

"Let's go find your safe house now," Katrina told me as we reached the car. "I'm ready for a shower."

"Thank God." I climbed in and dreamed about hot, running water the whole way there.

Chapter Fifteen

The safe house was in Encinitas, and the drive felt like it took an eternity. After living in Texarkana for a while, I decided I enjoyed life without traffic issues. It felt like we were on the road forever. By the time we navigated the traffic, the pedestrians, and the weird directions to the safe house, Aeneas had called.

Aeneas sent us a complete file on Noah that included a photo and even a credit report. I shot a copy over to Bartholomew so he could cross reference his files with the elves. I was pretty impressed with the report. Somehow, I'd been expecting them to be beautiful, arrogant people. Instead, they were more in touch with reality than I had imagined.

While I was impressed with how detailed the file was, I wasn't at all impressed with Noah. I understood why Iason dismissed him as a threat. According to the file, Noah was five feet six inches, one-hundred-and-twenty pounds, with red hair, green eyes, and no special abilities. His photo showed a clean-faced young man who looked to be about the same age as Bartholomew. For a twenty-year-old guy, he looked preteen. There was something sweet about his photo, almost innocent. Unfortunately, after a year on the job, I learned not to judge people by their looks. You never knew what was really going on in their heads.

When I finally hopped in the shower, I sighed in bliss. It felt amazing, and after I got out, I found the house really was stocked with any and every outfit one could imagine. I was learning that the Reapers had a very different definition of a safe house than most people. We liked our houses lavish and comfortable. This place was a hacienda-style ranch, with five bedrooms, three bathrooms, a huge kitchen, a three-car garage, and a huge backyard with a pool. The neighborhood was beautiful, and the grass had that manicured look most lawns had in Texas. I didn't know how, since I'd always thought California spent most of the year in a drought. Maybe they just watered their lawns a lot.

Around eleven in the morning, we made it to Noah's apartment. Katrina and I were dressed in bright sundresses with sandals. Katrina looked like a valley-girl ready for the beach. It might be her gift from War, but somehow, she always seemed to fit in. It didn't matter where she was. Nobody would ever question whether she belonged somewhere or not. On the other hand, there was me, who looked extremely uncomfortable and self-conscious all the time.

And I wasn't looking forward to chasing some kid around the neighborhood wearing a dress and sandals. Whoever came up with this master plan needed a demotion.

Aeneas's report said Noah lived in an apartment complex in Normal Heights on Cherokee Avenue. Bartholomew had sent us photos of the location courtesy of Google Earth and his skills at hacking local surveillance cameras. The apartment complex was pretty nice and in a decent neighborhood. Based on the file, Noah didn't work. He freelanced as a musician in different areas. That line of work didn't pay enough for him to afford this type of place. Something didn't add up. Bartholomew also reported Noah hadn't touched his debit card or credit card in two weeks.

"Any ideas for parking?" Katrina asked me after driving up and down the street for the third time.

"According to Bartholomew's photos, the complex has parking spaces in the back. Let's go there," I told Katrina as I scanned the pictures again. I had all the files printed when we were at the safe house. The office equipment at that location was better than Office Depot.

Katrina drove around the block and slowly pulled up to the complex. It was a gated area with apartments on the right-and-left-hand sides. From Aeneas's files, Noah's place was on the second floor. I wasn't sure how we were going to get in. My Intern training did not include breaking and entering—probably because a cop had been one of my instructors.

"Any ideas how we get in?" I asked Katrina after she parked in front of the gate. I hoped scaling the wall was not part of our mission today.

"I got some tools." Katrina reached in the middle console and held up a small pouch.

I blinked at her. Could we go back to the scaling walls idea? Because this one was worse. We could very well end up in jail after all was said and done.

Reluctantly, I got out of the car after I grabbed my phone and we walked toward the gate together. I kept watch while Katrina inspected the lock. Before Katrina could pull out her tools, the door opened. A young girl, maybe eight or nine, stepped out. Katrina held the door for her and smiled brightly.

"Never mind, Amy, I guess we can just wait inside for him." Katrina inched forward, holding the door open with her back. "Our brother has not been answering the phone for weeks and we finally got tired of playing games with him," she told the girl. I had a feeling the backstory was for my benefit as well.

"You have a brother that lives here?" It was more a question than a statement, but I didn't blame the little girl.

"Noah, in number 26D," Katrina told the girl. "Do you know him?"

"Yeah, I see him all the time. He lives across the patio from us," the girl replied. "Noah never said he had sisters."

"He is really private," Katrina told the young girl in a low voice.

"Yes, he is," the little girl confirmed with a nod. "I like Noah, but his new friends are weird." She glanced back and forth down the alley, her eyes showing the nerves she held inside.

"What do you mean by weird?" I asked her in my sweetest voice.

"They always wear black suits with dark sunglasses, even at night." The girl puffed her chest out. "Who does that? And they never talk. They give me the creeps." Once again, she looked around. "But Noah is not here, I haven't seen him in over a week."

"Are you sure?" Katrina asked her.

"Of course. When Noah is in the building, you can always hear him playing his sax from eight to noon." The little girl gave us a proud smile.

"How do you know this? Aren't you supposed to be in school?" I asked.

"I'm home schooled," she answered. "I get panic attacks and my mom prefers to keep me home to avoid the germ-infested kids. I'm off to see my grandma now. Bye." The girl skipped forward, smiling.

"There is something wrong with that kid," Katrina told me as she headed inside the gated complex.

"Besides a helicopter mom, no there isn't." I had heard of the crazy phenomenon, but I had never seen it. That poor kid needed to spend some time with kids her own age to balance her out.

I followed Katrina inside. The middle of the complex was a large quad area with some palm trees. I really liked the layout, but wondered how Noah could afford this place.

Katrina moved, not making a peep as she inspected all the doors. She pointed to one on the second floor and we moved quickly up the stairs.

Katrina inspected the area, which was a good idea. I couldn't see any of the neighbors, but that didn't mean they weren't looking through their mini-blinds.

"This is a really cheap door," Katrina said. "I could kick it down and it would probably be faster."

"Are you sure Constantine isn't your guardian as well?" I asked Katrina.

"I wish. He is awesome." Katrina spoke like a true Constantine fan.

"How about a plan B?" I whispered. "One that doesn't involve making a ton of noise and destroying private property." The last thing I wanted was Noah's neighbors calling the cops on us, and I had a sneaky suspicion they wouldn't be as quick as the little girl to believe our sister story.

"Fine." Katrina rolled her eyes and pulled the pouch from her pocket. I was a bit jealous. My girly-dress did not come with pockets. So not fair.

Bending down, Katrina got to work. Only a few moments passed before she stood straight and grinned. "Got it." Super Trooper sure had a lot of skills.

As I walked inside, the smell of dirt wafted to me. Even in the dark, I could see piles of it laying around the room. A terrible feeling anchored to my gut. The last apartment I went to that was in this condition, we found a half dead zombie-like human. I prayed we wouldn't find Noah like that, or worse.

The first room was a living room with a kitchen in the back. There was a hallway to the right that I assumed led to the bathroom. I walked towards the kitchen and Katrina headed to the bedrooms. On the fridge was a single photo of Noah and a very beautiful woman. I was pretty sure it was Genevieve because she looked so much like Iason.

"Isis, you need to come and see this," Katrina called.

"Please, God. No dead princess or zombie Noah," I prayed out loud.

I creeped towards the back, passing a plain-looking bedroom with a mattress on the floor. The next room was a small bathroom with no shower curtain. Strange. Shaking my head, I continued forward until I found Katrina in the last room of the apartment.

"Holy cow," I told her. The room was straight out of a CSI or Criminal Minds episode. "What is this?" I finally asked Katrina as my brain tried to process what I was seeing.

This was probably the master bedroom since it was bigger than the first. Unfortunately, Noah had turned it into a shrine to Genevieve. He had photos of her covering every wall. Strings hung from one wall to the other, connecting photos together. He even had an altar on the wall opposite from the door with a four-foot statue of Genevieve. The room screamed stalker, maybe even serial killer.

"I hate to admit this, but you were right, Isis. I'm afraid something bad has happened to Genevieve," Katrina told me.

I couldn't tear my eyes from the wall of photos. "This is insane. And I really don't get it. The princess is at least six inches taller than Noah," I said, pointing to a photo of them together. "I assume in order to make it to General in the elven Army, Genevieve had to be pretty tough. How could a scrawny kid like Noah kidnap her?" I asked. I knew people were capable of horrible things, but I had to be missing something.

"Weren't you the one telling me not to underestimate people?"

I narrowed my eyes at her. I just loved having my words thrown back in my face.

"True, but something is not right," I told her.

"That's the understatement of the year," Katrina replied as we both gaped at the psycho wall. "You take the left wall and I'll take the right. Maybe we'll find something that can help us if we look a little deeper."

Katrina moved forward and started searching the photos. With a shrug, I joined her. This was going to suck.

Chapter Sixteen

After searching Noah's apartment building, I realized cop-shows are not reality TV. They make everything look so easy and fast. In every show, the good guys entered a building or a house and in the first fifteen minutes, they find every bit of evidence they needed. By the time the show ended, they had the proof, a confession, and the perp behind bars. According to the magic of TV, it took them less than a week. It took us over three hours to find anything useful in Noah's apartment. It didn't help that Noah was a hoarder. The boy had boxes in every closet, under the bed, in every corner and crevice. You name it, that boy had stuff packed in it.

When we were finished inspecting, his poor apartment looked like it had been searched by angry drill sergeants. I was grateful Katrina knew what she was doing and made the job a little easier. It was Katrina that found Noah's journal, or his collection of journals to be more accurate. Katrina had flipped the mattress over and ripped apart the box spring. I wasn't sure which was more troubling: the fact that she looked there or that a grown man actually kept a journal.

However, Noah's journals impressed me. They were more like comic books than traditional journals. He was very visual and an extremely talented artist. Each chronicle had a different time period and length. We found the most recent journal, with his last entry being about a month ago. Based on his records, we deducted Noah was a creature of habit. He visited the same locations a lot. One of the most common in his book was Balboa Park.

"We can't just leave the place like that," I said as I shifted a pile of his logs to one arm and shut the door of his apartment.

"Yeah, I agree. Give me a minute." Kristina moved to the end of the hall and pulled out her cell phone. After a minute or two, she returned. "Called the clean-up crew. They weren't happy about cleaning an apartment, but they are on their way nonetheless."

I laughed and waddled down the stairs, holding the stack of journals in front of me. I shoved them in the back of the Caddy as soon as we got there and hopped in.

For rush hour traffic in San Diego, we made really good time. Katrina zig-zagged all over the place. I was edgy, while Katrina was full of energy. Missions were exciting to her. We made it to the park and Katrina was ready to get started.

"Based on the pictures, I recommend we start by the Rose and Desert Garden," Katrina told me, holding one of Noah's books.

The park was huge and divided into different segments. Katrina walked with a purpose, so I assumed she knew the place well. I had no clue where we were, but I slowed a bit to take it in. The place was beautiful. After being stuck in traffic with crazy drivers zigzagging all over the place, the calmness of the park refreshed me. I was surprised such a beautiful place sat in the middle of such a big city. I wondered if they had taken the idea from Central Park in New York City.

I followed Katrina, staying a few paces behind, just admiring the flowers and trees until she stopped abruptly. Unfortunately, I wasn't paying that much attention and slammed right into her.

"Ouch," Katrina told me as we both almost went down.

"Oh, sorry, Katrina," I told her, my face burning with embarrassment. "I got distracted."

"I completely understand," Katrina answered with a smile. "Does this place look familiar?" She pointed at an intersection in front of us.

I looked around, amazed how well Noah had captured every detail. I saw a street musician playing a flute by a bench near one of the corners. It was exactly like a few of Noah's drawings. The only difference was an older man with bleached blond hair and a bad tan stood in the corner where Noah would've been playing his sax.

"Should we talk to him?" Katrina asked me.

I shrugged, not seeing many other options. "Why not? What have we got to lose?" I stepped towards the musician.

We both strolled over, trying to blend in. The melody he played sounded complicated, which told me he was very talented. It almost sounded like a soothing lullaby, but I didn't recognize the beat. Maybe it was an original piece. That would be even more impressive.

"Hi. That is a lovely tune," I told the musician as we approached.

"Thank you." He smiled, then looked down at his case. I guessed if we liked it, he expected us to pay. Katrina dropped a twenty in and beamed at him. "Thank you, young lady. Very much appreciated." He flashed Katrina the biggest grin I had ever seen.

"My pleasure." Katrina told him in her most innocent voice. "We were looking for our friend and we were wondering if you had seen him. He normally plays in this area with his sax." She looked around the place for extra emphasis.

Our flute player went pale. He looked like he was ready to bolt. Katrina stood on one side of him to block his exit. I mirrored her posture on his other side. Just like that, he was boxed in. If he tried to move, either one of us were in the position to stop him.

"Calm down, we just have a few questions," I told the musician before he tried to run.

"I don't know where he is." The musician's words came out so fast and rushed I could hardly understand him. "He hasn't been around for over two weeks, so he abandoned his spot. It's all fair. Now the spot is mine." He held his chin up and gave us a hard stare, daring us to challenge him.

Street musicians had strict rules. Who would have thought? If poor Noah wanted his spot back, he'd have to fight this huge dude for it. Unfortunately, my money was on the flute player. Noah looked way too tiny to win a fair fight.

"So, you decided to claim his spot?" Katrina asked, glaring at him. "Did you steal his song, too?" Katrina asked the musician as she shoved up as close as she could get to him.

The poor man tried to take off, but I grabbed his arm, gave it a little twist, and held him in place. He looked around like he might find someone to help him, but the few people meandering through the park were too far away to be of any assistance to him.

"I didn't steal his song," the musician answered too quickly. "He was like the pied piper. People just flocked to him. I wanted to know how he did it, so I started playing his songs. Yeah, more people are stopping by to listen to me, but not nearly as many as he had." The musician stopped fighting and slumped his shoulders.

I felt bad for him, but I had a feeling Noah was using magic with his music. It takes one to know one. If he was using magic, it would explain how he could afford a place in San Diego without a regular paying job. I wondered what else Noah was getting from his elf side. It felt cruel to tell the poor guy that he would never be as good as Noah. Instead, I smiled at him and tried to calm him down.

"Thank you for your help. We really appreciate it," I told him as I pulled away.

"Yes, thank you very much and sorry to bother you," Katrina told him.

The musician's eyes widened more than I had ever seen in anyone. He had a vein pulsating in his forehead, and I was afraid he was giving himself an aneurysm. As soon as he was able to move, he took off with his flute and case. It looked like he wasn't taking any chances with us. In fact, he kept glancing behind him as he ran away from us. Poor guy.

By the time I turned around, Katrina was walking in the opposite direction. After a few seconds of watching the musician, I joined her.

"That was a waste of time," Katrina said without looking at me.

"Maybe, but at least we know where he was getting money from," I told her. "Every bit of info will help us fill in this weird puzzle."

"I can help you find Noah," an older lady told us. I had no idea where she appeared from, but she sat on a bench wearing a flamboyant dress, her wild, curly hair hanging loose around her shoulders, and her face covered in so much make-up I couldn't even imagine what she looked like without it. She appeared to be in her late fifties, and sat behind a small, tray table.

"Oh, really," Katrina told the lady as she walked towards her with her hands on her hips. "How do you know we are looking for Noah?" She stopped in front of the table and crossed her arms over her chest.

"Every other tough-looking stranger that stopped by this morning has been asking questions about him. Why not you?" she told us. "You are not fooling anyone with those silly dresses."

Who the heck was this weird old lady?

"Why should we trust you?" I asked her.

"I'm a voodoo priestess. I can help you," she told us with a wicked smile.

"Lady, that is not helping your case," I told the priestess. Katrina elbowed me in the ribs. "Ouch."

"So, what? You just thought you'd tell us out of the goodness of your heart?" Katrina asked the priestess.

I glared at her, but she avoided me completely. What was Katrina doing? This could be a lead, and she could ruin it if she kept talking like she was.

"Silly girl. Of course not," the priestess said. She pulled a cup from somewhere under her robe. "I will help you for a small price." She tossed the contents of the cup on the table.

I leaned forward and glanced inside. There were small objects resting at the bottom, but I had no clue if they were bones or rocks. I took a step back because I really didn't want to find out one way or another.

"Of course. Just a small fee," Katrina replied in a mocking tone.

"How about a freebie? On the house," she said. "Noah and your princess are in great danger. He has made a deadly pact and is in way over his head." The priestess angled her chin down and widened her eyes like it was time for her payment.

"That's it? That's your freebie?" I asked, not able to help myself. That was the most useless piece of info ever.

"Information is power," the priestess told me in a chilling voice. "Power has a cost. If you want it, you will pay." She smiled, a crooked, wicked-looking smile that had goosebumps running down my arms.

"I'm not impressed, but for five Benjamins you better make this worth my time," Katrina told the priestess, pulling out some bills.

"Make it ten and I will even tell you his shoe size," she said, her eyes ogling the money before her.

"Trust me, lady, I'm sure my team already knows that." I rolled my eyes. "Knowing Constantine, he probably had Bartholomew pulling his medical files from birth." The strange lady didn't smile at that, but Katrina sure did.

"Constantine? You work for Constantine?" the priestess asked with a shaky voice.

Katrina gave me an awkward look.

"Depends how many Constantines you know," I told the priestess. "Mine is fifteen pounds of pure fur," I finished, thinking the mental picture was pretty funny, however, the priestess must not have thought so since she looked a little green in the face.

"My apologies, Intern. I didn't recognize you," the priestess told me, this time not meeting my eyes. Was there a picture of me on a milk carton that I didn't know about? "Your boy is in serious trouble. He sold his soul to a demon and is now in hell." The priestess collected her cup, the weird bones, and her table.

"Hell?" I asked and turned to look at Katrina. "What do you mean by hell? Hell, like in Hell, Michigan?"

"Good day, Intern." The priestess stood and folded her table, tucking it under her arm. "I recommend you watch your back. There are dangerous forces at play." She took off, moving faster than I thought possible.

"Don't you want your money?" Katrina asked her.

"Only a fool would charge Death for information," the priestess yelled over her shoulder without slowing down.

"Isis, I need your reputation," Katrina told me in a serious tone.

"It's not my reputation that you need. It's Constantine. As you can see, he scares the crap out of everyone," I replied as I pulled out my phone. I dialed home, hoping the priestess was wrong.

"Did you find him?" Constantine asked without any greetings. I had him on speaker phone so Katrina could hear him.

"We wish," Katrina replied. "We met one of your fans," she added.

"That sounds like trouble," Bartholomew chimed in.

"It was. We met a Voodoo Priestess that claims Noah is in hell," I told the boys.

"Voodoo Priestess? That is absolutely trouble," Bartholomew told us.

"Isis, this is not good," Constantine told me. "You know what that means?" It could only mean one thing.

"I am afraid I do," I told Constantine. It was time for a visit to the devil. "Where is the entrance to the Cave here?"

"Why is it when something crazy is going on, Jake is always involved?" Bob jumped in.

"I think that is part of his job description," I told Bob.

"It's at La Jolla Beach," Bartholomew answered my question.

"You two need to hurry. Doors open at six," Constantine told us.

"What's the theme?" Katrina asked him. I guessed she was familiar with Jake and the Cave.

"Open mic. Be prepared to sing," Constantine answered. I could tell by his tone he wasn't happy. "Hurry up. We are running out of time and this is getting worse by the minute."

Before either Katrina or I could reply, Constantine had disconnected.

"That cat is never going to change," Katrina told me.

"Nope. He is always going to have the last word and end every conversation in the most dramatic way possible," I told her.

"Guess we are going to see the devil," Katrina told me with an irritated sigh.

"This day just keeps getting better and better," I told her. "Let's go. We need to find some Cave-appropriate clothes."

I had no idea what people wore for open mic, but I was sure my summer beach dress was not suitable for the Cave. We headed back towards our vehicle in silence.

Chapter Seventeen

It took Katrina forever to find a dress, which drove me crazy. Everything she tried on looked amazing, but it still took her thirty different dresses to find the right one—a long, black dress with slits running down both legs, lots of cleavage, and an open back. She also left her golden hair down, and it framed her face in such a beautiful way that if Jake was having a beauty contest today, she'd be a shoe in.

It didn't take me nearly as long as Katrina to find an outfit. I had two to pick from—a short, red dress, and a long, red dress that reminded me of Jessica Rabbit's dress. With my black hair, red always made a great statement. We had to be sexy enough to distract everyone from our real goal. I also kept my make-up light, that way if I started to sweat, I wouldn't have foundation running down my face. My hair went up in a bun, leaving me ready for a fight if one found me. While the Cave discouraged fighting, that had never stopped anyone from trying to kill there.

To make it to the entrance, we had to walk through sand. Normally, walking in sand relaxed me. However, when wearing four-inch heels and a shimmering gown, the sand becomes your worst nightmare. We took our shoes off and rushed to the entrance underneath the pier as quickly possible. Katrina led the way, but she crashed into a tall guy leaning against a pole and they both fell to the ground.

"Oh! Are you guys okay?" I asked them as I ran forward.

Katrina hopped to her feet first, brushing the sand from her dress. "I'm good." Her cheeks were bright red and she wouldn't make eye contact. "I think my feet got caught on my dress and I went down."

I didn't buy it for a minute, but I kept my mouth shut. Instead, I moved around her and held out a hand to the young man still on the ground.

"Let me help you." I told him. He grabbed my hand and pulled himself up. "Are you alright?" I brushed some sand from his suit jacket.

"Yes, thank you," he told me, trying to wipe sand from his coat without looking at it. He straightened his jacket and slowly faced us. "I'm used to women falling over me, but this is the first time one has taken me out in the process."

It wasn't hard to imagine women falling for this guy. He was tall, dark, and incredibly handsome. Jet-black hair glimmered on top of his head and he had the most enchanting grey eyes. I was sure he was breaking hearts daily.

"I'm sure they are," I told him.

He winked and smiled at me. A year ago, a hottie like him would have made my head spin, but after meeting Iason, his flirtatious behavior didn't even phase me.

"Let me guess. You are the new bouncer at the Cave," I said.

"Guilty. Is it that obvious?" he asked.

He was definitely new if he didn't realize Jake recruited his bouncers and body guards from the GQ catalog. There wasn't a single man in his service that didn't score over a fifteen on a zero to ten scale. These boys were meant to distract you and make you lose your common sense. I wasn't sure if he had female body guards, but the women at the club were just as gorgeous.

"Not at all," Katrina answered. "But it's the only logical reason why a man that looks like you would be standing under a pier in a three-piece suit." It was Katrina's turn to wink at the poor boy and look smoldering.

I had begun to wonder if I'd missed a training program on smoldering.

"Well, ladies, let's get this party going. It's going to be a fun night," Hottie told us as he stepped towards the end of the pier. I couldn't help but notice the repeat glances he kept giving Katrina. I chuckled to myself.

Katrina and I followed Hottie down the pier, getting our feet wet from the tide rising over the pier and wetting the boards. I was pretty sure his idea of fun was nothing like mine. I liked boring evenings at home playing my guitar, not running around the country chasing deranged kidnappers.

Hottie stopped in front of a curtain in between two of the wood beams. "Enjoy your evening ladies." He pulled the curtain back.

"You aren't searching us for weapons?" I asked him.

"With those dresses? You don't leave much to the imagination." Hottie gave us a long look up and down. "Anything you have hiding in there we could handle. Enjoy, ladies." He waved us in with a catty smile.

Weapons were not allowed at the Cave. The fact that I didn't require searching was a good reminder that I was currently half naked. This was not going to happen again. I definitely needed more clothes on. If my godmother ever saw me like this, she would kill me. Thinking about my godmother made my heart ache. How many other things hadn't she told me?

"Are you okay?" Katrina asked me after we crossed the curtain. She had already started down the stairs, and I'd stopped at the top.

"Yeah, sorry," I told her. "It's been a long day." That was another huge understatement.

"I understand, but I need you to focus," Katrina told me. "Put your game face on. This is the devil we are facing."

Should I tell Katrina I'd met Jake before? I decided I didn't need to, but she was right about one thing. I did need to focus.

"I'm good. Let's go." I gave myself a quick shake and followed her down the stairs towards another set of curtains.

The Cave was the kind of club that would make a Hollywood film director drool. Every night was different inside the walls. They had a new theme every night and changed the decorations to match each one. I honestly couldn't wait to see what they'd done for open-mic night.

Once we crossed the curtain, I decided this open mic must be for poets. There was a large stage at the far end of the hall, with a dance floor in front and cocktail tables circling it. The place looked more like it had once been a dance floor and they'd turned it into a theater instead of a regular club.

"Admiring the view?" Jake asked me from the side.

"It is always impressive," I answered with a smirk.

I had a tendency to forget that the devil was a fallen angel. Like most angels, he was magnificent. He had golden hair; piercing, blue eyes; and a look that could melt hearts—almost like a young Brad Pitt. He was wearing a fabulous Valentino suit to show off his muscles. I felt bad for the souls that fell under his spell because I was sure the price was high.

"Katrina, it's been such a long time," Jake purred.

"Jake," Katrina said, and somehow, she made that one word sound like an insult. Their eyes met, and I felt like I was watching a scene from one of those fighting movies where they circled each other, sizing each other up. It was uncomfortable to say the least, so I cleared my throat, hoping to ease some of the tension.

"Well, since you are here, can we get to business?" I told Jake, giving him one of my best smiles. "We are on a short deadline," I added

"Isis, dear, you are always on a deadline," Jake told me, but his eyes stayed on Katrina. "But you know the rules. No free talks without payment." He finally looked back at me.

"What's the catch today?" I wasn't sure what we were supposed to do.

"It's simple, dear. Get this crowd going wild and I'm all yours." Jake's eyes fell on Katrina when he said the last part. "You get to pick the song. Break a leg."

"Fine," Katrina said right before she dragged me away. I looked over my shoulder and Jake waved at me with a smile. Why was he so happy?

"What exactly are we supposed to be doing?" I asked Katrina as I focused my attention on the front of the room.

"Have you seen American Idol?" Katrina asked, all business-like.

I was ashamed to admit it. "Not really," I whispered. Katrina gave me a quick glance.

"No big deal," she said, a little calmer. "Basically, it's a singing competition, but your goal is to win the crowd and make them dance. Can you sing?" Katrina asked me as we made our way to the left side of the stage.

A large man with a clipboard stood at the front of the line. There were at least five people in front of us waiting. They looked too excited for my taste.

"What happens if we don't win the crowd?" I asked Katrina as I faced the crowd. They did not look happy.

"If you're lucky, you will get booed off the stage, but if you're really bad, watch out for flying objects." Katrina pointed to the closest table as she spoke. The collection of throwing knives and Chinese stars were impressive. These people took their singing serious. "How is your singing?" Katrina asked again.

"I'm okay, but I'm more of a musician than lead man," I told her as I analyzed all the different weapons sitting on all the tables.

I hadn't noticed when the next act had started, but it didn't last long. Some poor soul had tried to do an interpretation of Aretha Franklin's Respect and failed miserably. In less than twenty seconds, weapons flew, and screams erupted from the stage. My stomach turned.

Katrina sized up the other candidates and watched the crowd. Then, she turned to me. "What can you play?"

"Anything," I answered softly.

Katrina's mouth parted and her eyes went wide. "What do you mean anything?" she asked me, almost like she was analyzing me for the first time.

"I can play any instrument with very little practice now. Death's gift enhances our natural ability. I was a musician before joining her. She has made me out of this world amazing. I can actually induce certain reactions from people with my music." I held my breath, unsure how Katrina would take all this.

"This is awesome," Katrina told me as she gave me a huge hug. "I need you to pour your soul into this and make the people go wild. I got the singing part." Katrina flashed me an evil grin.

"Isn't that cheating?" I wasn't sure if I was supposed to use my gifts for a singing competition.

"Isis, you either do this or we don't get to talk to the devil today."

I hated it, but she was right.

"Fine, let's go," I told her.

She grabbed my hand and dragged me to the front of the line. The last two acts had gone up in flames. The remaining group appeared to be shaking, so they didn't argue when Katrina pushed passed them.

Katrina talked quickly to the large man with the clipboard. Up close, I realized he wasn't fat, but built like a linebacker with solid muscle. He had a baby face that did not match his lethal body.

After a few minutes, the linebacker handed Katrina the clipboard. She scribbled something on it, then shoved it in front of my face so I could read it. We were going to perform two songs: Wicked Games and Black Magic Woman. What an interesting combination, I thought.

We were on the stage before I had time to change my mind. Katrina walked towards the mic and I headed towards the band. I smiled at the guitarist who handed me his instrument. I hoped it didn't get damaged during this act. It was an expensive and very well-kept guitar.

Katrina glanced at me over her shoulder. I gave her a nod and she took the mic. She started with Wicked Games. No introductions were necessary.

Katrina was an incredible singer and she rocked the song like a pro. For most of my pieces recently, the intent has been to put people to sleep. This was the first one that I wanted them to dance.

By the time Katrina hit the second chorus, I was pouring all my energy into the music to make people move. I made the beats as sexy and provocative as possible. Wicked Games had a contagious beat that made you want to slow dance, so I was scared I put too much heat into it. People were dancing, though, and not only on the dance floor but also on the tables. The ones on the floor were so close they looked like one person.

Katrina sang to one side of the room, and when I moved to get a better view, I realized she was singing to Jake. I almost stopped playing. Had Katrina and Jake dated? That would explain the awkwardness between them. I didn't have the time to ponder their love lives, though, since Katrina cued the band to switch songs. If Wicked Games showcased Katrina's singing skills, Black Magic Woman put mine to the test. I just prayed I made Santana proud.

The rest of the song went by in a blur, and the crowd went wild the whole time. Before I knew it, Katrina dragged me off stage towards Jake.

"That was intense. Isis, you are phenomenal. We should go on tour," Katrina said, her words bouncing off the walls in her excitement. I barely heard her, though. Exhaustion had wrapped around me like a blanket. I wondered how much energy it took to create that level of magic.

"Katrina is right. You are amazing," Jake told me as we reached his table.

Katrina stiffened and sobered. She also got extremely quiet.

"How about business now?" I asked Jake. This situation was too uncomfortable for my taste.

"I don't know," Jake said in a mocking voice. "It's not like you won using only your talents." He looked me straight in the eyes as he leaned on his cocktail table.

"Whose fault is that for picking a musical challenge?" I crossed my arms in front of my chest and shifted my weight to one side.

"Why are you blaming me?" Jake said, framing his face with his hands to convey innocence.

"Oh, please. You know exactly what I can do, and you still asked for a performance," I told him. Why did the devil have to mess with me all the time? I was too tired for this.

"Isis is right," Katrina told him. "Your crowd is going wild. Now it's our turn." She narrowed her eyes at him.

"Fine, let's not get nasty now, ladies," Jake told us with a wave of his hand. I hadn't even realized his bodyguards were closing in on us. At his signal, they all stepped back. "Why do I have the pleasure of your visit?"

"We are looking for a half-breed elf named Noah," I told him quickly. "We were told he might be in hell." I wasn't sure if I believed the last part myself.

"Interesting. But what do you want from me?" Jake asked as he lifted his glass to his lips and took a sip. Although, I had no idea where the glass came from. I was pretty sure it wasn't there a minute ago.

"Can you confirm he is there?" Katrina asked him. "We really need to speak with him." She held his stare.

"Sorry, ladies. That is against the rules," Jake told us.

Katrina slammed her fist on the table and scoffed. "Seriously?"

"What rules?" I asked him.

"We value our clients," Jake told me. "If any of the living made a deal with one of my people, I don't intervene. It's a promise I keep to my people." Jake gave me another one of his irritating smiles.

"What does that mean? We didn't just rock your crowd for nothing," I told Jake. Inside, I debated whether or not I should choke him.

"I cannot confirm or deny if your little friend is in hell," Jake said, playing with his drink. "What I can do is grant you a pass, that way you can check yourself. I would start at the hotel and ask for Ralph." With a quick flick of his wrist, two gold cards appeared in his hand.

"Wait. What?" I asked Jake. I didn't want to go to hell.

"Don't tell me you are afraid of a little trip to hell," Jake teased me.

"That was way too easy. What's the catch?" Katrina jumped in, saving me from answering.

"Oh, come on. Why can't I just be friendly?" Jake asked, batting his eyes at me innocently.

"Because you are the devil and you always have ulterior motives," I told him honestly.

"True," Jake admitted, no longer bothering to try and look innocent. "The pass is only for three hours. The clock starts the moment you cross my threshold. You have to find your own way there and back. The catch is if you both are not out of hell before the three hours are up, your body and souls are mine. Happy hunting, ladies." Jake dropped the passes on the table, took his drink, and walked away.

"At judgement day, if Michael doesn't nail his ass to the cross, I swear I will." Katrina's voice held so much hatred it made me glad she was on my side. Before I could say anything, she marched toward the front door.

I grabbed the passes and followed her. I never thought I would say this, but I felt bad for Jake. Beware the wrath of a woman. Whatever he had done to Katrina was not good. The devil was screwed.

Chapter Eighteen

Outside the Cave, I started to freak out. I was Catholic. I couldn't go to hell. They might keep me there. I took a lot of deep breaths as we rushed back to the car. My heart rate accelerated to the point I thought I might pass out. Katrina unlocked the car and we climbed in as fast as we could.

"Isis, what's wrong?" Katrina asked me.

I couldn't talk. In fact, it took every bit of focus I had just to breathe. My chest felt so heavy I didn't know whether I had an elephant sitting on it or what. I needed a paper bag. Maybe some fresh air.

What I really needed was to not have to go to hell.

"Oh Lord, don't you dare pass out on me. Put your hands over your head and breathe."

I followed Katrina's instructions, breathing in slowly and blowing it out. I did it again and again. Five minutes later, my heart beat slowed down and I didn't feel like I was going to puke anymore, although my whole body trembled so hard my teeth chattered.

"Katrina, I can't go to hell," I finally told her, trying not to freak out again.

"Is that why you are freaking out?" Katrina asked me in a calm voice.

"Yes! I don't know how you can be so calm." The words rushed out of me. "You do know I'm a Christian. The only

Christian that has been to hell and back is Jesus. Do I look like Jesus to you?" I was pretty sure I sounded irrational.

"I hope not," Katrina answered me. "I'm pretty sure Jesus is a guy." She chuckled.

I didn't. Nothing about this amused me.

"Thanks, but not funny," I told her. At least she got me to calm down. "Why are you not freaking out?" I really wanted to know her secret.

"Isis, what do you think the devil and his demons let loose in the jungles of Korea, in the deserts of Iraq, in every major war we have ever had?" Katrina asked.

"The devil? I thought those wars were man-made." I had never thought about the conflicts from a supernatural scale.

"They are man-made and mostly orchestrated by War," Katrina said, looking straight ahead. "But in the midst of chaos, everyone takes advantage of it. I have fought more demons with human faces than I care to count. So has Bob. You should ask him one day." She looked at me daring me to question it. "This is just another mission. Yes, we are going to hell, but you are not helpless, so get a grip on yourself." Katrina focused on the road again.

I took a deep breath before talking. "I don't like it," I finally told her.

"You said it yourself. You are a Christian," Katrina told me. "Your Jesus didn't want to get crucified. He asked his father to take the cup away from him." I was surprised Katrina knew the story of the garden of Gethsemane. "Like Jesus, you don't have to like it. You just have to get through it." She smiled at me.

"You are taking this very well," I finally told her.

"Isis, I don't have a choice," Katrina told me. "If we fail, War could send me to hell to live, or any other horrible place for that matter. And it wouldn't be for a few hours, it would be for a decade."

"The real hell?" I asked her, and she just nodded. "Why is he so mad at you?"

That was a horrible punishment. She couldn't have done anything that bad.

"I accidentally started peace in the Middle East," Katrina whispered.

"What?" I didn't think I heard her right. "Is that even possible?" I was pretty sure she was messing with me.

"I had set up a meeting with all the leaders of the region in an effort to kill the leader instigating peace," Katrina said. "I didn't notice when the Chiefs changed seats, but I shot the dictator instead of the pacifist. The execution was flawless. I made it look like the dictator's troops had taken the shot. So, instead of war, I got unity." Katrina dropped her head on the steering wheel.

At times, I forgot the mission of the other horsemen was to bring death and destruction to humanity. Not sure why I was surprised about this.

"Oh, wow," I said, not able to come up with anything more elegant to say.

"Tell me about it," Katrina said, glancing at me. "Have you ever done something that goes totally against your Horseman's mission and purpose?" Katrina asked, hope filling her eyes.

"I have made lots of mistakes," I told her. "But at least I haven't brought anyone back from the dead. Granted, you can always fix yours and start a new war. If I become a necromancer, I'm pretty sure Constantine would kill me himself." I had a feeling it wouldn't be a quick death either, but I didn't say that out loud.

"Good point," Katrina agreed.

"We don't have a lot of choices here," I told Katrina, taking a few deep breaths. "If we don't find Noah, we might not find the princess, and then a lot of people risk becoming collateral damage. I'm terrified, Katrina, but at least you are going with me."

"You are not alone, Isis. Now let's get this show on the road." Katrina squeezed my hand for moral support.

I grabbed my phone from the back seat and dialed Reapers. Just because we had a pass to hell didn't mean I had a clue how to get there.

"What happened?" Constantine asked in his typical manner.

"We got a three-hour pass to hell," I told him as calmly as possible.

"In that case, you had better hurry. The Boatman's next pick-up near your area is at midnight," Constantine told us.

"Where are we meeting him?" Katrina asked, like this was a normal, everyday conversation.

"At Alcatraz," Bartholomew answered.

"Of course, it is," I said, rolling my eyes.

"We are sending instructions to George to have the plane ready," Constantine jumped in. "He will have your backpack ready as well."

What backpack was Constantine talking about? Who did I look like? Dora the Explorer?

"Ladies, be careful," Bob added. "Don't trust anyone there." The sound in Bob's voice made me wonder if he had ever been to hell.

"Isis, I am sending you instructions now. You don't have a lot of time," Bartholomew said. "After you land in San Francisco, it's a forty-minute drive to the coast, followed by a twenty-minute boat ride to the island. You better get moving."

That was a tight schedule. Bartholomew was right. We had better get moving.

"Go," Constantine ordered before disconnecting the call.

"No turning back now. We got this," Katrina told me.

"We got this, but we need to make a quick detour," I told her. "We are not going to hell empty handed." I sent a quick text before searching the GPS for my new destination.

It was a blessing Katrina drove like a Nascar driver. She made up the time we lost in our detour. We had a smooth flight and plenty of time to change into fighting gear. I was not heading to hell wearing a party dress. We missed the traffic in San Francisco, but Katrina still had to speed. I inspected the famous backpack during the drive and was not sure how any of the stuff inside would be useful. I also carried a box the size of a shoebox, only thinner. It was labeled Boatman. Then I had a giant chocolate bar for Fluffy. I sure hoped Fluffy had the biggest chocolate addiction in the world, because this bar was at least ten pounds. Even with all that, I was grateful the backpack still had enough room for my own stuff.

Bartholomew had secured a speedboat for us that was parked at the marina. I was hoping we had really good insurance on that thing, since I was pretty sure it belonged to us. We made it to Alcatraz ten minutes before midnight. Katrina got us to the island and I jumped off to tie the boat. I watched Katrina do it when we got the boat, so I figured it wasn't that hard. After a little trial and error, the boat was secured and we ran across the island. Fortunately, the Boatman made his pickup on this side of the island and we didn't have to go inside the prison.

"What is that sound?" I asked Katrina as I stopped running.

"What?" Katrina asked me when she realized I had stopped running.

"Can't you hear the screams?" They surrounded me, the noise coming from every direction to encompass me. I covered my ears, but still the screams got louder.

"No," Katrina answered, looking around. "All I hear is the wind."

"In that case, run," I told Katrina as I grabbed her hand and pulled her with me. We needed to get off this island now. Not all ghosts are friendly, and I was pretty sure I didn't want to get my butt kicked by an angry spirit. Getting these souls to their final home would require back-up.

We made it to the pick-up point just in time to see the Boatman pull up. Boats were not my specialty, but I had seen pictures of the time period and I was sure the Boatman was sailing an Ancient Galilee Boat. That thing was so old it probably took Jesus across the Jordan River. I had no idea how it was moving because there was no wind. I also couldn't see a motor anywhere and the people on the boat were not touching the oars.

Katrina gave me a worried look. I shrugged one shoulder. It was too late to turn back now, so I walked towards the ledge and smiled at the Boatman.

"Cutting it close, little sister," the Boatman told me in a raspy voice. He was covered in a deep hood from head to toe. The thing looked like it was made of wool. I wondered if he was itchy, at least until I saw his hands and noticed they were just bones. That explained the voice.

"Sorry. Traffic." I wasn't sure how you apologized to bones. "I have a gift from Constantine," I said, trying to change the topic. I took the box out of the backpack and tossed it to the Boatman. He caught it with one hand. If we had a company softball league, I wanted the Boatman on my team.

"The fur-man is always so thoughtful," he said to me. "Are you two just going to stand there? Let's go. We are on a tight schedule."

I gave Katrina one last look before following the Boatman's instructions. Katrina stayed close as we took a seat behind the steering wheel in the middle of the boat. The front half of the boat was packed with at least twenty souls. For the first time, I didn't want to have a conversation with these souls. I knew where they were heading and there was nothing I could do to help.

Katrina poked me in the ribs, dragging my attention to the Boatman who was bouncing for joy. "Please tell me we didn't bribe the Boatman with a mixed CD and some comics," she whispered.

Sure enough, the Boatman held his presents out, and Katrina was right. Was Constantine trying to get us killed?

"Have some respect, girl. Those are manga," I replied with a smirk. I loved the Japanese graphic novels.

"My bad, but we are still in trouble."

I couldn't argue with Katrina. I felt the same way.

"Time to party, my souls," the Boatman announced.

I don't know how, but the Boatman started blasting his new CD. This was insane. I was heading down to hell while listening to Cardi B's I like it like that. The Boatman was jamming, and he had all the souls jamming, too, their hands waving in the air.

"I'm impressed. Boatman can move," Katrina told me from the side. She was taking this trip much better than I was. "Disney could make a ride out of this. The ferry to hell with DJ Bag of Bones. I would be there every day." Katrina bobbed her head to the beat.

It was official. This was truly hell.

Within a few minutes, DJ Bag of Bones had us out of the harbor and into some fog. The temperature slowly changed, and everything got darker. I could still hear the Boatman singing, this time jamming to J Balvin's Mi Gente. A little creepy since he had a boat full of people he was dropping off to hell.

I wasn't sure how long we were on the boat or when I fell asleep, but a loud scream woke me. More came right after, piercing my head. I looked around and we were underground somewhere, the air so thick with smoke it was hard to draw in a breath. The boat had stopped at a pier and the souls were departing. I couldn't see where they were heading, but they just marched along. I started gagging when the smell of burning hair and flesh caught my attention. It was the worse smell I had ever experienced. It was rottener than the chicken plant in Hope where Eugene's lab was hidden.

"Here. Put this over your nose and mouth until we reach the hotel. It will diminish the stench," the Boatman said as he passed me a bandana. I noticed Katrina already had one on.

"Where are we?" I wasn't sure why I asked, but I needed to know.

"The torture chambers where the damned come to pay for their deeds." The Boatman stared at the souls. I shivered, wanting nothing more than to get out of there as soon as possible. "Here put this on. You must keep track of time from now on." The Boatman gave me the oldest looking watch I had ever seen. "Time moves differently here. We need to get going."

"Works for me," I told him as I put the watch on my right wrist. I figured there was no need to take mine off. "I guess it would be too much to ask for us to get a signal in here," I told Katrina as I looked at my phone on roaming status.

"Sorry, Isis, I don't think Sprint's long-distance plan covers hell," Katrina replied with a grin.

The Boatman made a quick left down a long river. The currents were calm, and the air was actually breathable. I took my bandana off and the Boatman went back to blasting his music. This time he had Nelly's It's getting hot in here.

Constantine must have made the CD for the Boatman, which meant he had way more jokes than I'd guessed.

"Play it loud, Boatman!" a voice screamed. Katrina and I both jumped up to find the sound.

A young man was riding down the river in an inner tube with a drink. I wondered if I was imagining it because his drink even had a paper umbrella in it.

"Hold it down, my man," Boatman screamed back to the young man floating away.

"Who was that?" I asked, my voice a little shaky.

"Jose," Boatman replied. "He used to be the Intern in Europe. It was a rough death for him. Glad he is back to his normal self again," he told us.

"Wait, this is Death's Intern's afterlife?" Katrina asked the Boatman and then looked at me. Did she really think I had a clue what was going on here?

"Welcome to the River Styx, little cousin," the Boatman told her, his voice much too happy.

"I definitely chose the wrong Horseman," Katrina told me. "I get to spend my afterlife frozen in ice waiting for the end of times and you get to chill in an inner tube drinking frozen drinks. How is that fair?"

"Our life span is a lot shorter," I told her.

What I didn't tell her, though, was of all places to spend my afterlife waiting for judgment day, no part of hell would be my first choice.

"Isis, you are nuts," Katrina replied. She tried to glare at me, but we both just ended up laughing.

"Ladies get ready. We are almost at your stop," Boatman announced.

No turning back now. Katrina and I did a quick inventory check. Just because we were in hell didn't mean we were planning to stay there.

Chapter Nineteen

Boatman slowed down and maneuvered his ancient boat up to a rickety, old pier.

"What is that thing?" Katrina asked Boatman.

"That offense to the world of architecture is Hotel California," Boatman told us.

"Of course, it is," I told them. Who said demons didn't have a sense of humor.

Boatman was right. That thing was truly hideous. It looked like a castle, a fort, and a horrible misshapen mansion had a child and that thing came out.

"I know we are in hell, but we have standards." The Boatman turned his back on the hotel as he spoke. "Somebody should put that thing out of its misery and burn it down." He was seriously disgusted by it. "Okay, ladies, off you go. You got thirty minutes, hurry back."

"Thirty?" I asked the Boatman. "What happened to three hours?" That was not enough time to do anything.

"We need time to recon the area and sneak in," Katrina added.

"Little sister, thirty minutes is plenty." Boatman was staring down at me. I forgot the man was technically a skeleton. I had never been intimidated by glowing socket balls before. He turned his glare towards Katrina and I was grateful. "Your three hours includes transportation. There is no need to sneak around. This is hell. The living radiate like an atomic bomb. Everyone knows you two are here. Besides, I got things to do. I'm the DJ for the pre-Halloween party for the Interns. I can't be hanging out with you all day. I got music to prep." I wasn't sure how, but Boatman snapped his fingers and kicked us off.

"I'm glad he has his priorities straight," Katrina whispered to me as we walked up the dock.

"Tell me about it," I replied back.

We moved towards the hotel following a yellow path. Like Dorothy, we were not in Kansas anymore, but this was a yellow brick road. I had a horrible feeling this design was not a coincidence. Unfortunately, when I looked down, the yellow brick road turned into a road made of human skulls.

"Holy crap!" I screamed as I jumped off the trail. Katrina looked down and followed suit.

"I'm confused. How is this supposed to get humans to give up their souls to demons or the devil?" Katrina asked me as we started walking parallel of the path.

"If you make it this far down, I have a feeling your soul is already theirs," I told her.

"Remind me to shoot the devil when we see him again," Katrina told me with an evil smile.

"Will do." I was not arguing with her. This place was awful.

We decided to jog the short path from the pier to the hotel's entrance. The sooner we got this done, the sooner I could take a bath with bleach and disinfect myself. We crossed a small bridge at the entrance to the property that was over a moat. They had a moat? Did they think somebody was actually planning to storm their castle? This was ridiculous. I looked over the edge of the bridge, probably because I was a sucker for punishment. I almost puked and Katrina had to pull me back.

"You have to be kidding me! Boiling blood?" I looked at Katrina, and I knew my eyes were wide and my face was pale. I had to look horrified, but who could blame me? The place was right out of a horror film.

"Come on. Let's get this done," Katrina said as she pulled me further up the path.

We made it to the front door in one piece. I half expected gargoyles to open the door. Instead, a very handsome bellboy opened the door for us. He didn't speak, just smiled and waved us in.

"Should we be worried? That was too easy," Katrina asked me.

"I haven't stopped being worried," I replied. I had Don Henley's song playing in my head and it was on constant replay.

"If Boatman is right, and I'm sure he is, they are expecting us. This is a horrible trap," Katrina finished, and her voice was almost giddy. "Let's not make them wait."

Katrina was way too excited to face evil. I didn't feel the same, but I still followed her inside. The place was even gaudier on the inside than the outside. All the walls were red and weird pictures hung in the most random places. Gold chandeliers were scattered in the large lobby. At least there was a reception area to the left of the place. To the right, a huge collection of leather couches was strategically organized. I was expecting demons with tails and horns everywhere. Instead, it looked like a Victoria Secret runway show was going on in this place, if Victoria Secret allowed men to model. Half-naked young girls and boys were everywhere, with older, but gorgeous, men and women in suits. I had no words.

"Remember, we are on their turf. They can change their appearance to look like anything," Katrina told me in my ear. "Don't be fooled by it."

"Hi. We are looking for Ralph," Katrina said to a young man behind the reception desk.

"Hi. He is over there," the young man with perfect teeth and amazing jet-black hair replied. "He has been expecting you."

"I am sure he has been. Thank you," Katrina told him. She turned to me and said, "Are you ready for this?"

I thought for a minute. There was no need to pretend I wanted to be here, so I told the truth. "Nope, but we don't have a choice."

We walked towards the center of the leather couches. I was wondering where the hotel did their shopping because those couches were great quality. As we got nearer, the crowd parted for us, leaving a path directly to a blond man sitting on the largest seat I had ever seen. I had a feeling this was how Moses felt when he parted the Red Sea. In awe, but totally terrified.

I stopped and stared at the man at the end of the path. If that was Ralph, he didn't look like one. He looked more like Ryan Reynolds with blond hair and black eyes. A weird look, especially since I had a huge crush on Ryan. Ralph looked menacing, so he was ruining it for me.

"Ladies, so nice of you to join us," Ralph announced with a booming voice. "We have been expecting you." He waved his hand at the crowd and slowly got up from his throne. It looked like he might just make a whole production out of this.

"Sorry we are late," Katrina said. "We were admiring the place." I had no idea what she was talking about.

"Oh, yes. Isn't it magnificent?" Ralph told us. "Don't you agree?" The rest of the pretty people became bobble-head-dolls and started nodding up and down non-stop.

"I don't know. It's a bit gaudy," I told him, toning it down a bit. I actually thought I'd never seen something so overdone in my life.

"Let me guess. You must be Isis," Ralph told me. I was pretty sure he knew exactly who I was. "The boss said you would be the one with the mouth and the pretty blonde would be the muscle." He eyed Katrina and I like we were lunch. It was interesting Ralph called Jake boss and not his highness. I would ponder that later.

"In that case, introductions are not needed," I told Ralph as I made plans in my head to choke Jake to death. "Obviously, you know why we are here, so where is Noah?" No need to play games. I wanted to leave as soon as possible.

"No foreplay? That's a shame," Ralph answered, licking his lips. I was starting to feel sick to my stomach again. "My pet is gone. Sent him to Haven yesterday."

"What?" I screamed. I felt like I was having an out of body experience. "Are you kidding me? Why didn't Jake just tell us that?" Jake was definitely going to die a horrible death when I got ahold of him.

"Oh, come on now." Ralph answered in a very condescending manner. "Do you bore your boss with all the dreary details of the job?" Ralph glanced between Katrina and me.

"I guess you haven't met Constantine or you would know the answer to that." I took a deep breath to calm down. "Let's go, Katrina, this trip was a waste," I told her as I grabbed her arm.

"Don't you want to know if the princess was with him?" Ralph asked sweetly as the rest of the crowd snickered.

"Are you planning to tell us?" Katrina asked as she looked around the room, assessing the crowd.

"Of course, sweetie. I'm here to help." Ralph walked around his throne like a model strolling a cat-walk.

"Okay, I'll play." I wrapped an arm around the front of Katrina to hold her back. I had a feeling she might kill Ralph if she got her hands on him. "Was Noah here with the princess and is the princess okay?" I glared at Ralph but made my voice sound as bored as possible.

"Much better," Ralph answered. "Yes, the princess was here. She is in great health, for her condition that is. A bit on the sleepy side."

Katrina and I exchanged glances.

"What condition and what have you given her to keep her sleepy?" Katrina asked Ralph this time.

"Ladies, if you don't know, I shouldn't be the one to ruin the surprise," Ralph told us in a mocking tone.

"Spill it, pretty boy. You know you want to," Katrina replied.

"She is pregnant. Exciting." Ralph clapped his hands.

My mouth dropped open, and so did Katrina's.

"Is that even possible?" I asked Katrina.

"It is now. The power of elven blood," Ralph answered for her.

"Why are you so helpful?" I finally asked him.

"I have nothing to lose. You are never leaving here," Ralph said, his voice filled with confidence. I felt like I was in an Austin Power's movie and the villain just revealed his big plans. That never ended well for the villain.

"I'm sorry. I thought we had three hours?" I asked Ralph.

"Oh, you do." His voice was so charming, I almost believed him. "You see, the boss said to be helpful and sociable with his guests. He never said anything about us not trying to keep you. It's up to you to find a way out." Ralph rubbed his hands together like an excited child. "If you can, that is."

"Constantine said not to trust anyone in hell," I told Katrina.

"There is a reason they are in hell to begin with," Katrina told me. "Sorry, sweetie, we can't stay. Got a date with Boatman," she told Ralph, doing an awesome Southern accent. I didn't know she could pull that off. Katrina grabbed a 9mm from her back and pointed it at Ralph.

"Are you serious, little girl?" Ralph raised his brows. "Do you honestly think a gun can hurt us?"

The room erupted into laughter, which gave me plenty of time to flip my backpack around and pull out my toy.

"A gun? No, probably not. But maybe this," I told Ralph as I aimed my super soaker at him and fired.

Ralph had no idea what hit him. His laughter stopped and screams filled the air. Smoke billowed out of him as I took aim at the first couple of men rushing towards us.

Somebody should have told Ralph never to underestimate his opponent. The guys burst into flames and the smell of burning flesh filled the air.

"What in the hell is this?" screamed one of the guys.

"Holy water," yelled Ralph, his eyes now wide with terror.

Half of Ralph's face and body were melting. He had probably been a really strong angel back in the day because his face was starting to heal, unlike his entourage who were falling apart. I was sending silent thanks to Father Francis. It was good we'd had time to run my errand, even though I felt terrible for texting him so late since he had been two hours ahead in Texas. However, he hooked me up with one of his friends in San Diego to make sure we had what we needed for the trip.

"Katrina, we need a door now," I said, my tone filled with urgency. I had two large containers attached to my water gun, but they were not going to last forever. I was making every shot count.

"Got it," Katrina said behind me. I couldn't turn around to see what she was doing. "Time to take cover." Katrina jerked me to the side in front of a large pillar.

Before I could ask any questions, Katrina blew up an entire wall and the entrance of the hotel exploded. All the boys in front of the blast were thrown at least twenty feet in the air. Even Ralph was tossed aside.

"Katrina, I said door. Not to take the whole place down," I told her as I looked over her shoulder at the massive damage she had created.

"Sorry. I wasn't sure how C4 would react in hell, so I added more just to be on the safe side," Katrina told me, looking at the ground. "Let's get out of here." She dragged me to my feet and we started running.

"You will never leave here alive," Ralph screamed. "Release Fluffy," he screamed at his flunkies.

Katrina and I scrambled over debris. Pieces of the ceiling started to fall off as the walls on both sides collapsed. I flipped my backpack over again, grabbed the large candy bar, and handed it to Katrina.

"I have no idea what Fluffy is, but we are going to need this," I told her as I tried to readjust my bag and water gun. Just as she took it, the ground started trembling. "Oh God. Are we having an earthquake?"

"Not this time, just Fluffy." Katrina pointed over her shoulder.

"What?" I asked and looked where she was pointing. Fluffy was Cerberus, the three headed hound that guarded Hades. He was huge, angry, and dripping saliva everywhere. "I don't think we have enough candy there," I told Katrina. We needed a small dump truck to feed that thing.

"We don't need to feed him. Just distract him," Katrina told me as she grabbed my shoulders and held me still.

Not sure why she was holding me. We needed to get out of there.

"Calm down, Isis. When I say go, run like your life depends on it. Just wait for my cue." Katrina was full of jokes today. Of course, our lives depended on it.

"Hey, Fluffy. Catch," Katrina yelled at the massive beast that was the size of an F150. Katrina took aim and I thanked God for her super trooper strength. She launched that bar like a missile. Fluffy didn't think twice and followed the chocolate. "Isis, go!"

Katrina didn't have to tell me twice and it was the fastest sprint I had ever done in my life. If somebody would have timed it, I would have beat an Olympic record.

"Boatman, go!" I screamed with the little air I could find.

Fortunately, Boatman didn't need a lot of instruction. He had the boat moving before we reached the pier. Katrina and I jumped on as soon as the boat was near us. We landed horribly, but I didn't care.

"Is there any way to make this go any faster?" Katrina asked Boatman as she watched Fluffy heading our way.

"Of course, dear." Boatman reached underneath his steering wheel and the calm boat reacted like a speed boat.

Katrina and I dropped to the floor and took deep breaths. I was leaning on Katrina when the boat slowed down.

"We are here," Boatman announced.

Katrina and I looked over the sides of the boat and saw nothing.

"Here, where?" I asked him, confused.

"Home," he said with a smile.

"Home? We can't stay in hell," I told him. Had he lost his mind? "You are supposed to take us back."

"Sorry, little sister, this is a one-way trip," Boatman said. "You got to take the elevator to Haven, right over there." He pointed to a wall of rock on the edge of an island.

"Hold up," Katrina jumped in. "What do you mean you can't take us? Boatman, we can't go to Haven. That is the one place I'm not allowed to visit without permission. I don't even know who to request permission from. Trespassing on Haven is a death sentence."

"There is an elevator to hell in every Haven? Why didn't we go that way?" I asked the Boatman. My patience was gone, and I was ready to kill him.

"Sorry, that's also one way," Boatman answered in a calm tone. "You either have payment or the appropriate clearance to use it. Come back and visit, little sister. Loved what you did with the place." Boatman started laughing and couldn't stop. He pulled up to the island and I hopped off. Katrina followed, but a lot slower than I would've liked. We waved at Boatman, but he didn't see since he was still cackling.

"Who has a one-way elevator?" I asked out loud.

"Seriously, that's the part you care about?" Katrina demanded.

I couldn't blame her. She didn't understand and she probably never could.

"Isis, we are stuck in hell. To make matters worse, if we find a way to get out of hell, we are going to die."

Katrina started pacing and I made my way towards the wall of rock. If Boatman was right, I should have access to this freaky elevator. I was feeling like Willy Wonka with his crystal elevator. I stood two feet from the large rock formation and couldn't figure out how it opened, until I looked to my left. Next to the large rock and hiding by a small stump was a scanner. The same kind we had at Reapers. I placed my hand on the screen and the little machine scanned my finger print. I turned to watch the large rock formation open in the middle.

"Time to go home," I told her as I entered the elevator.

Katrina looked stunned for a second, but it didn't stop her from rushing inside right as the doors started to close.

Chapter Twenty

For an elevator in hell, this one wasn't very impressive. It looked like a regular elevator. The only difference was, instead of numbers for the floors, there were pictures. We only had two pictures that were lit up. One had an image of cowboy boots, while the other was a penguin. By process of elimination, the penguin had to be Antarctica—where the Intern named Bob was stationed. I was pretty sure he was the only other Intern not changing cities every six months. I pressed the cowboy boots and "God Bless Texas" started playing. The music selection impressed me.

"Isis, are you going to explain why you can open a magical elevator in hell and know the correct button to a Haven city?" Katrina had leaned against the far wall, crossed her arms over her chest, and didn't look the least bit happy.

"Easy. Because according to Constantine, I'm in charge of the Haven in North America, which happens to be Texas," I told her as I leaned against the wall as well, but I didn't look miserable. In fact, my jaw hurt from grinning.

"What?" It took Katrina a minute to process that information and her head snapped in my direction when everything clicked. "Death's Interns run the Havens?" She didn't sound very convinced.

"Trust me. I can't believe it either." At least we were on the same page for this.

"Texarkana is the new Haven. Crazy," Katrina said. "Wait, isn't that where the zombie apocalypse took place last May? Did you start that?" Katrina looked a little too happy for my taste.

"Yes, we did have a zombie episode, but no, I didn't start that," I told her, a little offended. Hadn't I explained the whole idea of bringing people back from the dead? "You can thank Pestilence and her horrible hiring practices for that one." I shook my head just thinking about Pestilence. That woman was nuts.

"I can see that. She is a special one." Katrina smiled at me.

"I had hoped by now the situation would be forgotten, but there is this crazy girl selling zombie apocalypse t-shirts all over town." It was time to find that girl and burn her supplies.

"Oh, you have to give her credit. She has an entrepreneur spirit, or maybe it's a morbid sense of humor." Katrina held back a smirk, although not very well. "Either way, she is hustling. Don't hate on her." She grew quiet for a minute before she started bouncing around the elevator. "Does that mean you know who is selling the dancing robots? I'm on the wait list and it is going to take at least six months to get one." She put her hands in a praying gesture in front of me.

"You are in luck. I'm sure Bartholomew can move you up the list," I told her.

Katrina dove in and wrapped me up in a hug.

I patted her back. "You are way too happy about this."

"According to the order, I can customize my robot." Katrina's words came out so fast I almost couldn't understand her. She was also jumping up and down and wouldn't stop. "I want grenade launchers in mine." Katrina spoke like a true soldier.

I opened my mouth to reply, but my phone beeped. And it kept beeping, every notification I'd missed while in hell was coming back.

"I guess we have left hell," I told Katrina as I looked at my phone. "Oh, not good."

"What happened?" Katrina asked, getting closer to look at the phone with me.

"It's three p.m. on Tuesday. We lost at least nine extra hours," I told Katrina. My phone was set to military time so there was no confusion if it was morning or afternoon. Before I could start complaining, the doors of the elevator opened.

We stepped out to a large lobby area, rundown but still beautiful. The tall windows let plenty of light in, which only confirmed the time of the day.

"Do you know where we are?" Katrina asked, checking the place out.

"Downtown in the old Union Station building," I told her. "I have been here before. It's hard to forget. For the first time ever, I'm grateful it is closed down." How would you explain to a bunch of commuters that you just came from hell? No need to panic.

I looked around, hoping to see a trail or something confirming that Noah had been here. Unfortunately, tracking was not my expertise, so I settled for calling home.

"Isis!" Bartholomew answered, overly excited. "Hold on. Why does your phone put you in downtown Texarkana?" I could tell by his voice how confused he was.

"Don't tell me that lazy Boatman dropped you off at that stupid elevator?" Constantine hissed.

"You knew about this little ride?" I asked him, making sure my voice was flat and definitely not amused.

"Of course, I did. What kind of guardian would I be if I didn't?" Constantine answered. "I hate that elevator. For decades, the only active button was Antarctica. Nobody ever risked landing in Bob's territory that way. Those stupid penguins will blow you off the map."

Antarctica Bob had combat trained penguins? That was insane.

"Boatman took a huge gamble taking you there, unless the word is out that Texarkana is the new Haven," Constantine continued.

"They know, Const," Katrina told him. She was a brave woman calling him that. "The demon Ralph sent Noah here."

"Oh great. This is going to suck," Constantine replied.

"Tell me about it," I added. "Bart, we need to do something about this door. We need surveillance monitors. Pretty much we need everything. We can't have an entrance from hell unsupervised." I was not happy about this new development.

"Good point, Isis," Constantine agreed. "Bartholomew, buy the building. Make them an offer they can't refuse and expedite the process. Get Shorty to add some men to the location."

Constantine was such an overachiever. I asked for a couple of doors and now we owned the whole building. If I thought about it, though, he was right. We shouldn't take any chances.

"That's perfect," Bartholomew added. "Shorty needs a location for all his recruits. Now he can have a whole block." Bartholomew's voice was filled with happiness.

"Sounds like a project for Bob," Constantine added. "He will make sure to get that place fixed and in working condition." Constantine didn't have to say the rest—that Bob would establish rules and guidance to keep everyone within military standards.

"Great plan guys, but can we get a ride," I said, ready to head home so we could have this conversation in person.

"Shorty is right around the corner. I'll have him head your way," Bartholomew told me. "Glad you made it home, Isis. We missed you."

I loved Bartholomew. He was the sweetest kid ever. I was glad he passed that horrible stage he had in May.

"Miss you, too, big guy." I meant those words more than he knew. "I hope you guys have some food for us. We are starving." My stomach grumbled as soon as the words left my lips.

"We got you. Bob should be back from Walmart by the time you guys get here," Bartholomew told me. "Constantine left to inform Abuelita and Eric that the hell door is activated. This is going to be fun. Safe travels with Shorty and see you soon." Bartholomew hung up before I could reply. That boy was spending so much time with Constantine that he'd started picking up his bad habits.

"Ready?" I asked Katrina.

"Should I be worried about Shorty?" Katrina asked me with a smirk.

"Nah, Shorty is the real deal," I told her. "He is about five feet four inches, and maybe one-hundred-and-twenty pounds soaking wet. Shorty knows everyone and has more connections with the transient population than anyone in the four states area. If it's moving in town, Shorty knows about it. He is officially our eyes and ears in the underground." I had to admit, I really liked Shorty, although he could be a bit shady.

"Sounds like a great asset," Katrina said, impressed.

"He was my first informant," I told her. "Actually, he is my only informant. Everyone else works for him. Shorty is also Bob's best friend, so Shorty is family."

"I don't get it, he sounds legit. Why the warning from Bartholomew?" Katrina asked as we made our way towards the front door.

"Shorty drives like a bat out of hell," I told her, not liking my recent hell memories. "Would you do us the honor?" I asked Katrina, pointing at the door. I wasn't even going to try since I knew she could get that thing open faster than any crook in town.

"Oh, he can't be that bad." Katrina said as she bent over to work on the lock.

"You will see," I said and left it at that. She could make up her own mind.

In less than five minutes, Katrina had the door opened. We stepped outside the building and I realized how much I had missed Texas. The weather was warm, but not too hot —perfect for a fall day.

I glanced at Katrina to comment on the weather when she pulled me back.

"Isis, watch out." Katrina still held my arm when a large F-250 truck stopped in the same spot I had just been standing.

"Boss lady, where you been?" Shorty screamed from the driver's side.

"You were saying?" I asked Katrina.

"Never mind. I take it back. He is a menace," Katrina told me, shaking her head.

Shorty ran over to our side with a huge grin on his face. I couldn't blame him for being a speed-demon. I blamed Constantine for giving him a tank to drive around town.

"Ready, boss lady?" Shorty asked. "Who is the beautiful flower with you?" Shorty asked me as he stared at Katrina.

I had to swallow the bile down. Could he be any more pathetic?

Katrina, however, gave him a sweet smile.

"Back off, Shorty." I poked him in the chest. "Don't be fooled by the looks. She could be your mother."

"No worries, boss lady. I like me a cougar." Shorty made some weird growling sound, and I almost smacked his shoulder. Maybe I should have. It might have brought him back to reality.

"Down, puppy. This cougar might cut your throat." Katrina patted his cheek. She walked around him and climbed in the truck.

"Boss lady, I think I'm in love," Shorty told me as he ran back to the driver side.

If Shorty was in love, I was going to be sick. This day just kept getting worse and worse, and it wouldn't end. Things were becoming more surreal by the minute. I gave myself a quick shake and headed towards the truck. I was hoping I could take a nap before I had to run around like a maniac again, but I had a sneaky feeling that wouldn't happen since we were running out of time fast.

Chapter Twenty-One

A drive with Shorty was like taking a roller coaster ride through traffic. He didn't slow down for anything. Shorty treated traffic signs like small suggestions—nothing to be taken seriously. I made the fatal mistake of asking him once why the cops never pulled him over. According to Shorty, since they were all on the same side, they gave him a pass. He kept control of the underground and the cops left him alone, and he thought that was a great deal. Unfortunately, the rest of the citizens probably didn't feel too safe with him on the road.

Shorty got us to Reapers in record time and I was so happy to be home, I didn't even mind when he almost ran over three pedestrians on New Boston Road.

As soon as we got out of the car, Katrina and I headed inside. Constantine gave marching orders to Shorty to start recruiting for Union Station. When the man had a mission, it was even more dangerous. He might run over more people to get it done faster.

Normally, I would give the new guest the full tour of Reapers. Today, though, I was just too tired, so I quickly pointed at the different areas on the first floor. Katrina stopped by the vehicle area and smiled.

"You are right, a 50Cal won't work on this baby," Katrina told me as she pointed at Ladybug.

I smiled back, and we headed to the loft. We walked in to find Bob busy cooking, Constantine shouting orders at his headset, and Bartholomew typing away. It was business as usual. I was so overwhelmed with joy, tears ran down my cheeks.

"Isis, are you okay?" Bob asked when he saw me. He walked over and wrapped an arm around me, holding me away from him so he could inspect me.

"I just missed you guys," I told him as I pulled him in for a huge hug.

"We missed you, too," Bob said, hugging me back. "I told Constantine that it was a bad idea for you to go to hell." Bob didn't release me until I stopped shaking.

"It was a huge waste of time," I replied.

"Wow, you two look like crap," Constantine said from the kitchen counter. When had he moved from the computer area?

"Well, it's nice to see you too," I told him as I let go of Bob. Then, I walked over to Constantine and rubbed his head.

Constantine swatted my hand and said, "Girl, you are about to lose that hand if you don't stop now." I knew he didn't mean it. His threats usually came in the form of a hiss, and he almost sounded playful.

"Mission accomplished. We own Union Station," Bartholomew announced as he made his way towards the kitchen area.

"That fast?" Katrina asked him.

"When money is no problem, you'd be surprised how quickly things get done," Bartholomew answered.

"Great. I'll head over now and meet Shorty with the crew," Bob told us. "Some renovations will need to be done, but we can make it barracks-style and give some of the team a place to live." I could tell Bob's mind was already racing.

"That's a great idea," I told him, wondering why we had never considered doing something like this before.

"First things first. You two need to eat," Bob said as he grabbed two plates of food and set them on the table. "I got you black-bean tamales, rice, and beans from Abuelitas. Horchata for Isis and iced tea for Katrina. Horchata has milk so I figured you wouldn't be drinking it anyways."

As always, Bob thought of everything.

"You remembered," Katrina said as she placed her palm over her chest.

"You were the first vegan person I had ever met. Hard to forget," Bob told her.

Katrina gave Bob a small bow in return.

It was a cute scene, but I was starving. I took my place at the table and started eating. Katrina joined me, and Constantine jumped on the kitchen island and stared at me. Bob waved at everyone and headed out the door. Bartholomew went back to his computer station after making sure I didn't need anything. I felt spoiled, but after three days of running around, I didn't mind.

"I don't understand," Constantine said. "You had a state-of-the-art plane that came with a bed. Why do you look so beat down?"

"It's hard to rest when you are stressing," I told him in between mouthfuls.

"We were trying to plan and develop strategies," Katrina added, trying to help me.

"How did that work out for you two?" Constantine asked, his tone condescending.

"Obviously not very well," I told him. "We lost almost half a day and the only thing we confirmed is that Noah has the princess and that they are in town." I stabbed my tamale, letting some of my anger out.

"Easy, tiger. That poor thing didn't do anything to you," Constantine told me, pointing at my destroyed tamale. "Besides, it wasn't a total loss. Now we can focus our efforts, instead of having you two crossing time zones over and over."

Constantine had a point.

"How hard can it be to find someone in Texarkana?" Katrina asked as she sipped her tea.

Constantine and I looked at each other.

"You'd be surprised how hard it is. Especially if they don't want to be found," I told her, remembering our experience with the witches and the accountant. This could be a nightmare.

"One thing at a time," Constantine told us. "You both need a bath. You stink of Sulfur and who knows what else." Constantine shook his whiskers as he looked at us.

I took a sniff of my clothes and realized he was right. I couldn't believe Bob gave me a hug when I smelled so bad.

"Oh, a bath sounds great, but I can take a quick shower instead. That way Katrina can jump in after me." I knew Katrina had years of training in the field, but I was sure she was ready to get clean.

"No need," Constantine said. "Katrina can use my room. We have baths ready for both of you."

"I made some calls, and we will have our architects and engineers come out next week," Bartholomew announced. "We have plenty of room over at Bob's apartment to build more rooms on that side of the building." Bartholomew pointed at the empty space across from us on our level. The walkways around the perimeter on the second floor were used for running only. I never considered adding more rooms on that side.

"We're becoming a boarding house for Interns. Lovely," Constantine added, shaking his head.

"I like it," I told the boys. "I'm heading to soak. Katrina, when you are done, I'm sure Constantine will show you his room." I had never been inside Constantine's room, but I was too tired to wait for Katrina and check it out.

I put my dish in the sink and headed towards my room with my glass of Horchata. When I flipped my light switch, jazz played from the stereo. I smiled. Bartholomew's little trick would never get old. I wanted to take a detour towards my bed. Knowing how bad I smelled stopped me, though.

When I walked into the bathroom, it smelled like rose petals. I dropped my clothes on the floor, afraid to add them to the dirty clothes. Those things just needed to be burned. I slowly climbed in the hot water and sank in. My muscles instantly relaxed. I hadn't realized how tense and achy I had been until that moment. I closed my eyes and let the hot water soothe my body.

I fell asleep in the tub. No big surprise there. At least it was only for two hours, so the day wasn't wasted. By the time I walked back in my room it was past six. Death sat in my chair, reading a cooking magazine. With Bob being super-chef, I started getting cooking magazines to keep up with him. I was impressed how many recipes and really good articles they had.

"Hi, Death," I told her. Having Death show up in my room was no longer a surprise.

"Hi, Isis. Glad you are back," Death said as she put the magazine down. "How did it go?" Death wore a brown Calvin Klein two-button suit jacket with matching pants. I didn't know how she made everything look good. I had tried a similar outfit for a mission recently and I looked like a librarian turned serial killer.

"I found out you can't trust demons. Not to mention they are condescending and rude." I left out the few chosen words I was actually thinking.

"It is in their nature to feel superior to others," Death answered. "They are the fallen ones, remember. Anything else?"

Death was really good at accepting people and things for who they were, nothing more and nothing less. Constantine was the same in that regard.

"Is it possible for a vampire and an elf to have a child?" I asked Death. That was really driving me nuts.

Death tapped her chin. "It hasn't happened before, but that doesn't mean it is impossible," Death finally told me.

"Elves are special creatures, so their powers can disrupt even the natural laws of the planet." She paused for a few moments. "Isis, this changes everything. If the princess is pregnant, she is in real danger. People will kill for that child. You need to find her first." Death got up from her chair and stepped towards the door.

"When you say people, you mean others besides the vampires and elves?" I had a feeling things had just gotten even more complicated.

"Unfortunately, yes," Death answered from the door. "If the princess is able to carry this child and gives birth, this could change the supernatural world. You are looking at a child more powerful than both the elves and vampires combined. It is in our best interest that Genevieve raises her child, got it?" Death left without waiting for my answer.

Why did everyone want world domination? I rubbed my face and decided it wasn't worth thinking about. I was sticking with plan number one: find the princess. Everything else could wait. I dressed as quickly as possible and rushed back to the loft. Everyone was gone except Constantine.

"What happened to everybody?" I asked him as I headed towards the kitchen.

"Bartholomew is taking inventory of the arms room," Constantine answered before he went back to licking his paws on the back of the leather couch. "He wants to place another order today, so he is checking his supplies. Katrina finally went to shower and hopefully, nap. She was talking to War, who wanted to send a squad of Rangers to help with the search," he added, almost as an afterthought.

"Oh, yeah, that would work. They will blend in perfectly in Texarkana," I told him as I grabbed a nectarine from the fruit basket.

"That's what she told him," Constantine added. "It took a while, but she finally convinced him. Bob is still with Shorty. Eric stopped by and he is working on filing a missing person's report for Noah and Genevieve. Lastly, you got a call from Abuelita. She wants you to stop by," Constantine finished, looking proud of himself.

"Wow, everyone is really busy," I told him, feeling a bit lazy for napping in the tub.

"Girl, please. For the last two days, we have been sitting on our butts waiting for you to call." Constantine shook his head. "It is about time people start working around here. Now go check on Abuelita and see if she has some news. I had given her an update on the situation. Maybe she heard something." Constantine had always been great at giving orders, but I didn't always appreciate them. Today, I couldn't be more grateful.

"On my way, boss." I gave him a quick salute and headed towards the door.

"Isis," Constantine called right as I reached the door. "Glad you are back."

I smiled. He wasn't a sensitive type, so what he had just said was huge for him.

"I'm glad to be back," I said as I walked out the door.

Chapter Twenty-Two

I drove to Abuelitas and was amazed when I saw the parking lot full, which was strange for a Tuesday night. A line of people waited at the door and cars were lined up around the building. I parked in the only empty place, and it was almost parallel to the road.

Abuelita's restaurant was named Abuelitas and was located on Highway 82 in Nash. It was less than a five-minute drive from Reapers, which made it an easy stop for TexMex food. Abuelitas was also the only restaurant that openly catered to the supernatural community. Which meant the regulars were a mixed crowd. I used to be a waitress at Abuelitas when I first got to town. Now I just helped out when she needed me. With my salary at Reapers, I didn't need the extra income.

I walked around the back of the restaurant, avoiding the angry line of people outside. I didn't want the poor people to think I was cutting. The backdoor to the restaurant led directly to the kitchen. Abuelita's kitchen was almost bigger than the dining area because she took pride in her space. There were always more pots on the stove than any five-star restaurant could manage.

"Isis, what took you so long?" Abuelita asked as soon as I made my way around the stove.

"I fell asleep in the tub. Long day." No need to lie, Abuelita knew exactly what I did.

"I heard. Are you okay?" she asked, putting down the large spoon she was using to mix a pot of beans.

"I'm fine. Maybe my ego is a bit wounded," I told her as I started mixing her pot of chicken tortilla soup. Her soup smelled so good, at times it made me rethink the idea of no meat eating.

"How can your ego possibly be hurt?" Abuelita asked. She gave me a quick inspection with her eyes and then went back to mixing.

"I don't know. I figured that after a year, I would be better at this job," I admitted. "Somehow, I thought we would go down to hell, find this boy, and be done with this mess," I told her as we moved closer to the front of the restaurant.

"You went to hell?" Gabe asked from the bar area. "Please tell me you are kidding," he added.

Gabe was our resident angel. Tall and handsome with fabulous blond hair and gorgeous eyes. Once I found out the boy was an angel, my poor crush died a horrible death.

"I wish," I told him as I walked over.

"Well, look who decided to join the party," Angelito said from my right side.

Abuelita had added a drive-thru window to the restaurant, and Angelito managed both the register and the drive-thru.

"I know I'm hot, but you don't have to stare," Angelito told me. "How about giving us a hand since you are here?"

I wouldn't admit it out loud, and hated to admit it even in my mind, but Angelito was hot.

Angelito was Abuelita's grandson and her pride and joy. He was about six foot one, one-hundred-and-eighty pounds of solid muscle, had dark hair, hazel eyes, and the most flirtatious smile I'd ever seen. Unfortunately, he knew the affect he had on girls—a fact that always gotten him in trouble. I was only a few years older than he was, but I had a hard time seeing him as an adult. Angelito fell in the same category as Bartholomew: a younger brother.

I glanced around the place and it was wild. "Where do you need me?" I asked him. When family needed helped, you just rolled up your sleeves and jumped in.

"If you could take orders from the people waiting in line outside, that would be a huge help," Angelito told me as he pointed at the door. "Ana is working the dining area."

I looked over Gabe's shoulder and found Ana working the registers. Ana was one of my favorite people in town. She was a five-foot-four brunette in her late twenties, but somehow still managed to look younger than me. She was cute and probably the friendliest person I had ever met. Ana and her boyfriend were the only humans that worked here.

I waved to her over the crowd and she waved back. I couldn't believe it, but I felt at home when I grabbed a pen and paper and headed out the bar door to take orders.

"It's about time you got here. We missed you," Ana told me as I walked by her. We did our ritual hip-bump as I passed her.

"Been traveling the country," I told her with a wink.

Ana smiled and headed towards the kitchen area. I was impressed how well she adjusted to being the only human working with so many supernatural creatures.

I gave the crowd my sweetest smile and started taking orders. Luckily, some of the people in line wanted their order to go. I wasn't sure why they didn't do the drive-thru, but I was afraid to ask. There was an air around some of them and I was tempted to use my third eye to check. I crushed that idea quickly after remembering my last experience with the vampires. Last thing Abuelita needed was me going all psycho and chopping her clients to pieces.

Time moves fast when working hard. We had less than twenty-four hours and I was praying for a miracle. I took careful inventory of everyone I saw, hoping to find Noah, but no luck. After an hour of taking orders, the place had finally settled to a more manageable pace, so I left Ana to handle the floor. She really didn't need me anymore.

"Where did all these people come from?" I asked when I headed behind the bar again, not directing my question to anyone specific.

"According to grandma, we should thank you for the booming business," Angelito answered.

"Me? How?" Angelito always blamed me for all crazy things that happened in Texarkana. Some were my fault, but I wasn't sure how this weird phenomenon had anything to do with me.

"He is technically right," Gabe jumped in.

That was odd. He never agreed with Angelito, which meant I was in trouble.

"How?" I asked again, this time giving him my evil stare.

"Down girl," Gabe told me, raising his hands in a sign of surrender. "This is what happens when a town becomes a Haven. Technically, you're the reason that people are moving in by the truck-load." Gabe glanced at the crowd.

"Are any of them humans?" I was hoping most of them were, or the number of people I was going to be responsible for had grown exponentially.

"Some, but not many," Abuelita said from behind me. I jumped. I hadn't even heard her walk up.

"It has been a long time since we had a Haven in North America. The word spread very quickly," Gabe said with a smile. "I'm proud of you, Isis. A lot of them are refugees looking for a safe place."

"Don't give me that much credit," I told Gabe, feeling a bit ashamed. "I had no idea what a Haven was until Saturday, so it wasn't like this happened on purpose." My hair had come lose from my ponytail, so I tried to fix it— anything to keep my hands busy.

"Would you have moved if Constantine told you about it?" Abuelita asked as she gave me a careful look.

My eyes went to the ceiling as I thought about that. "No, I guess I wouldn't."

"In that case, this is your doing," Abuelita told me and kissed my forehead. "We are here to help. You are not alone. Constantine said you are starting a registration center for all the new people. I'm letting him use the restaurant in the mornings. I figure it will feel safe for everyone and nobody will question all the people coming and going." Abuelita gave me a quick hug before heading back to her stoves.

I had to hold back the tears of joy. "Thank you, Abuelita," I told her, my voice low.

"Honey, we are family. You know that."

"Well, that is one problem solved," I told the group. "Now we just need to find Noah and the princess," I added, my voice losing all remnants of hope.

"What does he look like?" asked Angelito from the window.

"Hang on. I have a picture." I pulled my phone out and showed the group.

"Hey, he was here this afternoon," Angelito said with a bright smile.

"How could you possibly remember him after all the people you've seen today?" Gabe asked. I had been about to ask the same question, but he'd beaten me to it.

"Easy. He was waiting at the door when I opened this afternoon," he answered with another brilliant smile. "Hard to forget him. He paid with a brand-new Benjamin and looked spastic. He also ordered food for at least five people." Angelito went back to taking orders at the drive-thru.

"Well, at least we know he is in town and hopefully, hasn't left again." That was the best news I had heard all day.

"He is not going anywhere," Abuelita added. "If everyone is looking for him, Haven is his only safe place."

Hopefully, she was right. It would make things so much easier.

I said my goodbyes and headed home. My tub nap was great, but it hadn't helped as much as I thought, and I was crashing fast. I needed a good night's rest or I'd never be able to think straight. We could start fresh tomorrow.

Chapter Twenty-Three

It was a blessing that by the time I got back to Reapers the loft was empty. I grabbed a glass of milk and headed to my room. I admired Katrina for not drinking milk. That girl had a huge amount of willpower. I would probably die if I went vegan. With Bartholomew having a gluten intolerance and me not eating meat, our meals consisted of everything covered in cheese. Veganism would make my lifestyle very difficult.

I woke up before five and I felt incredible. My body rhythm was still off from all the jumping around, but after seven full hours of sleep in my own bed, I felt like I could conquer the world. I got dressed and went out for a short run. I missed the feel of the wind in my face. Plus, I just loved fall in Texas. You could still wear shorts and not freeze to death when you stopped running.

I made it back to Reapers before six feeling pretty good about myself. I walked into the main floor and found Katrina beating up the punching-bags like they were terrorists. I was afraid to ask what crime the poor bag had committed. To avoid her wrath, I strolled towards her, making as much noise as possible. I wanted to make sure Katrina heard me coming and I wasn't sneaking up on her. Last thing I needed was Wonder Woman unleashing her powers on me. I was afraid Katrina would shoot first and ask questions later.

"Is it dead yet?" I asked her as I approached.

"Almost," she replied without looking.

Katrina gave the poor thing a round house that was impressive. I made a mental note never to get in a kickboxing match with her. She was lethal.

"Now it's dead." She snickered.

"How high can you kick?" I asked her, keeping my distance.

"About this high," Katrina said as she demonstrated. It was not fair. She could deliver a perfect kick to face level without struggling.

"You are dangerous," I told her.

"Not enough if my boss thinks I need a squad of Rangers for back-up." She started punching the bag again.

"Are you sure that's it?" I asked her before I walked around her and took a seat on the weight bench.

"What else could it be?" Katrina asked without looking at me.

"Did you tell War that Noah was in Haven and that I'm in charge of it?" I asked her casually.

"Yeah, I gave him the details in my daily report..." Katrina trailed off and met my eyes. "What are you trying to tell me?"

"You know as well as I do that the Horsemen have a very weird relationship, almost competitive." I started telling her. "Isn't it convenient that War wants to send more of his troops here once he finds out his top General has permission to enter their only restricted area? Think about it, Katrina. How would it look if War is the one to stop this mess in Death's territory? That's bragging rights forever. He won't let her forget the Dark Ages." I stretched my shoulder as I spoke. Being next to Katrina was making me feel lazy.

"That is twisted but so like him." Katrina took a deep breath and came over to me, then she took a seat on the ground and faced me. "Am I overreacting?" Katrina asked me.

"Yes, and I understand," I told her. "I'm sure he is still upset with you, but he is not going to send you to hell. He would have done that already. He is trying to maximize this situation. Trust me, Pestilence does it all the time with Eugene."

"We are just their pawns," Katrina told me.

"It's not personal, just the job description of an Intern. Why do you think we get paid so well?" I replied, and we both laughed.

Our celebration was cut short when Eric came rushing through the pedestrian doors. He was so focused he didn't even see us as he ran up the stairs. I gave Katrina a quick look.

"That's not a good sign. Let's go," I told her, and we both ran after Eric.

By the time we reached the loft, Eric was pacing back and forth. I was surprised to find the boys up already. Granted, they all still wore their pajamas, but at least they were awake.

"Eric, slow down and repeat everything you just said," Constantine told Eric as we walked in. Constantine stood on the kitchen table watching Eric. "Some of us don't 'habla crazy.'"

From what I could tell, Constantine was the only one that looked fully awake and he still couldn't follow Eric. Not a good sign.

Bob and Bartholomew were in the kitchen. As we went in, he handed Katrina a large mug of coffee, then he gave Bartholomew and me cups of hot chocolate. I did a double take to make sure Bartholomew was actually wearing a Onesie. Yes, he was, and he was rocking that thing. It even had the footie-sock-thing.

When I looked back, Eric was taking some quick breaths, probably to calm down. He turned in our direction and his mouth dropped when he saw Katrina. After spending the last few days with her, I was used to boys drooling over her. Katrina was awesome. She gave Eric her best Farrah Fawcett wave and the poor boy almost swooned.

"Eric, today. Focus, boy," Constantine yelled at him.

I grinned. For some reason, I loved watching Constantine yell at others. Probably because he was always yelling at me and it was nice to have a break.

"I'm sorry," Eric said, his eyes still on Katrina.

"Hi, I'm Katrina. I'm War's Intern and I'm old enough to be your mother." Katrina knew how to crush a man's dream.

Bartholomew and I worked hard not to laugh.

"Really?" Eric asked, confused.

Katrina just nodded and smiled. I had no idea which part he was asking confirmation for.

"Now that we've settled that, get to the point, Eric," Constantine growled.

"Sorry," Eric said as he ran his hands through his hair. "We got problems. A group of vampires checked into the hotel at the convention center last night. They have taken the entire top floor." Eric had his hands on his hips when he finished. He was doing his Peter Pan pose.

"Which convention center?" Bob asked.

"The one on the Arkansas side," Eric replied.

"How many convention centers do you have?" Katrina asked us.

"Two. One on the Texas side and one on the Arkansas side," Bartholomew added. "Don't ask why. We are still confused about that." Katrina smiled at Bartholomew when he finished. He really did look adorable in his onesie.

"That's the other problem," Eric continued.

"We have more problems?" I asked him. Eric sure knew how to ruin a morning.

"An elf delegation checked into the other hotel at the other convention center." Eric started pacing the room again.

"That took them a while," Constantine told us. "I was expecting them yesterday."

"Why yesterday?" Katrina asked before I could.

"We figured out both groups were tracking the jet," Bartholomew told us. "As soon as you made it to hell, Constantine told the pilots to head home. So, the only logical location for them to pick up your trail again was here," Bartholomew finished with a grin.

"Why wouldn't they follow the plane?" Katrina asked.

"Our pilots and the jet are stationed at Miami," Constantine added. "Most influential people in the supernatural community know that information. As soon as the plane headed back to Florida, they probably stopped tracking it." Constantine took his favorite Sphinx pose.

"Do you think this means they know we are here?" I asked Constantine.

"It is hard to tell," he answered. "If they just got here, they are probably getting their spies in place to search their area." By his tone, I could tell Constantine was not happy.

"It sounds like we should save them the trouble," I told the group. "It's time to remind our guests this is Haven and they'd better behave." I gave Constantine a wicked grin.

"It's about time we go on the offense. Just try not to turn every vampire into dust," Constantine told me. "It doesn't foster good will if you kill them all."

Constantine made a great point. Which meant I needed to do something to control my third eye.

"Okay, what am I missing here?" Eric asked, looking lost.

"Isis is only able to see the vampires' true forms," Katrina told him. "From what I gathered, it's horrible and she goes straight into fight mode. Last one that got near her she cut to pieces and he evaporated into a cloud of ash."

Did she need to give him that much detail?

"Ouch. Vicious," Eric told me.

"You have no idea how hideous and evil they look," I said, trying to defend myself.

"True," Constantine added. "The younger they are, the more monster-like they are. The older ones almost look human, though, so be careful," he said the last part almost like a threat.

"Random question number fifty-five," Katrina said, raising her hand. At least she knew how to get the attention of a group. "Aren't people going to notice all these weird strangers in town?" Katrina asked us.

That was a good point, and one I hadn't even thought about.

"I doubt it," Eric replied. All eyes went to him as we waited for him to continue. "Thanks to Constantine's Halloween parade, the city is packed with all sorts of weird, freaky people. They will fit right in." Eric narrowed his eyes at Constantine.

"No need to give me that look," Constantine said, as sweet as pie. "The new coven in town wanted to make a Halloween celebration and asked about the parade. Now that we have close ties to the Order, I figured it would be a great peace offering," Constantine finished.

"Is that the only reason?" I asked Constantine, not believing this noble gesture of his.

"And they have a giant float of him," Bartholomew added under his breath.

"Now I believe that part," I told him.

"How could I punish them for having great taste?" he asked. "You should see the float. It's almost identical to me. I've never seen anything like it. Well, unless I look in the mirror, that is." He started purring like a mad cat.

"Well, that's my cue to leave," I told the boys. "Katrina, would you like to join me in welcoming our new guests to Haven?" I figured Katrina had enough anger inside that she could hurt anyone.

"It would be my pleasure," Katrina replied with an evil smile.

I was glad she was on my side.

"Eric, please keep us posted if you find anything else on Noah," I told him.

"I will," Eric told me. "Isis, be careful. These are powerful beings." Eric frowned.

I just smiled back at him. No sense in him worrying. I was worried enough for the both of us already.

"Now that we settled that, we'll run and take a shower before making our house call," I told the boys.

Katrina and I headed towards the bedrooms. I stopped in the middle of the hallway, feeling like an idiot.

"Katrina, I'm so sorry. I should have offered earlier. I have a closet full of clothes you can pick from," I told her, trying not to sound creepy.

"Thanks, Isis, but it's all good," Katrina told me as she headed towards Constantine's room. "Bartholomew contacted my team when we went to hell. They mailed him my clothes and other gear. He thinks of everything," Katrina said, more than impressed.

"He is good like that," I told her. "Okay. See you in a few." I entered my room and got ready for the day.

Chapter Twenty-Four

Katrina and I took Ladybug to the convention center on the Texas-side. The Hilton Garden Inn Hotel was attached to the convention center and from what I'd heard, the chef in the restaurant was world class. I wondered why the vampires didn't pick this one instead.

When we went inside, Katrina used her gorgeous looks to get the whereabouts of the elves from the front desk boy. I felt bad for him. He didn't have a chance at resisting her. It was almost painful to watch.

According to Katrina's new fan, a group of elves was hanging out by the pool outside. We made our way towards the pool, admiring the décor of the place. It was a lovely place as far as hotels went. By the time we reached the pool, we found Iason chilling beside the water, sitting with an elder version of himself.

"They take their sunbathing seriously," I joked with Katrina.

"Tell me about it," Katrina replied. "Looking at them makes me want to go on a diet," she added.

She had a point. The pool was surrounded by beautiful people. Counting Iason, the other guy in the chair next to him, and the bodyguards, there were at least seven elves in the pool area and they all looked amazing. I also noticed we had more trees around this part of town. That reminded me, I needed to check the area around Reapers for our trees. I was hoping they were back as well.

"By the way. I have been meaning to ask, where are their pointed ears?" I whispered.

"You will only see it with your third eye, but I don't recommend it," Katrina replied in a low tone. "Their true forms can be as overwhelming as the vampires, but not for the same reason."

I made a mental note not to look at them with my third eye. I wasn't ready for more overwhelming visions.

"What a surprise to find you all here in town," I told the group in my loudest voice as we walked up to them. The five elves standing around all tensed up. It made me curious to see what kind of weapons they were carrying under those fancy jackets.

"We are enjoying the Texas climate," Iason said with a smile. At least he wasn't in full glamour mode. "We were told it's fabulous this time of year. What do you think, Father?" Iason asked the man sitting next to him.

I had to do a double take to make sure I wasn't imagining things. The elven king was gorgeous, and way younger than I imagined. I was expecting some old, crippled guy who could barely move. This king looked like he had just stepped off of a runway and graced us with his presence. No wonder humans fell prey to these beings. They play with our emotions. Who could resist them?

"Not bad at all for almost November," the king replied with a sexy voice that made you think of Elvis Presley. That was too weird and definitely not fair. "How could we help you ladies?" he asked us.

"Oh, we don't need anything, sir. We were in the neighborhood and decided to come over and personally welcome you to Haven," I said in my sweetest voice. "We weren't expecting you," I added, just in case they missed the sarcasm in my voice. I didn't want them to think I was glad to see them.

"You hadn't checked in, so we decided to visit," the king said in a condescending tone.

"I wasn't aware I was supposed to check in," I told him, putting my hands on my hips. I could play sassy with the best of people. "Did you get that message, Katrina?" I asked her in my calmest voice.

"Not at all," Katrina replied, not bothering to look at the elves. "I was under the impression we had three days. Last time I checked, we still have the rest of today." The last part Katrina directed at the elves.

"We are talking about the safety of my daughter. I will not leave that in the hands of children," the elf king told us. I felt like he was staring down at us. How was that possible when he was sitting down?

"That's funny. Last time we spoke you didn't think your daughter was in any danger," I told the king. He could play concerned dad with someone else.

"The safety of my daughter was the reason we started all this," the king said to me. "I recommend you find her quickly. If the vampires get their claws in her, we will destroy everything in our path to get her back." His eyes were wide and crazy, and he rolled his hands into fists.

"Let me remind you, sir, that you are now in Haven and not in your own territory," I told the king, putting as much strength into my words as I could muster. "I recommend you follow the rules of Haven and stay on your best behavior. I will do everything in my power to protect the citizens of this city. Don't force my hand or I will make you an example of what Death's wrath is like." I had no clue if I could carry that threat out, so I was hoping they wouldn't try me.

"Young lady, those are some bold words," the king told me. "Are you planning to enforce the same rules with everyone?" He angled his head up towards me and crossed his arms over his chest.

"Trust me. Your buddies down the road will be getting the same speech shortly." I was pretty sure he knew the vampires were in town.

"As long as the rules apply to all, it will be our honor to follow them," the king said, bowing his head. "Now, I recommend you hurry and find my daughter." He turned his face to take in the sun again.

Iason gave us a little wave and winked at me. He almost looked proud of me. Elves were strange beings. I gave Katrina a look and we left the pool area. Based on the king's behavior, we had been dismissed.

Katrina and I headed back towards Ladybug, neither of us saying a word. I wasn't sure how many people were reporting back to the king and I didn't want to take any chances. We made it back to Ladybug in time to see Shorty pulling up next to us.

"Boss-lady, big Bob said I would find you here." He jumped out of the truck.

"Why didn't you just call me?" I asked him.

"And miss seeing your lovely face this morning? Never," he replied, but he wasn't really talking to me. No, he stared hard at Katrina.

I shook my head. "Well, Shorty, here I am," I told him, waving a hand in front of his face to get his attention. "What do you need?"

"Right." He shook himself and turned my way. "We found our guy," I wondered when poor Noah became public enemy number one to the underground.

"Are you sure? Where?" I asked Shorty. We never found people this quickly. I was amazed. I gave Katrina a surprised look.

"We added extra people around the downtown area, now that the gates of hell have relocated there," Shorty told us like it was a natural thing to have an elevator to hell in his neighborhood. "A couple of the ladies saw a guy that matches his description entering the lofts downtown." He beamed, tucking his thumbs in the pockets of his jeans.

"Which lofts, Shorty? Downtown is exploding with those things now." I wondered if lofts were the new rental term.

Nobody called the housing downtown an apartment anymore. They were lofts, plain and simple.

"The City Hall ones," he replied. "We can't guarantee if he is still there, but he went in last night."

"That's a great start, Shorty," Katrina told him sweetly.

He grinned, and I thought he might fly away under her praise.

"Are you up for a little detour?" I asked Katrina.

"Best lead we've had," Katrina answered. "It's not like the vamps are planning to do any sightseeing during the day."

"Wait. We have vampires in town?" Shorty asked, looking around nervously.

"Yes. They are staying at the other convention center," I told him. "Make sure to warn everyone you have in that area and pull back at night. I don't want any accidents happening." I really didn't want any of our people to fall for their tricks and end up becoming someone's dinner.

"Boss lady, that's too easy." Shorty grinned. "Anyone we need to worry about in this one?" He pointed at the hotel.

"We got elves in that one," I told him. "They are just as dangerous as the vampires. Make sure people watch, but do not engage. Got it?" Most people never paid the transient population a lot of attention. I didn't want them to become collateral damage in case a war broke out in town. For the Reaper team, they were family.

"Boss-lady, are you going to be okay?" Shorty asked, concern etched into his tone.

"I got Super Soldier with me." I pointed at Katrina. "I'm pretty sure she can take them."

Katrina gave Shorty another million-dollar smile and he took a step back.

"If the boss-lady is looking at you for back-up, it means you are a bad ass," Shorty told Katrina. "Cause the boss lady is as tough as they come. I can't mess with you. You could kill me with a spoon." He gave Katrina a quick bow and headed back to his truck. "Call if you need me, boss lady!" he yelled right before he took off.

"I knew you were pretty tough, but how bad ass are you?" Katrina asked me. "If being told that I'm tougher than you makes me hard to date, you are the Queen B."

"Get in the car before I leave you here," I told her, and she started laughing.

If she could make jokes again, I knew she was at least in a better mood. However, I wasn't sure I liked the jokes when they were at my expense.

Chapter Twenty-Five

The drive to downtown from the Hilton's convention center was an easy one. At this time of the day, most people were at work or school. Texarkana also didn't have a traffic problem. We just had crazy drivers that refused to follow traffic signs, and Shorty was the main culprit. The way people were driving today, I wondered if Shorty had opened a driving school in town and nobody told me.

I had Katrina call Bartholomew for me on our way to the City Hall lofts. I wanted him to check the records of the building for anything unusual and find out who the current residents were. I was pretty sure Noah didn't have friends or family in town.

It took us less than ten minutes to get to the loft. The building was located right behind City Hall on the Texas side. I wasn't sure why anyone was nervous of downtown. That part of town had more cops roaming the area than anywhere else, a fact that made me jittery. Last thing we needed was to get arrested for trespassing.

Since Ladybug stuck out a little too much for me to park in front of the loft, Katrina and I parked behind the TRAHC building and walked over. We made our way to the building as casually as possible. Katrina looked around, pretending to be a tourist. I knew better, and I could tell she was memorizing the area in case a quick escape was needed. We made it to one of the side doors of the loft building, hoping we hadn't attracted too much attention.

"Boss lady," a male voice I didn't recognize called from across the street. Katrina and I had to struggle to see him. The guy came from the shadows of the building and made his way towards us.

"He is good at camouflage. That boy should be in the army," Katrina told me under her breath.

I had to agree with her. Our informant was great at hiding.

"Hi. Do you have anything to report?" Shorty had given me a specific script to follow when I interacted with his team. I made sure to stick by it. It made them feel better. I thought it was a bit crazy, but who was I to judge.

"Our guy came in last night," our informant said after he crossed the street and joined us. He was average height and build. Nothing distinct to make him stick out in a crowd. I knew the dirty clothes and greasy hair were a disguise since he smelled of Dove soap. Bob had very strict rules for those who worked for him. "I have been watching this door on and off. We were supposed to get more people to watch the other side, but right now we are short due to the new mission."

Hell's door was starting to affect our information flow.

"Did you see anybody else with him?" I asked our stealth informant.

"Nobody, boss lady," he answered, his eyes roaming. "A few of the ladies saw him walking down Texas Boulevard yesterday afternoon, but he was alone then, too. Should we be looking for someone else?" he asked me in a concerned tone.

"Yeah. He should be traveling with a pretty girl, probably blonde, maybe around my height," I told him, and he studied me carefully. Those were vague descriptions, but I had no idea in what condition the princess was in.

"I will pass the word around, boss lady," he told me.

I knew the whole underground would be looking for the girl hanging out with Noah. At least they only had orders to observe, otherwise poor Noah would be going down. He had better pray we don't tell them to attack.

"Thank you. Great work," I told the informant. "We are going in to check it out. If you see anything strange heading our way, call me." Last thing I wanted was to be trapped in a loft downtown with creepy demon-worshippers.

"Will do, boss lady." Our informant crossed the street and disappeared back into his hiding place.

"Oh yeah. That takes skills," Katrina told me. "If he needs another job, I'll take him. And I mean that, too."

"Good luck taking any of them away from Shorty," I told her. "He is a better recruiter than the cigarette companies," I admitted.

It was true. Shorty had a talent like nobody else to get people to follow him into crazy schemes. Which explained how he managed to get people to volunteer to guard the gates of hell.

"I can take him," Katrina joked.

I had to smile. I would pay good money to see a fight between those two. Shorty was a tricky one.

That got me thinking. I pulled my phone out and called Bartholomew, hoping he had some good news for us. "Bart, we are here," I told him when he answered. "Please tell me you got something." I was hoping our boy-genius extraordinaire wouldn't let me down.

"You have one apartment empty right now, 2C on the second floor," Bartholomew informed me. "Everything else has been filled for over six months. Nobody has any supernatural connections and nothing unusual in their homes." That was a good sign and helped narrow our options.

"Sounds like a great place to start. Thanks, Bart," I told him.

"Okay. Call me back and let me know what you find," Bartholomew said before he hung up. He didn't even wait for me to agree. I really needed to talk to him about manners.

"Well, 2C is our destination," I told Katrina. "The door is all yours." I pointed at the door handle.

"Too easy," Katrina replied.

Katrina walked over to the door and pulled out her little pouch of tools. I followed her and then leaned against the wall, looking as innocent as possible. I wondered how many doors Katrina had picked in her life, because she was really good at this. In less than three minutes, she had the door unlocked and was heading inside. I followed her like we were on our way to her place.

Katrina rushed up the stairs and headed straight for 2C, but I took my time inspecting all the other doors in case someone decided to join us in the hallway. By the time I made it to Katrina, she had the door unlocked and opened.

"Has anyone ever mentioned to you that you are a menace to society?" I told Katrina jokingly.

"My soldiers tell me that every day," she replied.

I followed her inside and found a pretty nice size loft. Unfortunately, the place was deserted other than a single sleeping bag shoved against the far wall and an empty container of food from Abuelitas.

"That's odd. Where is the rest of the food?" I asked Katrina.

"What food?" Katrina asked me, looking around the large room.

"Angelito told me Noah had ordered enough food for five people," I told her. "This container is just for one. Why would he keep this and not the others?" I asked her, pointing at the container.

"Isis, I don't know if I want to know what you are thinking," Katrina told me, scrunching her face when she looked at me.

"It's just curious," I said, holding back a little. I would hate to scare her with my theories.

"Go ahead, tell me. I'm afraid I'm thinking the same thing," Katrina finally said.

"You do agree this is odd, that mousy, little Noah can be man-handling a trained soldier by himself, right?" I said, hoping Katrina would confirm my suspicion.

"Yes. It is almost impossible," Katrina admitted.

"What if he had her drugged?" I added. "You heard that creep Ralph mumbling about sleep. It's the only thing that fits. Noah couldn't carry a grown woman alone. Who is helping him? Who was he buying all the food for and where are they keeping Genevieve?" The questions poured out of me so fast I couldn't keep up with them all.

"You know if we had all the answers to those questions, we wouldn't be standing in this empty loft by ourselves," Katrina said, opening her arms wide and gesturing to the room.

"True," I told her, rubbing my eyes with my palms. "I just hate this feeling that we are three steps behind."

"I agree with you but stressing about things we can't control is not going to help us," Katrina told me. "We just need to find him before they move again."

I pulled out my phone and called Bartholomew.

"Any luck?" Bartholomew asked.

"Besides a sleeping bag, the place is empty," I told him, my voice pouty and pathetic.

"Well, you'd better hurry. I got some news from Constantine." Bartholomew was a little too serious for my taste. "The witches reminded him that the borders between the worlds will be thin tonight due to Halloween. This will make it easier for things to cross over to our world."

"Thanks, Bart. No pressure at all," I told him.

"You got this," Bartholomew added with way too much energy. At least he had confidence in me. "I'll keep scanning the police monitors and cameras around town.

I'll let you know if I find anything. Good luck out there." This time I didn't wait for him to hang up. Instead, I disconnected the call as soon as he finished talking.

"More good news?" Katrina asked me.

"The usual. Supernatural barrier between the worlds will be thin tonight so we need to make sure nothing crazy happens," I told her, trying to imitate Bartholomew's voice.

"Wow. Here I was thinking nothing ever happens in Texarkana," Katrina told me.

"As I was told, that was true until I moved in." That didn't make me proud, either. For all I knew, I was responsible for the drop in the price of real estate here.

"I believe that," Katrina replied, smiling. I was glad she could smile at everything. "Did I ever tell you the last time I was in Texarkana?" she asked me, looking around the loft.

"Why were you here?" I couldn't even imagine that.

"I was inspecting the Depot," Katrina said, lost in her thoughts. "That was over twenty years ago. The downtown, of course, is still about the same, but everything else has grown and expanded. I never would have imagined that," Katrina told me.

"I'm glad it has, and I would like to keep it that way," I told her.

"In that case, let's visit some vamps," Katrina said, facing the door. "Lead the way, sheriff." She had jokes today. Heck, I had a feeling she had jokes every day.

I shook my head but led us out of the apartment. Katrina locked the place back up and we headed to visit our favorite vampires at the Arkansas-side convention center. We had too many creepy beings in town all at once. Texarkana was about to have a Halloween they would remember for ages.

Chapter Twenty-Six

House call number two was Vampires-R-Us at the Holiday Inn Express Convention Center. I had never been to the hotel before. The closest I got was when I had to pick up a few souls that got lost at the attached water park. I didn't know what had been worse: the kids screaming because of the ghost or the ghost screaming about the kids. They just kept feeding the frenzy. It took me over three hours of chasing the poor souls around the park. It was so loud, I couldn't command them to stop, so I finally tackled one to the ground. Thankfully, Bartholomew had disabled the park's security cameras, because according to him, watching me running around in circles had been hysterical.

"Are you ready for this?" Katrina asked me.

We had been sitting in the parking lot of the hotel for at least five minutes. I had checked all my pockets ten times. My scythe was inside my cargo pocket for easy access, but I was nervous. I wasn't sure which part scared me more: facing the dark side of the vampires, or that it didn't bother me killing them. My stomach churned and I felt nauseous. I had to swallow several times before I could speak.

"I guess," I told Katrina, staring at my hands.

"Here. Wear these." Katrina handed me her aviator sunglasses.

"Thanks, I guess," I told her, not sure why she gave them to me.

"They won't be able to see your eyes through the glass," she told me. "They will also help you avoid making eye contact with them and going serial killer on their asses."

I shrugged, not thinking her theory would work, but I also had nothing to lose by trying it.

"I hope you are right," I told her as I put her sunglasses on. I got a quick look in the mirror and realized Katrina's glasses were stylish. They even made me look good. "Let's do this before I chicken out," I said, hiding behind her bad-girl sunglasses.

We walked in the hotel like we owned the place. The layout of most hotels was easy to navigate, but to make sure we didn't look out of place, we had Bartholomew send us the blueprints. We walked by the reception desk and waved at the young lady on duty. She gave us a cheerful smile and waved back.

"Do we need to have Bart disable the cameras?" I asked Katrina as we reached the elevator.

"No need," she replied. "I'm pretty sure our buddies took care of that already. They are not interested in having a record of their people coming and going." Katrina sounded pretty sure of herself and I hoped she was right. The last thing I wanted was to make the front page of the Texarkana Gazette or the most views at the TXKTODAY for going nuts on the vampires. I was sure Death would kill me if the headlines read "Reapers Employee Goes on Killing Spree."

"Last chance to change your mind. I can go alone if you want," she said, giving me an out.

"I can't hide in my own town. It doesn't give the impression of a tough sheriff," I told her.

"That's my girl," Katrina replied and stepped in the elevator as soon as the doors opened.

The elevator ride was too short, and we arrived on the last floor of the hotel to find it very dark. I looked around the hallway and all the curtains were shut. Most of the hallway lights were off, and with my sexy-aviator glasses on, everything had a creepy glow to it. We made our way to the exclusive suites at the far end of the hotel. I was hoping to reach the door and just knock. Instead, we found two huge linebackers standing guard in front of the door.

"At least we know we are in the right place," Katrina told me before strolling over towards the guards. I followed slowly behind, keeping my eyes low to the floor.

"Hi, boys. We are here to see your boss," Katrina told them in a bubbly voice as she stopped in front of the linebackers. "He is expecting us."

"His emperor is not expecting any visitors at this time," tall, mean, and muscular on the left said. I couldn't get a clear look at his face, but his body was huge.

"Get lost," the second one added. He was also huge, but maybe a smidge smaller than his buddy.

"Not without talking to your boss," Katrina told muscle-tag-team.

"I. Said. Get. Lost," number two repeated, this time enunciating all of his words. Did he think we had a learning problem?

"Oh, cut it, pretty face. Your mind tricks don't work on us," Katrina told him. "Tell your boss the dynamic-Interns are here, and we are not leaving without talking to him." She sounded sweet but stern as she came up beside me, raising her brows in question.

"I'm good. Just busy counting the patterns on the carpet," I told her with a smile. "Why are they not moving?" I asked her in a softer tone.

"They can communicate telepathically with their masters," Katrina answered, not taking her eyes off the twins. "The older ones need very little sleep. Which in turn gives them the power to sustain their children during the day. I'm pretty sure this entire floor is packed with vamps," she told me.

I couldn't help it, I shivered. We needed to get out of there before I flipped out.

"The emperor will see you now," linebacker on the left said. "You have five minutes. Don't make us drag you out," he growled.

"You wish," Katrina replied as we walked in the room.

The suite was gorgeous. Just as I was about to take my sunglasses off and inspect the room more thoroughly, my eyes were drawn to the two figures sitting on armchairs in the middle of the room.

"Ladies, what a surprise," the male on the right told us. I glanced in his direction and my eyes were drawn to his face. Somehow, I avoided the eye contact, but the pull was almost irresistible.

"I'm impressed, little one. You are stronger than I thought," the man told me.

Great, another creep trying to push his powers on me, I thought.

"Let me guess. You are the emperor," I told him. I inched forward, putting me right in front of Katrina, and I felt her tense as I took my glasses off. I couldn't afford to look weak, though. I wanted to protect my city. "I'll make this quick. You are now in Haven and I expect you will follow the rules of the land. You know the consequences for disobeying," I told the emperor, staring him in the eyes.

It was the strangest thing I ever saw. He looked human, but he also shifted to his beast form. Not for long, it was a quick effect. It was like watching a flip book as someone turned the pages. The quick changes were starting to give me a headache, but at least I wasn't terrified. His human body was handsome, mature, and absolutely elegant. If it wasn't for the monster popping out, he looked the part of the emperor. He studied me as much as I studied him.

"I'm impressed. You have incredible self-control," the emperor told me. "You were right about her, Arthur. She is different," the emperor told the other guy sitting next to him.

I did a quick take to confirm it was his heir sitting next to him. Arthur gave me a small smile.

The emperor cleared his throat. "As impressive as you might be, I don't like being threatened."

"Not a threat, sir," I told him, acting as professional as possible. "We had a deal, and I still have at least eight hours left. So, the fact that you are in my town with an army of vampires can't be a coincidence. I run this place and I will do everything in my power to protect it. You are welcome to stay as long as you keep your kids in check." I put my hands on my hips and narrowed my eyes a bit. No way would I back down, and he needed to know that.

The emperor smirked. "Does every visitor in your town get this welcoming speech?"

"Gave your in-laws the same speech already," I told him as sweetly as I could without being fake. "Don't make me regret it." I turned around and started to walk away.

"Reaper, the clock is ticking," the emperor said. "If you don't find her soon, we will tear this town apart to get her back."

"Yeah, yeah. I've heard that before," I told him, not bothering to turn around. "Enjoy the water park. I'll call you all later tonight," I added as we walked out.

I sounded a lot more confident than I felt. I passed both mini-trolls without looking at them. Katrina was not far behind me. I made it to the elevator in record time. By the time Katrina joined me, I had pressed the button and the elevator had arrived. We didn't say a word until we were out of the hotel. My head was pounding from staring at the emperor and probably the fact that he kept trying to use his powers on me. I rushed to Ladybug and leaned against my vehicle, breathing deeply.

"Isis, are you okay?" I heard TJ's voice ask me.

TJ was my favorite cook at Big Jakes. He was six feet tall with the best mocha complexion I had ever seen, and fabulous brown hair to boot. TJ had the ability to make every girl stop and stare at him. And of course, he didn't even have to try.

"I'm good," I whispered, not turning around. I leaned over Ladybug and cradled my stomach, pretty sure I was about to puke.

"Food poisoning, we think," Katrina told him. "Hi, I'm Katrina." She stuck out her hand. "Isis's new friend," she added, although I didn't know why.

"Hi, Katrina. TJ," he replied, shaking her hand. I was glad I didn't have to do the introduction. "What are you guys doing here?" TJ asked Katrina.

"Would you believe we were getting a membership to the waterpark?" Katrina asked him.

"Not at all," he said.

I slowly turned around and leaned my back against Ladybug. TJ didn't disappoint. He looked fabulous in his Big Jakes shirt.

"Why are you here?" I asked him.

"Delivering," he said, pointing to his shirt. "Some big-wigs are in town and wanted food. For the money they paid, we would deliver to New Boston." He gave me the sexiest smile ever. "Are you going to tell me why you are here, or is this top-secret Reapers business?" He chuckled. Although, if he knew how accurate his statement had been, he might not find it funny.

"Reapers business, but I need some help," I told TJ. "I have a hypothetical question. If you wanted to hide in Texarkana, where you would go?"

"The mall," TJ replied.

Katrina and I looked at him with blank stares.

"Why?" I asked him.

"It's climate controlled. They have bathrooms, and you have plenty of stores to go in and out of." TJ told me as he ran his hands through his hair. I was pretty sure he had no clue how hot he looked right then. "Besides, nobody ever buys stuff at the mall now a days. It won't be unusual to have a random guy hanging out at the food court for hours playing on his phone." TJ's theory was solid and made a ton of sense. The mall would be the last place I ever thought to look.

"That's a pretty good idea," Katrina told him. "And since you're full of great ideas, where would you hide a girl you're keeping as a hostage?"

"Oh God, Isis. Who is missing now?" TJ turned his full attention on me. "You do know you spend most of your time looking for missing people."

I thought about that for a second. TJ was right, but I didn't want to admit it out loud.

"It's all good, TJ." I gave him a hard stare, trying to look convincing. "We don't think she is in danger. Just being held against her will." My voice cracked right at the end, so I didn't sound convincing at all. I sucked at lying.

"Is that really the best you can do?" TJ asked me, and even Katrina shook her head.

"Hey, I'm trying here," I argued. "Back to you, wise guy. Any ideas?"

"I would have pulled a Dogma," TJ said.

Why was TJ so cryptic today?

"Fine, you got us. What does that mean?" Katrina asked, and I was grateful.

"Are you serious? You two haven't seen the movie Dogma?" TJ asked us. Neither Katrina nor I had seen the movie, which I found out when we both shook our heads. "Make a note. You are watching it with me," TJ told me, and I could feel the heat pool in my cheeks. "I hate to ruin the ending but here it goes. God came down to earth and one of the fallen trapped him here by putting his human form in a coma."

I scrunched my forehead. That movie sounded weird, and I had no idea how it pertained to the princess being kidnapped.

"You would put the person in a coma?" Katrina asked.

"A coma might be drastic," TJ replied. "I would just find a way of hiding them in a hospital. Nobody ever checks those."

"That is brilliant," I told him.

"Thank Kevin Smith. I'm just copying him." TJ was even cuter when he was being humble.

"We might just do that," Katrina told him.

"I've got to go," TJ told us. "Ladies, fun talk. Weird, but fun. Isis, stop by the restaurant. You need some fries," TJ told me as he walked towards his car.

"Are fries code for something?" Katrina asked me as we watched TJ walk away. He had a really nice butt.

"Nope. Just fries," I told her, but Katrina did not seem convinced. "Let's get out of here," I told Katrina as I hopped into Ladybug.

The vamps and elves were right about one thing. We were running out of time.

Chapter Twenty-Seven

TJ's mall idea might be crazy, but we had no other leads, so it was somewhere to start. On our way to the mall, we called the boys for an update. I told Constantine TJ's theory and he agreed it was worth checking. Constantine sent Bob to check the hospitals. Since Bob volunteered at both hospitals, the homeless shelter, and even Saint Edward's Outreach Center, he was Reapers Good Samaritan. I was starting to wonder if we kept Bob gainfully employed.

Katrina and I were tasked with checking the mall, as well as Walmart Super Center on the Texas side. That alone could take us forever. That Walmart was a giant rectangle with tons of stuff everywhere. Searching the mall and Walmart sounded as exciting as hanging out with the vampires. I was starting to believe Bob got the easy assignment. Technically, though, Eric had the easiest assignment. He had to check all the jails. As a cop, that wouldn't be very difficult for him. All he had to do was check computer records, which was almost cheating. Why didn't I ever have those kinds of missions?

After three hours roaming the shopping centers, we made it back to Reapers with nothing to show. Unless you counted extreme mental exhaustion. I really hated shopping and shopping centers. I was also traumatized about some of the things you saw in those places. The latest was tan colored skinny jeans, or maybe they were leggings. It should be illegal to wear them. The rest of the world should not have that image imprinted in their brains for all eternity. Regardless of your size, a pair of pants that made your legs look like a raw Pillsbury biscuit was never the way to go.

Katrina and I walked into the loft of Reapers looking beat-down and depressed. Bartholomew and Constantine were so focused on the computer screen they didn't even glance in our direction. Maybe they had found a new lead. Otherwise, we'd all be going in blind.

Finally, Constantine met our eyes. "With those looks, let me guess. You found nothing."

"Oh no. We found tons of stuff. Just nothing useful," Katrina told Constantine.

"Next time I want to hide, I'm doing it at Walmart," I added as I took a seat at the kitchen table. Katrina joined me with a loud thump as she dropped in a chair. "That place was nuts. How can the noon crowd be just as weird as the midnight crowd? Why?" I wanted an explanation about the mysteries of the world. Why were some Walmart customers totally out of control?

"Why do you think I refuse to go there?" Bartholomew chimed in, but his opinion didn't count since he couldn't handle crowds, anyway. Walmart was a nightmare for him any day, but I decided not to point that out.

"Avoid it, Bart," I told him, then I sighed. "Please tell me one of you found something." I hoped they did. At least then someone's afternoon would have been productive.

"I tapped into some of the security cameras downtown," Bartholomew said. "I have several shots of Noah walking around down there, but they have no rhyme or reason. He is just walking in circles." Bartholomew glared at the screen, then turned the same unhappy look on us.

"Let me see," Katrina told him as she walked over to the computer area.

My stomach chose that moment to grumble so loudly I'd be surprised if the room hadn't heard it, so I went to the fridge and opened it, searching for something to eat. As soon as I opened the door, Bob walked in the kitchen.

"Isis, please grab the glass dish on the top shelf," he said from the doorway.

I shook myself. Did Bob somehow rig the fridge and when someone opened it, he appeared? I almost laughed at the ridiculousness of my thought, but somehow, I controlled myself.

I pulled the dish out, not sure what Bob had made. He stepped into the kitchen and started opening cabinets. I had no idea what he was looking for, but Bob moved with a purpose. He handed me a few cans of veggies. Hopefully, he was about to make some lunch because I was starving. He piled some clean dishes and food items on the kitchen island, and then he looked up. I followed his gaze to find Eric walking in the room.

"No luck with the jails," Eric announced.

I felt like somebody had kicked me in the shins after I'd already gone down.

"Great," Constantine said. "Okay, Chef Emeril. Do you have an update for us?" Constantine asked Bob, who was busy gathering more ingredients.

"Checked Saint Michael's and found nothing," Bob answered, not looking happy at all.

"What about Wadley?" Constantine asked him.

It took Bob a minute before he answered. "Unfortunately, she is there," he said, not looking at the group.

"That is awesome," I told him.

"Not really. She is in the ER." His shoulders deflated,

"They have her connected to a lot of tubes," Bob told us. "They have no idea what is wrong with her, but she is not waking up."

"We need to get her out of there now," Katrina told us from the computer area. "The medicine they are giving her is keeping her unconscious. She is an elf. Human medicine is not good for her." Katrina really knew how to quiet a room.

"What do you suggest we do?" I wasn't sure if I was ready for the answer.

"We break her out," Katrina said.

"What?" Eric said.

"You can't be serious," I told her.

"How?" asked Constantine.

"Easy. We create a Trojan Horse," Katrina said, like that made all the sense in the world. "We just need an ambulance and uniforms. We can walk in through the main door of the ER and get her out."

"It sounds like it's time for me to get going," Eric told us. "I don't need to be an accessory to a crime." Eric waved at us and headed out the door.

"Isis, what else can your music make people do?" Katrina asked me.

I watched Eric leave, longing to follow him. But I knew I couldn't, so instead, I took a deep breath. "I guess almost anything if I can add the right emotions to it." I didn't need much energy to create a 'stay away' song. "Normally, I just have people fall asleep or stay awake. Those are two things we can't have going on in an emergency room." Last thing I needed were a bunch of dead people due to a lack of treatment by comatose caregivers.

"True. Both of those things would be bad," Katrina admitted. "How about making people dazed and confused for a few minutes?" A gleam brightened her wide eyes.

"Maybe," I told her. "I will need to create it." It wasn't like I had a huge collection of mind-controlling tunes laying around.

"Good. Now that we have a distraction, we just need an ambulance," Katrina told us.

"I got that," Bartholomew announced.

"Are you planning to buy one?" I asked him, my chin touching my chest as I crossed my arms over my stomach.

"Nah. No time," Bartholomew replied. "I know a guy who works at Lifenet. He owes me a favor."

"Do I want to know why an EMT owes you a favor?" I asked him, sounding very big-sister like.

"It's probably safer if you don't know," Bartholomew told me in a shy voice.

I shook my head but let it go.

"Can your person get us uniforms as well?" Katrina asked Bartholomew.

He nodded. "I don't see why not."

"I think we got everything, then," Katrina said. "I'll put some make-up on before we leave so we look like professional paramedics."

I didn't have the confidence Katrina did, but it didn't matter. This was going down whether I was ready or not.

"I like it," Constantine said. "But you need to be out of the downtown area before the parade starts at seven. I recommend you leave within the hour. Bartholomew, make sure to have your friend bring the ambulance ASAP," he ordered.

"Boss, what if they recognize me?" Bob asked Constantine.

"No worries. We will give you a face mask and a hat," Katrina told him.

Bob looked anything but convinced.

"Trust me. It will be fine. I'm going to check my kit and see if I have face paint with me. I usually keep some in my rucksack," Katrina added and headed out the door.

"I hope this works," Constantine said as he went back to helping Bartholomew.

"Bob, what is going on? You haven't been acting like yourself since Kansas," I asked him in a soft voice.

"Nothing. I'm fine," he told me without meeting my eyes.

"You are a terrible liar." I walked around the kitchen area and blocked his path to the sink. I figured he would talk to me or I wouldn't let him cook.

"Isis, I need to get this done and we don't have a lot of time," Bob told me. "Besides, shouldn't you be making music?" Bob might be right, but I wasn't letting him off the hook that easy.

"Not moving. If you don't talk, I'll blame it on you if I'm late." It was a low blow but I didn't care. I was worried about Bob and he was being ridiculous.

"Fine," he said reluctantly. "You heard Katrina say we served together," Bob told me, and I nodded. "Well, I was technically War's gunner." My eyes got really big when Bob said that. "He didn't look the same, but his voice never changed. I will never forget his voice." He shivered. "The day I got hurt, we were in a convoy and we got attacked. It was my job to protect the General and he got shot right in front of my eyes. For years, I have been carrying the shame and guilt of letting my hero die." Bob paused and clenched his fists. "You don't understand how it felt to find out he is alive. Isis, I tried to kill myself—more than once I might add —because I thought it was my fault he died, and now it turns out he never did."

When he stopped, I didn't know what to say.

"You are allowed to be pissed," Constantine said as he jumped on the island. I didn't realize he was listening to us. "The Horsemen are not human. For most of them, they don't understand human emotions or attachments. War has died thousands of times. It's how he can start fresh in a new place with a new face. The fact that he chose you as his witness says a lot about your character and he trusted you."

I could tell Constantine's explanation did not help Bob, and it definitely did nothing for me.

"Constantine, it's still pretty crappy to do something like that," I told him.

"I don't disagree," Constantine said. "Why do you think I work for Death? Everyone is not indispensable." Constantine put his paws over Bob's hands.

"We all have crosses to bear, but you don't have to do it alone," I told Bob. "You have a family now. Besides, if War tries that crap again, he will have to deal with Death and me." I leaned in and gave him a huge hug.

"Thank you, Isis," Bob told me. "I'm more afraid of you than Death. You are accident prone." Bob gave me a forced smile.

I punched him in the shoulder in a playful gesture. "Are you going to be okay?"

"I guess you are not the only one who needs to learn to forgive and let go of the past," Bob told me.

"Ouch. Low blow." Did he have to go there? I was trying to be supportive. We were not talking about me and my godmother drama.

Bob met my eyes. "I'll promise to let go and forgive, but only if you do the same."

He had a point. How could I ask him to do something if I wasn't willing to do it myself?

I nodded. "Fine. We will do this together," I reluctantly agreed. I didn't want to forgive my godmother yet. There was still too much anger, and I felt like being petty for a while, but I would try.

"I love it. Beautiful. So much healing going on," Constantine jumped in. "But you are running out of time. Take your skinny butt to your room and get to work. Bob, you need to get ready as well. Best way to heal is to keep on moving. So, move." It was official. Constantine only allowed fifteen minutes for a pity-party. After that, it was work time.

I marched to my room to get things going. I didn't want to get yelled at again by my evil fur-ball dictator.

Chapter Twenty-Eight

Preparation for Operation Body Snatch did not take long. We were out of Reapers in less than forty-five minutes with sirens blaring from the ambulance. That part was really fun. Normally people didn't jump out of my way when I drove—not like they do with Shorty. Having traffic clear out was pretty exciting. Bartholomew's friend called in the emergency for us and Wadley was ready. I just hoped we didn't go to jail for impersonating EMTs.

Bartholomew had given us headsets to communicate with each other and him. They were a better version of the ones the secret service wore on TV. They actually blended in, so nobody would be able to tell we were wearing them. Katrina and Bob had earplugs on their other ear for protection. The plan was to roll Katrina in as our victim and have her set off my recording. According to Bob, the princess was in one of the first beds in the ER area. We should be able to make the grab quickly.

Bob drove down like a true paramedic, as fast as possible without looking suspicious. We parked by the ER and rushed to the back to get Katrina. We had her secured on the stretcher to avoid too much attention. Unfortunately, as soon as people saw Katrina, they were going to panic. She might have done too good of a job with her make-up because it looked like half of her head was missing. At first, I wanted to call a real ambulance for her.

"Everyone ready?" Bob asked as we pulled the stretcher out. I was grateful Bartholomew's friend explained the procedure to us.

"Not at all, but we don't have a choice," I replied.

"That's the spirit, Isis," Katrina mumbled from the stretcher. "Now let's go and steal us a princess."

I rolled my eyes. She was way too excited about this. I took a deep breath, gave Bob one last worried look, and we pushed her inside.

The next three minutes were straight chaos. I had a new appreciation for how much coordination hospital staff needed to handle every case that rolled in their door. From the moment we rushed in, nurses and doctors scrambled from every direction to reach us. It made me wonder if having a person die in their facility affected their rating, kind of like when hotels had bedbugs. When the doctors directed us down a hallway, I met Bob's eyes, unsure what to do.

"We're getting close to the target," he murmured.

"Katrina, in five," I whispered to her.

We needed to set off the recording as close as possible to the princess. I didn't want to disrupt any other areas of the hospital if it wasn't necessary.

"Bart, we're ready for you to cover us," I said in a soft tone.

"You are clear to go. All the cameras and security feeds within a five-block radius are mine," Bartholomew replied. "Hurry up."

He didn't need to add the last part. I had been feeling the pressure since we pulled in the ambulance bay.

Katrina turned the recording on and the effect was mesmerizing. Creepy as hell, but still mesmerizing. I had picked a classic Santana for my base and as the music played, everyone within hearing range swayed to the beat. Eyes went blank and drool dripped from the corners of their mouths. I prayed nobody had any brain damage from this. It would make me feel horrible if I accidentally took out some of our top professionals in the community.

"Let's go everyone. I don't know how long it's safe to keep them this way," I told Bob and Katrina.

Bob released Katrina from the stretcher, and both of them pushed it towards the princess.

"Isis, we need to work on your intent," Katrina told me. "This might be too powerful for humans." She pointed at the patients on the beds, all of them swaying and drooling as well.

"Hey! It's hard to judge what dazed and confused feels like," I replied.

Katrina and Bob found Genevieve and were unplugging her from all the machines and IVs. I didn't want anyone else to join the drooling party, so I kept watch. I turned to monitor one of the corridors when I saw Noah. I didn't think twice before I took off after him. When he realized I was heading his way, he started running as well. Unfortunately, we kept the music low to only impact the ER area, and Noah was not close enough to hear it. Which led to me having to chase him down hospital corridors like a maniac.

"Isis, where are you going?" Katrina asked through the headset. "We're almost done here."

I knew we were on a timed schedule, so if Katrina said they were almost done, that meant we had less than two minutes.

"Stick to the plan," I told her as I ran. "I saw Noah. Get the princess to the ambulance and I'll meet you outside."

"Copy that," Katrina replied.

Noah ran fast for such a scrawny boy. When I caught up with him, I planned to have a long conversation about deals with demons and trips to hell. It still pissed me off that I'd risked my soul going down there for the fool in front of me.

Noah took a sharp turn and I followed, not too far behind. But by time I made the turn, he was gone. The hallway I stood in had doors on both sides, but they were all closed. Where did he go? I didn't know, but I was willing to search every door if I had to. I pulled one door open. Nothing. Another. Nothing again. So much for getting lucky and finding him in the first couple doors I tried.

"Isis, where are you?" Katrina said in the ear set.

I took a deep breath. "I lost Noah," I told her as I checked another room. "I'm looking in the rooms near where he disappeared. He has to be in one of them." And when I found him, I was going to shake the hell out of him.

"Another one," Katrina said.

That got my attention. "Another one what?"

"We lost the princess," Katrina said, her tone soft but tinged with uncontrolled anger.

"What?" I yelled, and the sound echoed in the hall, along with the sound of my footsteps as I ran as fast as I could towards the ER.

"Someone stole her and the ambulance," Katrina continued. "When Bob and I managed to get the stretcher in the ambulance, they took off."

If this wasn't Katrina's idea of a sick joke, we would all be dead.

"I'm on my way," I told her.

It didn't take me long to make it to the ER. I headed straight outside to stare at the empty space where our ambulance had been. Katrina paced back and forth, and Bob had his phone to his ear.

"This can't be happening," I told Katrina, throwing my hands in the air.

"Bart, please tell me you got something on your videos," I asked him over the headset.

"Sorry Isis, I wasn't watching that side after I started the loop," Bartholomew responded. "I'll need to look at the footage to let you know." He sounded about as worried as I felt.

"We need to get out of here before people start asking questions," I told Katrina as Bob made his way back to us.

"Way ahead of you," Bob told me as he pointed to the road. Shorty was rushing at us at full speed. I couldn't have been happier to see him.

"Bart, you need to let your friend know his ambulance was stolen," I told him, my stomach nauseous from the humiliation swirling inside me.

"Already submitted the report and sent an APB to Eric," Bartholomew replied.

Even better. Eric would never let me live that down.

Shorty did one of his classic screeching stops in front of us. Katrina and I jumped out of the way to avoid getting run over. I wondered if Shorty understood the purpose of his brakes. One of these days, I needed to check with Bartholomew on how much money we were spending in vehicle maintenance for Shorty. That poor truck took a lot of abuse.

We hopped in the truck as quickly as possible and Shorty took off.

"Boss lady, what do you need us to do?" Shorty asked.

I smiled, more than grateful he didn't bring up the obvious—that we'd lost the princess.

"Shorty, I saw Noah at the hospital. I'm pretty sure he is on foot. We need people combing the city for him," I told him. I was pretty sure Noah knew who took the princess. "We also need to know if anyone has seen the missing ambulance," I added, more as a prayer than an order.

"I texted you the plate number," Bob told Shorty.

"We are on it," Shorty told us.

"Once War hears about this, I'm going to be spending the rest of my days as a Private doing guard duty in Guantanamo Bay," Katrina told us, an air of resignation in her tone.

"War doesn't need to hear anything," I told her. "This is a small set back. We still got time. We got this."

Hopefully, I sounded more confident than I felt, because I had a feeling we didn't have this at all. Silence enveloped the truck for the rest of the ride.

Chapter Twenty-Nine

Constantine stood on the kitchen table when we walked into Reapers. He looked at least twice his size, I could've sworn he was foaming at the mouth. Could a five-thousand-year-old cat get rabies? I feared we were about to find out.

"Somebody, please tell me what happened!" Constantine yelled. "It was a simple operation. I leave you alone for ten minutes to talk to the boss and you lose the princess. How is that possible?" Constantine paced the length of the table, which looked a bit crazy since he was so huge right now.

"Constantine, it is my fault," I said, trying to save the others from his wrath.

"Of course, it is!" Constantine roared. I was not expecting that one. So much for reverse psychology. That did not work on this cat. "It's your fault, and Bob's fault, and Katrina's as well." He hissed at us.

Several seconds passed, but I knew Constantine hadn't finished his lecture. Bob, Katrina, and I were ready for it when it came, all of us standing at parade rest against the glass wall. I guessed our military training had kicked in.

"Isis, what possessed you to take off after Noah in the hospital?" Constantine asked me, sounding a little calmer. Before I had time to answer, he turned to Katrina and Bob. "And you two—how could you load the stretcher in the ambulance before securing it? Honestly, people, if I didn't know any better, I would think you were all working for the other side." We all looked at the ground. "Bartholomew, please give me some good news," Constantine let out a long sigh, then glanced at Bartholomew.

"I got a shot of the guy who stole the ambulance," Bartholomew told us. "It is a bit hazy and is going to take me some time to clean up." He let out an impatient snort, showing his frustration.

We all pooled behind him so we could see what he was looking at. Maybe Bartholomew's news would stop Constantine's lecture. What was I thinking? I knew better than that.

Katrina leaned in and analyzed the shot. "You might be in trouble, big guy," she told Bartholomew. "I have seen this before." Katrina pointed at the image of the guy in the video. "See how he is blurry, but everything around him is in focus."

We all leaned in to get a better look. Sure enough, it looked like someone had added a fancy Hollywood special effect to the screen.

"What are we looking at Katrina?" I asked on behalf of the group.

"Magic," Katrina answered. "Unfortunately, you only see this used by dark wizards," she added as we all stared at the screen.

"Please tell me it's not the guy from Redlick. That man hates us," I said, praying it wasn't our friendly dark-wizard chef. I couldn't blame him for hating us. Bob and I had kicked down his door and interrogated him in his kitchen.

"Nope. Not him," Bob answered. "Our buddy is much taller and muscular. This guy, even with the spell, looks scrawny." Bob had an awesome eye, so I trusted him.

"Not to mention, he needs some sort of demon connection to pull it off," Katrina added. "That is not an easy trick. It is one thing to fool the human eye, but cameras are a whole different ball game. They normally are not tricked by the glamour of certain spells."

Just great. Maybe we should just go around using our phones everywhere, then.

"That's a start," Constantine said, most of the anger evaporated from his tone. "Bartholomew needs to cross reference all dark wizards or any wizards that might have a tie to demons and their locations. We need to know how many are hanging around Texarkana and haven't checked in."

Constantine was truly going to enforce checking in with us from now on. I felt bad for violators. Their fine would be outrageous.

"Any luck that maybe one of our friendly guests have stolen Genevieve from us?" Katrina asked with a light in her eyes.

"Unfortunately, no," Bartholomew answered. "I have been monitoring both locations." He pointed at a couple of monitors on the wall. Bartholomew had images from both convention centers. "I have also tapped their rooms and been listening to all conversations they've had. Nothing exciting has been going on." I had no idea how Bartholomew did all that, and I really did not want to know.

"I'm running out of ideas," Katrina said and dropped to the leather couch.

"Everyone, wait. We got something!" Bartholomew yelled. He adjusted a couple of speakers from his computer station and pressed a few keys on his keyboard. Multiple speakers blared the same voice.

"Meet me at seven forty-five tonight downtown at the Perot Theater parking lot if you ever want to see your precious Genevieve alive. Bring one million dollars in gold. No negotiations. Don't be late." The voice stopped, leaving us all staring at each other.

"Find out who the hell that was!" the emperor screamed from one of the speakers.

"Trace that call and get my security now. I want that bastard dead!" the King of the elves shouted from another.

"What just happened?" I asked the group. "How did our lives just get more complicated?" This day just went to hell in a hand basket, and after personally visiting hell, I could use that expression with ease.

Bartholomew turned the volume down on the speakers. Both parties were screaming orders at everyone, which made for madness in our computer room.

"Good news. At least we know where to find the princess," Constantine said. "The bad news is, it's right in the middle of the parade route. We are going to have vampires and elves in the middle of humans, witches, and who knows what else." He paused for a minute to lick his paw. "At least he didn't say we lost the princess."

I had to agree with Constantine. That was definitely one piece of information we didn't need getting out.

"Bartholomew, any way you can trace that?" I asked our super genius.

"I'm trying, but considering I have no idea what phone they called, it might take me a while." Bartholomew sounded disappointed. "Not to mention it was a recording, so it might not do us any good to bother tracking it down." He shrugged.

"How do you know it was a recording?" Katrina stiffened on the couch, concern etched across her crinkled forehead.

"Because I have the same program," Bartholomew told her.

"Isn't it weird they are asking for a ransom now?" Bob asked us.

"This is not about the money, or they would have asked for it a long time ago," Constantine said. "They want everyone at the same location at the exact same time. I hate to admit it, but they are smart. Sounds like we don't have a lot of options. We are going to the parade,"

Constantine announced. "Bartholomew, we need to get the float ready."

Bartholomew gave Constantine a nod.

"Hold up," I told Pinky and the Brain over there. "We have a float in the parade? Really? When were you two going to tell me about it?" I planted my hands on my hips and stuck my chin out. What were they trying to do, get us kicked out of town?

"It was a contingency plan, just in case we needed it," Constantine replied. "Guess what? We need it." Constantine's tone left no room for arguments.

My phone went off before I could ask any more questions about the mysterious float. My caller ID said Abuelita, and my heartbeat went wild. We couldn't handle any more drama today.

"Hi, Abuelita. What's up?" I answered, trying to sound cheery.

"Dear, I know you are busy, but you have a visitor at the restaurant and he really needs to talk to you." Abuelita's voice sounded shaky with nerves.

"Somebody wants to see me at Abuelitas?" I repeated, more for the benefit of the group standing around me. "Are you okay?"

"I'm fine dear. Just startled." That was not a good sign. Nothing ever bothered Abuelita, which made me worry about the identity of the guest.

"Who is over there?" I whispered. Not sure why. It wasn't like they could hear my side of the conversation. At least, I hoped they couldn't.

"Jake is here, honey. Please hurry." Abuelita disconnected after that. Was she hanging out with Constantine as well? Why didn't anyone ever wait for me to say goodbye? In the grand scheme of things, I was obviously, focusing on the wrong thing, but it still bothered me.

"Isis, who is at Abuelitas?" Bob asked me.

"None other than Jake," I told them.

"Isis, you can't go," Bob told me. "It could be a trap."

"I don't have much of a choice," I replied.

"Isis, you can't trust Jake," Katrina added. "Regardless of how sweet and caring he sounds, he will always let you down." Katrina frowned and her eyes went to the floor.

I understood her concern, and I knew something had happened between them, but I didn't have the problem Katrina had with Jake. I probably never would, either. He never sounded sweet or caring to me...

"I'll be fine," I told the group with a smile. "He probably has a legit complaint about his hotel. Our insurance covers that, right?" I asked Constantine.

The rules of the job were that the Interns took all customer complaints. Not the first time Jake had complained. It was the first time Jake had come to my territory, though. He would make me take a horrible trip to the Cave to humiliate me before he whined about anything. It gave him more amusement that way.

"You tell that two-timing, cheating devil that we are not paying." Constantine scoffed. "The moment his demons announced their intentions of keeping you down there, our clause to respect their property was negated. So, no! He can pay for the repairs of his hideous building."

With Constantine on the roll he was on, it was probably a good thing that Jake had asked for me. I could easily picture Constantine scratching his eyes out.

"Got it. We are not paying," I repeated his instructions. I didn't need him mad at me again. "Let's divide and conquer. You guys get the float ready, and I'll meet up with the devil," I told the group.

"I got a few databases I want to check for our mystery dark wizard," Bartholomew reported.

"Bob and I will handle the float," Katrina told me. "I want to make sure we have plenty of ammo for our new little friend." Katrina flashed an evil smile.

I had a feeling between her and Constantine, a lot of people were going to suffer today.

"Sounds like a plan," I told her, trying not to sound concerned. "Please pack me some extra ammo, too," I told Bob. I didn't know how long my meeting would last, so I had to be sure I'd be ready for whatever might happen at the parade.

"Not a problem. We got you covered," Bob told me with a smile, but I could tell it was fake. Probably because he hated Jake, so it made him angry anytime I had to go see him. Honestly, though, he was taking it well compared to other times.

"I'm going to change out of this uniform before heading out," I told everyone as I headed to my room. The last thing I needed was the devil making jokes about what I wore to see him.

As I left the room, Constantine went right back to barking orders. I didn't blame him. We had less than three hours before the parade started. This little meeting with Jake was happening at a horrible time. Leave it to the devil to mess with my schedule.

Chapter Thirty

No offense to the devil, but I trusted him as far as I could throw an NFL player. That translated to not trusting him at all. I dressed in my combat gear, black top with black cargo pants, and silver-toed combat boots. In general, my work arsenal consisted of a few paintball guns with Eugene's special recipe, a machete, and a regular gun for blowing up windows and vehicle tires. This time, I added my new scythe to one of my straps. I was starting to feel like Batman with a utility belt, way too much stuff attached to my body.

I pulled into Abuelitas' parking lot and the place was deserted. I didn't think she would close the restaurant because of the parade. Maybe Jake was responsible for this phenomenon. I didn't believe Abuelitas' clientele would be afraid of the devil.

Considering the place was empty, I parked right in front of the door and walked in. Abuelita was waiting for me inside, and Jake sat at a table in the back, drinking Horchata and eating chips. The laid-back décor of the restaurant clashed with his fancy, white suit, although he looked rather comfortable sitting there.

"Where is everyone?" I asked Abuelita.

"He paid me to close early," Abuelita told me, looking over her shoulder at Jake. "Be careful, dear. I'll be in the kitchen." Abuelita gave me a tight hug, and that hug told me if I said the word, she'd send the devil to hell in flames. She was loyal to a fault.

I smiled and squeezed her back, holding on to her for a few extra seconds before I let her go and stepped towards the devil. She gave me another quick look before walking around the bar and disappearing into the kitchen. She wouldn't be far away if I needed her, so that helped calm me, and somehow, I even found the confidence to hold my shoulders high as I sauntered to him, a sway in my step much similar to Katrina's. I didn't have time to dally, so I took the seat in front of Jake without waiting for an invitation. This was Abuelitas, not the Cave, so I would play by my own rules.

"If you are here to complain about your stupid hotel, Constantine said we are not paying," I told Jake as I crossed my arms and leaned back in my chair, doing my best imitation of the Godfather.

"That monstrosity! Please, Isis." He shook his head and chuckled. "I should give you a present for blowing it up. Hell is bad enough without adding that eyesore to the mix."

"Why would you ever let anyone build it, then?" I asked, even though I knew the question wasn't important at all. "And why are you here?" I added. There, that one was definitely important.

"You heard the saying, when the cat is away, the mice will play?" Jake said, shaking his Horchata and taking a sip. "Would you like one? These are delicious." Jake pointed to his drink.

Before I could reply, Abuelita was in the room bringing me a Horchata, a bowl of chips, and guacamole.

"Here you go dear," Abuelita told me as she placed the food on the table. "Would you be needing anything else?" Abuelita asked Jake.

Abuelita hardly served her customers, but that didn't mean she wasn't the perfect hostess.

"No, thank you. Everything is perfect," Jake told her like he'd read my thoughts.

"I'll be in the kitchen if you need me." She narrowed her eyes at Jake, letting him know she would go to bat for me if need be.

When Abuelita was gone, Jake added, "She really cares for you."

"I have a great support system," I said and I meant it. I was blessed to have them. "So, why are you here?" I didn't have the time for a social call.

"Back to business, of course," Jake said with a smile, dipping one of his chips in my guacamole. I wondered if he was trying to get killed by Abuelita. "It appears my mice have been very busy lately," Jake added, staring out the window.

We were silent for a minute. I wasn't sure what he was thinking, but I decided not to waste the opportunity to enjoy Abuelita's chips. Her homemade salsa was to die for, but the guacamole was sinful. I had no idea how she made it and I didn't even care because I would never be able to make it myself. I was savoring my piece of heaven when Jake started talking again.

"Do you know the rules of the game?" he asked me.

"I barely know the rules of my job. I am pretty sure I have no clue about yours," I told him between mouthfuls of chips.

He laughed. "Eventually, you should give in and read your manual."

"At this point in time, I will need to find it first," I said, trying to chew and talk.

"You are a stubborn girl at times," Jake eyed me carefully. "Our rules are simple, Isis. We don't interfere directly with human affairs," he said. "We can whisper to them, entice them, bargain with them, or even give them gifts. You would be surprised what humans would give for a little bit of comfort or power. Easy way to pass the time until judgement day gets here. I worked too hard and lost too much to lose the earth now. It seems after all this time, I underestimated the cunning of my own people."

"Let me guess. You are not behind all this," I said, and the words came out a little more sarcastic than I intended.

"Why would I give you a pass to hell if I was?" Jake asked.

"To have your minions capture me." I glared at him. It was still a fresh wound, what could I say?

"You were in no danger. All you had to do was summon me." Jake snapped his fingers when he spoke.

"What do you mean by summon you?" I asked, leaning into him.

"You know. The way people summon demons. How else?" He spoke to me as if I had a clue in the world about what he referred to, which I didn't. It kind of pissed me off.

"Dude, really?" Did he honestly think I had any idea how to do that? "You do remember I'm Christian? Summoning demons is pretty much forbidden. Where would I learn how to do that?" I said, and my voice echoed around the room, but I couldn't help it. Jake had lost his mind.

"Constantine should have shown you," Jake answered.

"You obviously don't know Constantine that well." That cat would be damned before he trusted the devil for backup.

"True," Jake conceded. "I'm glad you both got out. How is Kat?" he asked in a gentle tone.

"Ready to kill you, but I'm sure you knew that," I told him. I really wanted to know what had happened between them. It had been bothering me since I saw them together at the Cave. I wouldn't ask Katrina, but I figured the devil would be a safer bet. Before I could talk myself out of it, I asked, "What happened between you two?"

Hopefully, I hadn't pushed my luck too far.

"What do you think happened?" he asked instead.

I rolled my hands into fists. Why couldn't people just answer a question?

"A really ugly breakup." That was my first guess.

"You could say that," Jake told me. He was quiet for a minute and I thought he wasn't going to say anything else, until he did. "I was ordered to stay away or pay the consequences." He gave me a sad smile. I couldn't believe it. He actually cared about her, at least it looked like he did. I had to take that with a grain of salt, though. The devil was a master at deceiving people.

"Oh, please. Do you actually expect me to believe someone threatened you and you were afraid of them? Who was it, Jesus?" I had a hard time thinking anyone else could be that powerful.

"It wasn't me who was going to get hurt," Jake told me, and my stomach dropped.

The idea of someone I cared about getting hurt because of me was unthinkable. I actually felt sorry for Jake.

"Does she know?" I asked.

Katrina was miserable, and she deserved to know the truth.

"No, and she won't," Jake added in a stern tone. "Now stop playing matchmaker and let's get to business." He gave me a hard look.

I nodded. "Alright. Give it to me, then." No need to push my luck more than I already had.

"The earth is mine, Isis, and I'm not planning to lose it—especially to one of my own. I need you to stop this mess and get Ginny back."

Was Jake actually trying to give me orders?

"Hold up now," I said, my voice way too loud for the small space. "Two things. One: you do know I don't work for you, right? I already have Constantine for that, and I don't need another one of him in my life." I huffed. "Two: how do you know Genevieve?"

"No, you don't work for me directly," Jake told me. I opened my mouth to reply, but he raised his hands, stopping me. "Everyone has emissaries on earth. Consider yourself mine. This is just me whispering in your ear. I could get closer if you prefer." The last part came out in a silky tone that sent shivers running down my spine.

Damn the devil, I thought. Damn him all the way to hell.

"Stay on your side of the table and whisper from there," I told Jake.

Unlike Katrina, falling in love with the devil would never be in my hand of cards.

"That's what I figured," Jake said. "And yes, I know Ginny. How do you think she met Arthur? Only at the Cave would those two species ever cross paths."

Now he really had my undivided attention.

"You set this whole thing up?"

"I would love to take all the credit, but I introduced them a few times and gave one hell of a reference letter." Jake cleaned his hands, which made me think our meeting was almost over. "I never expected for them to fall in love. That was a plus."

"Why? What do you get out of that relationship?" I pushed, and maybe a little too hard, but I really wanted answers and Jake had never been this helpful.

"Ginny is one of my favorites. She manages my personal garden in hell," Jake said. Her father is an arrogant bastard. He needs a little humbling."

I chuckled. That was hilarious coming from the devil.

"Now I need you to get her back," he said.

"Yes. You keep saying that, but how and why?" All these backstories were fabulous, but I needed real, hard facts now.

"Simple, Isis. Everyone picks a player to represent them on earth. Up to this point, I have stayed out of it because the outcome didn't affect me." Jake sat up straight and stared at me. "This game has gone too far, and the end could bring about a war I don't feel like playing in. Tag my dear, you are my representative. You will find your little friend Noah and his partner in the housing project in front of your airport. They are in the second to last house at the end on the right-hand side." Jake stood up and straightened his lapels.

"Are you serious? You knew all that information the whole time?" I said in a growl, almost pounding my fists on the table. I was going to kill the devil.

"Not the whole time. Your boy just moved to Haven recently," he said in a calm voice. "I have spies everywhere. Unfortunately, nobody has seen Ginny since you lost her. I recommend you hurry before those two move again."

"Wait. Let's get something clear. I am not your emissary or representative," I said, needing Jake to understand.

"Whatever you say, dear," Jake said, hearing me but not really listening. "Let's just say I have a bet and my money is on you. Do try not to blow up the whole town. I like Texarkana being Haven now. I can actually get really good TexMex again. If it makes you feel better, call the info my apology for your incident in hell. Now we are even." He walked around me and touched my shoulder. "Isis, your friends are right. Never trust a demon," he purred.

"Including you?" I asked.

"Especially me." He gave me a sly smile. "I need your expertise today, but trust me, I will do whatever it takes to get your soul. So, be careful." He fixed the bottom of his suit, then walked out the door.

"You get all that, Abuelita?" I asked her as I got up from my chair.

"He is right about not trusting him," Abuelita added as she came to the dining area.

"So, do I go to the airport?" I asked.

"Do you have a choice?" Abuelita frowned at me.

"Nope," I said because there was nothing else to say. We were out of options.

"In that case, you better hurry."

"Great," I told her and gave her a hug.

"I'll call Constantine and fill him in," Abuelita told me. "Isis, be careful. There are powerful forces at play," Abuelita added. Her words sent goosebumps dancing down my arms. Nervous energy bounced through me, and I didn't know if I had the strength to finish this. But I knew I had to try.

I jumped in Ladybug and headed to the airport. We didn't have a lot of time, so I texted Bob to meet me there with Katrina. Abuelita could fill them in on the details.

Chapter Thirty-One

The Texarkana Regional Airport was less than fifteen minutes away from Abuelitas. A small blessing. Bob texted back to wait for him. I figured I would recon the area, then wait outside for the cavalry. It was dark when I made it to the airport, but I got there in record time. Worry chewed through my stomach. I had to spy on a dark wizard that consulted with demons—definitely not the most appealing decision I'd ever been forced into making.

Ladybug could be recognized by any supernatural being in the area, too, so parking on the same street was out of the question. I decided to park in the airport parking lot, then made my way to the location Jake had described. I had never noticed these houses before, and they were pretty nice. I hoped the neighborhood had insurance against dark wizards and demons because they were going to need it.

Either everyone was at the parade or hiding somewhere, but the neighborhood was empty, which made things a little creepier than I liked. I walked around the house and looked through the windows. At least that was my intent, but all the windows were covered with aluminum foil, which was crazy. These people could work for ADT because they took security seriously. I thought I saw some lights coming from one of the windows on the far end, so I made my way in that direction and reached the window. I was pretty impressed with myself until I heard a tree branch snap. Spinning around, the last thing I saw was a two-by-four by my head.

My head pounded, and when I tried to open my eyes, I couldn't see anything. They were covered with some kind of dark material. After I got control of my racing heartbeat, I took an inspection of the rest of my body, which wasn't easy not being able to see it. I couldn't move my hands or feet but to wiggle them, and I could feel a rope digging into them when I tried. Well, that was just great. I wouldn't be getting away by running that was for sure. Something was also covering my mouth, and it felt like duct tape from the texture of the material. I could also tell I was on the ground on my side, like I'd been thrown there like a sack of potatoes.

There was good news, though. I was pretty sure I found the bad guys. Either that, or I found a serial killer, and neither of those things was good news for me.

"David, what are you going to do to her?" a male voice asked. He had a soft voice, too. Almost feminine.

"I told you already, we need a sacrifice to bring the boss over," David answered, at least I assumed it was him.

"What exactly do you need for a sacrifice?" the soft-spoken male asked.

"Blood, Noah. It always requires blood. Why is that so hard to understand?" David yelled, and his voice was rough, almost cold.

"You can't kill her. She works for Death," Noah said, almost panicking.

It took me a minute to put it all together. I was their sacrifice. Me. I sure hoped Noah would be a little more persuasive with his whole "you can't kill her" talk.

"We are not going to kill her, just take some blood from her," David told Noah.

And that didn't make me feel any better at all. In fact, I could feel my heart beating through my temples and my ears were ringing. I needed to get the heck out of this place, and fast.

"David, nobody was supposed to get hurt," Noah said, almost pleading. "The plan was to save Genevieve from those evil vampires. Not to start a war. She will hate me when she figures out what happened. I just wanted her safe." Noah sounded like he moved farther away when he finished speaking.

The good news about being bound was your other senses become sharper. Of course, that only happened after the panic went away and some form of rational thought kicked in. I was able to notice when Noah and David got closer or farther away from me. Not that it did me a lot of good.

I really needed to start paying attention when people told me to be careful.

"Noah, this is for the greater good," David said in a soft tone, as if he was trying to calm Noah down. "Do you really think the princess wants to have a monster of a child? We are helping her as well as humanity. When the boss takes his rightful place next to God, people will come to see the error of their ways and repent."

Oh my God! David was nuts. I didn't need a PhD in psychology to diagnose this looney-toon. He was going to set lose a demon on earth with my blood, and he thought somehow that would get him to heaven. That man needed a new bible to read. His was a little distorted.

"I don't know. This is getting out of control," Noah said, this time a little closer to me. "And who are those guys you gave Genevieve to? Where did they take her? They looked dangerous. What if they hurt her?" At least Noah was focused on the safety of the princess.

"Everything is under control," David told Noah.

"No, it isn't," Noah snapped. "Everything is not under control. Nothing is going according to the plan. Where is

Ginny?" Noah sounded angry, finally.

"Shhh, keep your voice down. You are going to wake her," David told Noah.

Unless they had a collection of prisoners, I assumed they were talking about me. I made sure to relax as much as possible. I wanted to appear like the people that were sleeping on sandy beaches, without a care in the world, which was really hard when listening to people planning to bleed you to death.

"Oh, please. Like it makes a difference. You are planning to kill her anyway."

Thanks, Noah, I thought. Way to make a girl feel better.

"Either way, I'm sure her friends will be here shortly," David told Noah. "I don't need them listening to our plans. They might try something stupid to stop us."

"Of course, they are going to try to stop us. So is half of the world," Noah told David and he sounded far away again. That boy was making me dizzy with all his moving around.

I wasn't sure if they could see me or if they were paying any attention to me, but I needed to do something. My hands were in front of me, so obviously these two were not criminal masterminds when it came to prisoners. They didn't even bother tying my arms to my body. I didn't want to draw too much attention to myself, but I needed to check if they took my weapons.

Beep. Beep.

An alarm system went off somewhere. The beeping sounds grew louder and louder with no sign of stopping anytime soon.

"Sounds like we have more visitors," David told Noah, a little too much happiness in his tone. That explained how they had known I'd been on the perimeter.

"Oh no. There are two of them and they are carrying guns," Noah said, panic filtering through his voice. He definitely hadn't been made for combat.

"Noah, relax and come over here," David said. The sound of his voice was menacing. If I was Noah, I would go the other way and get away from him.

"This is no time for you to be playing with your weird cauldron. We need to leave or get help!" Noah shouted.

"That is exactly what I'm doing," David said softly. "Thank you, my boy. Your services are no longer needed," David said.

"What? Ahh!" Noah screamed.

I couldn't take it anymore. I pulled my blindfold down, which happened to be a horrible mistake. It gave me a front-row view of David stabbing Noah. It was a good thing my mouth was gagged, or I would have screamed. David was nuts if he had no issues killing his own people.

"Your blood is not human enough to call on a full demon, but it is good enough for a beast," David told Noah, pulling the blood-covered knife from Noah's chest and dropping it in the cauldron.

This was going from bad to straight hell. A hell-beast on earth was not a good plan. I didn't care if either one of them saw me. My wrists were too tight for me to break loose, but I could work on my feet. I took a quick inventory and my guns and machete were gone. I could feel my scythe inside my cargo pocket, though. I guessed nobody had been scared of a metal tube. If only they knew. The cauldron started boiling. Noah had dropped to the floor, alive but bleeding. David started mumbling some weird words as the front door burst open.

My eyes roamed the room. It looked like we were in the living room, but it was empty except for a large, black cauldron in the center which was facing the door. Either David was overly confident, or he was dramatic. Either way, it wasn't a good plan.

Katrina and Bob rushed in, weapons at the ready.

"Don't move!" Bob shouted at David.

David didn't listen. Instead, he backed away from the cauldron.

Fog lifted from the cauldron and claws wrapped around the top right before the head of a beast appeared. It looked like a giant, mutant lizard with bulging eyes and the body of a tiger.

"Oh, that is not good," Katrina said and opened fired. But the bullets didn't even dent that thing.

"Isis, where are you?" Bob shouted as he scanned the area. The stupid fog had hidden me completely.

I managed to get my feet untied, then rubbed against the floor to pull the gag from my mouth. Before I could yell, David yanked me up by my hair. I looked at his hands and my eyes went wide. He had another knife in his hands. Where the hell did he get all the knives?

"What a beautiful scene. You will all die together," David announced as he dragged me across the room. The smoke hadn't hidden that side, which allowed me a clear view of the pentagram on the floor. This fool was serious about his sacrifice.

"This meddling girl will be the perfect offering for my king," David added.

I rolled my eyes at his dramatics, but at least I knew what Ralph's career aspirations were.

I was not planning to let psycho David drag me in that corner. My hands were tied, but everything else was working. I stomped my foot on top of David's and he screamed. I wondered how much silver was inside my boots, because I heard his bones crack. Before he recovered from the pain, I slammed the back of my head into his face. That hurt like hell, especially after the head injury I had recently received. David was probably a great dark wizard, but he sucked at fighting. Luckily for me, that was my specialty, and after the head to his face trick, he let go of my hair. I ran forward and turned to face him, only to find him bent over, nursing his bloody nose.

My head was still spinning but I stayed standing. I managed to focus enough to kick David in the groin, then followed it up with a knee to the face as he was going down. He dropped like a rock. I kicked him in the ribs one more time for good measure, then pulled the gag out of my mouth while looking for my friends. The other side of the room looked like a tornado had hit it. Half a wall was missing, and the door was ripped to pieces.

"Isis, we could use your help here!" Katrina yelled from across the room. The beast had both Bob and her cornered. The bullets were of no use, so they were using the rifles as clubs.

I grabbed David's knife and used it to cut my ropes off. I was wondering which one of them tied my ropes. Probably Noah because it looked like a Boy Scout knot and he definitely had the appearance of a Boy Scout.

I rushed over to help Bob and Katrina as I pulled my scythe out. They were pinned in a corner and the beast's back was towards me. Trying not to make too much noise, I took a huge leap and brought the scythe down the middle of the beast. A normal scythe would get impaled on its target due to its weird shape and the way I was using it. Of course, I didn't have a normal scythe and this thing went straight through the beast and down the middle. I was expecting to get covered in blood or green slime, like in most monster movies. Instead, we were showered in ashes. The beast was gone, and the room suddenly fell silent. I leaned on my scythe and tried to catch my breath.

"What took you so long?" Katrina asked me.

"Me? I thought you two were here to rescue me?" When had the tables turned to make me the one doing the rescuing?

"It appears we were the distraction until you got ready," Bob added. "Next time, do it a little quicker."

"Of course. What was I thinking?" I told them as we smiled at each other.

"Where is the wizard? Katrina asked.

"Over there, in the corner," I totally forgot about David. We walked in his direction.

"You will never take me alive," David said in an evil voice right before he pulled another knife from his jacket and stabbed himself. "You are too late. The plan is in motion. The end is coming," David gurgled as he fell to the floor and died.

Why couldn't evil villains die quietly?

"I got this," Katrina told us as she ran toward the kitchen.

I raised my eyebrows toward Bob, but he just shrugged. I guessed we'd find out where Katrina went when she came back.

"I don't know about dark magic, but he had a talent with knives," I told Bob.

"Who is that?" Bob asked as he scanned the room.

"I almost forgot. It's Noah," I told Bob as we rushed over to him. "Knife boy over there stabbed him first. Is he dead?"

I wasn't sure how I felt about Noah, but I didn't want him to die.

"Not yet, but you better put pressure on that wound soon," Death said over my shoulder. After the crazy day I'd had, her appearance didn't even startle me.

I shook my head and turned, but Bob had already gone to work covering Noah's wound. From the looks of it, he didn't need my help yet.

"Look out, Death," Katrina said as she crossed the room at full sprint carrying a bucket full of water.

Katrina dropped the entire bucket of water on David. Death looked at me and all I could do was shrug. I had no clue what she was doing.

"I'm not taking any chances that his blood activates his stupid ritual," Katrina told us. "Let's see how well the magic works with everything smeared." She clapped her hands together and crossed her arms over her chest, admiring her work.

We waited a few seconds and the only thing that appeared was David's soul. Death walked over and grabbed him. David screamed—something I'd never seen happen before.

"Normal reaction of the damned," Death told me. "You are running out of time. Don't let them kill Genevieve in Haven. If her blood is spilt during Halloween, it will open the doors to hell. I'm kind of busy today, Isis. Make sure that doesn't happen."

"Is it me, or does this just keep getting worse by the hour?" I asked Katrina and Bob.

"You know the drill, and it is never easy with the Horsemen," Katrina told me. "By the way, Death's red dress looked great with her blond hair."

That took me a minute to process. For me, Death had a black business suit that looked fabulous with her Jimmy Choo shoes.

"Time to go," Bob announced.

"We can't just leave Noah here to die," I told him, surprised Bob would suggest leaving now. He'd never been one to be cruel.

"Of course not." He glared at me. "But obviously, we can't take him with us and we can't call the cops. I gave him an elixir to dull the pain and I texted Abuelita. She was already heading this way with Angelito to find you since you didn't check in. They will take care of him and clean the place."

Bob made sure Noah was comfortable before he stood. I found my weapons thrown in a pile by the kitchen counter and retrieved them.

"How are they going to clean this place up?" I asked Bob as I looked at the missing wall.

"Due to the black magic, they will need to blow the house up," Katrina told me. "It's like having a meth lab. Nobody will ever be able to live here again."

I guessed Jake had been right. We were blowing up Texarkana one house at a time.

"Hurry," Noah mumbled in his pain-induced state. "The ransom was a rouse to get everyone to the Perot. They are going to release more beasts there and spill as much blood as possible," he got out right before he passed out.

That was all the motivation we needed. All three of us ran out the door. I prayed Noah would be okay and hoped Abuelita would arrive quickly because we didn't have time to wait. We had to save the princess.

Chapter Thirty-Two

As everyone kept reminding me, the clock was ticking. Instead of running to get Ladybug, I jumped in The Camaro with Katrina and Bob. I guessed being undercover was out of the question when you were short on time. Bob was driving as fast as Shorty. He took a left on East Broad Street and gunned it for downtown. For some reason, most parades in downtown used the Beech Street Church's parking lot for staging. Today, that was perfect, since it faced Saint Edward Church.

"I need to make a call," I told Bob. "Do we have any more water guns in the trunk?" I asked him as I dialed.

"We took them out after the zombies," Bob answered without looking at me. "How many do we need?"

I loved the fact that he didn't care why I asked, he was going to make it happen.

"As many as we can get," I told him. "We are going to need them at the float," I added for clarification.

"Got it. I'll have Shorty get them," Bob told me as he called Shorty on his phone.

"I feel like I should call someone," Katrina told me from the front passenger seat.

I smiled at her but wasn't sure she could see me since I was sitting in the back behind Bob.

"Hi, Father Francis," I said when he finally answered. "Sorry to call, but I need your help." I wasn't sure how to break the news to him.

"Of course, you need my help, Isis. You are the only person I know who is always in trouble," Father Francis told me, more jokingly than upset. "What is it this time?"

I held my breath, pretty sure he wasn't ready for this. "Father, in my defense, trouble finds me," I told him. I was sure he was rolling his eyes since Bob and Katrina were shaking their heads in the front of the car. "We are expecting to have hell beasts and potential demons on the loose in town. Could you meet us at the parade staging area?"

"What?" Father's voice cracked when he spoke. "Oh, Jesus. I'm on my way." I heard him say a few more prayers before the call disconnected.

"Bob, hurry," I said from the back. Today, I didn't mind being a back-seat driver. We needed to get to that parade an hour ago.

Bob violated a few traffic laws getting us to the staging area, but he made it look easy. He had to take some detours since some of the roads were already closed off. I was surprised at all the people walking towards the parade.

When we pulled up, the staging area was packed with people getting their floats ready. The parking lot of the church was actually a full city block that had been turned into a parking lot. We had to park on the street opposite from Saint Edward due to space being taken up by all the floats and the foot traffic of the pedestrians walking by. I had no clue where Bartholomew was with our float.

"Got it," Bob said to his phone. "Bartholomew is across the parking lot on the other side facing Saint Edward."

I had to give Bob credit. He was efficient.

We took off running through the street because there was no way to go straight through the parking lot. We found Bartholomew standing on top of a sixteen-foot-long float. It was decorated as a stage, with musicians and dancers. Bartholomew was dressed in a black suit with a loose white tie and sunglasses.

"Bart, who are you supposed to be?" I was wondering if I had missed an important memo.

"The Korean sensation. The one and only, PSY," Bartholomew answered, demonstrating PSY's famous dance moves from Gangnam Style.

"Look at you, big boy. That's what I'm talking about it. You got moves," Katrina told Bart, giving him a high five.

"Are you planning to do Gangnam Style for the whole parade?" I asked, afraid for Bartholomew's health.

"Of course not," Bartholomew replied. "We are going to do New Face, and I Luv It. Trust us, Isis. We got this."

"You speak Korean?" Katrina asked Bartholomew.

"One of many languages I know," Bartholomew answered, not being arrogant, just matter of fact. "Ladies, got to go. I need to check with the coordinator on our time." Bartholomew took off in a hurry.

"Isis, I'm here," Father Francis came up behind me. I raised my eyebrows, surprised to see him still sporting his priest outfit. I was sure it had a formal name, but it just looked like a man dress to me. However, I had no plans of telling him that.

"Oh, thank God, Father," I told him, giving him a huge hug. I wasn't sure if he was going to be so happy when I told him what I needed him to do.

"Isis, I don't like that look," Father Francis told me as he looked down on me. After all, he was taller than me by a few inches, and I blamed that on his perfectly combed white hair.

"I promise I'll go to confession when this is all done," I said, but I might need two sessions after all this. "We need you on the float with holy water shooting at demons, okay?" The words rushed out of me.

"Do I need to get the water?" Father Francis asked.

I leaned in and gave him another hug.

"Not at all, Father. We will get your ammo for you," Bob told Father Francis. "Ladies, I recommend you head to the drop-zone. We'll handle the float," Bob told Katrina and me.

"Who's driving?" I asked Bob.

"I am." Eric ducked underneath Bartholomew's dancers to get to us.

"Now it's a party," Katrina announced.

I glared at her.

"Here. I had to stop by Reapers on my way here." Eric handed us our headsets. "It seems Bartholomew got a little too happy about his singing debut and forgot a few key items. Make sure to hit the button on the headset to speak. Hit it a second time to disengage," he told us as he looked at all the people getting ready to perform. "I'll make sure Bartholomew wears his. You better get going."

"Follow me," I told Katrina as I took off running down Fifth Street towards the Perot Theater parking lot on Main Street.

It took us longer than I expected to get to the Perot. The streets were packed with protestors, as well as people there to watch the parade. It was almost equal on both sides. I had never seen this many people at a parade downtown. Unfortunately, the crowds just kept getting bigger. If they let a hell-beast loose on this crowd, it was going to be a massacre.

"I need one of those," Katrina told me in the headset.

I turned to look in the same direction as her. There was a street vendor selling zombie apocalypse t-shirts. I wanted to scream. I was never going to live that down. The worst part was the t-shirts were actually cute.

"Ladies, we are rolling," Bartholomew told us over the headsets. "At this rate, we should be at your location at exactly seven-forty-five."

I glanced at my watch. We only had fifteen minutes, which was no time at all.

"Katrina, I'm not finding anything out of the ordinary," I said as I pointed to the crowd. "Unless I open my third eye, I can't tell the difference between humans in costume or wild demons." And I really didn't want to do that.

"Isis, please don't do that," Katrina told me as she came to my side. "Vampires will be showing up soon, if they aren't here already. I don't need you going Darth Vader on me and killing everyone."

Katrina had a valid point. Luckily, she smiled when she finished speaking because I really didn't like the Darth Vader comparison very much.

"Let's split up and see if we can cover more ground," I told Katrina, and we both went in opposite directions.

The parking lot to the Perot was very small. It was already packed with cars, street vendors, and people. The only good thing about it was it had a great view of the parade going by and a terrible view of the side of the Perot. The parking lot didn't even face the front of the building. I had no clue why our thieves had picked this location. We searched everywhere and every once in a while, when the crowd cheered for a float, we stopped.

The protestors were standing on the Perot side of the streets, waving their signs. I wished they would listen to their own message and head home.

On our side of the street, we had all the party people. Suddenly, the crowd went wild, and that included the protestors.

"Isis, you are not going to believe this," Katrina told me over the headset.

I looked at the approaching float and it was a giant replica of Constantine. My jaw fell open and I had no words. The giant thing opened its mouth and started doing Rap God.

"Constantine, where are you?" I said to my headset. I was pretty sure that was not a recording. I got nothing back from Constantine, but I did spy our drone flying above us. I might choke that cat the next time I saw him.

The crowd clapped and danced like Eminem was actually on stage. It didn't help that right behind Constantine's performance came Bartholomew with his half naked dancers. When had they lost their clothes? To make that float even crazier, Bob stood there in his military fatigues playing the drums and Father Francis pretended to play the base while wearing his priest robe.

I shook my head. It was a scene right out of Wayne's World.

"Isis, six o'clock on the staircase. I found our princess," Katrina said as she tried to make her way across the crowd.

I looked over and saw a dark figure carrying the princess up the fire escape of the Perot.

Things were not any better on our side of the street. Our new favorite guests were heading our way. The elves were coming on my right, and they were in full glamour. They had the crowd staring and drooling as they walked. Unfortunately, they were also armed for battle. On my left, I had the vampires closing in. I was glad they were far away because Katrina was right. I was ready to turn them to dust. It was going to be a race to see who got to the princess first. I ran across the street in front of Bartholomew's float. Thank God Eric was driving and saw me coming. A quick glance back showed me Katrina had made it across the street, but she'd been stopped by two full-sized hell beasts.

"Guys, we have a problem here," Katrina told us.

I almost laughed. That was an understatement.

Katrina had picked up one of my machetes from The Camaro and was going to town. Too bad all she was doing was making the thing angrier.

"Bob, we could use some help here," I told him as I worked to get my scythe out.

"We're on it," Bob replied.

Bob and Father Francis pulled super soakers from behind the drum-set and lit the beasts up. The water hit one beast and the thing screamed and smoke billowed from it, but it didn't go down. I had high hopes that the sight of a burning hell beast would scare the humans away, but no. They were clapping like it was part of the show.

"Constantine, we need to get these people out of here," I told him over the headsets. I knew he had eyes on us.

"Too easy," Constantine said. "I hope everyone has earplugs with them." I had no idea what he was talking about, but everyone jumped on the line and said yes. "I did a few modifications to one of your songs, Isis. This should do the trick." Constantine blared the music from the drone, the tune of Ludacris's song, Move Bitch, get out the way, but with my beat for keeping people away.

I wasn't sure if that was the effect we were looking for, but all the humans started running in every direction like all hell had broken loose. Technically, I guessed it had. I jumped on the float to avoid getting run over. Even the dancers took off from the float. I had no idea where they were running to, but they were moving.

"Guess that worked," I told Constantine.

As soon as I had a clear space, I ran across the street to help Katrina, ready to attack with my scythe.

"Isis, get up there. We got this," Katrina ordered.

I looked up and realized our sweet, little princess was giving her captors one hell of a fight. This was definitely not a ransom pick up, but a sacrifice. By the look of the fight, the princess woke up just in time as they were planning to bleed her to death. She was keeping both the guy and the knife he was holding away from her stomach.

I didn't have enough time to climb the fire ladder before Genevieve fell over it. I had a flashback of when I accidentally pushed Teck down the fire ladder in New York City. My heart stopped, and I didn't know what to do. Before Genevieve became one with the pavement, she was snatched midair by something I couldn't recognize.

"What the hell? What was that?" I screamed to no one.

"Isis, that was some form of hell-man," Constantine told me. "You better hurry. He is heading towards Union Station."

Of course, he was. This night was making all my nightmares come true.

"Constantine, what should I do about these two hell beasts?" I didn't want to leave my friends behind, especially as two more beasts appeared.

"Get my sister, Reaper. We got this." Iason appeared on my right.

"Not if we kill them first," Arthur told Iason.

I didn't care who was going to kill what. I took off after the princess. This was the second time in one day someone stole that girl from us, and it would damn sure be the last time.

"Constantine, warn the team at Union Station that they have company coming. I'm on my way," I told Constantine as I ran down Main Street.

Chapter Thirty-Three

After months of nonstop running, sprinting down a couple of blocks was no big deal to me. Doing it while holding a scythe was a different story. I wasn't sure why I didn't collapse the stupid scythe to pocket size instead of carrying it like a javelin. I blamed my high stress level for my lack of rational thoughts.

I made it to Union Station to find Shorty and three other guys blocking the entrance for the beast. The beast was in the middle of the street with the princess over his shoulder. I looked around the area and I couldn't figure out where all the cops were. We were downtown next to the police station, after all. I should be able to hit a cop by accident. Unless it was the fact that Constantine blasted my tune in a half mile radius.

"Listen, you freak. Drop the princess and you won't get hurt!" Shorty shouted at the hell-man.

The hell-man carried the princess like a sack of potatoes. She looked so limp and unresponsive, I hoped they hadn't hurt her beyond repair.

I wasn't sure if man was an accurate description for that thing. He had wings, a tail, fangs, and really bad skin that resembled scales. For lack of proper words, I was sticking with hell-man. He turned so fast that he sent me flying with his tail. I had no idea that thing could be so strong. I landed against Shorty's truck with a bang, and I was pretty sure I dented the poor thing. If this kept up, I was going to be bruised all over and I probably already had brain damage from all the hits to my head. I got up and faced the hell-man, who now stood between Shorty and me. At least I managed to hold on to the scythe when he threw me.

"Did I hurt you, little Reaper?" the thing said to me. "You poor little thing. What? You don't recognize me now? It has only been a day." The thing actually cackled, and the sound echoed through the street. It sent shivers down my spine.

I stared at the thing but couldn't find any recognizable features. "We met somewhere?" I finally asked.

"Oh, now you are hurting my feelings," the thing said, mocking me. "You don't recognize me from Hotel California." The thing smiled at me and it had the most disgusting teeth I had ever seen.

"Guess fresh air doesn't agree with your complexion," I told the thing. If he was one of Ralph's people at the hotel, ouch. The good looks had completely vanished. Why would anyone agree to work for a demon to look like that?

"Anyway, you heard my colleague. Drop the princess," I said, not in the mood for chit-chat.

"You are too late, Reaper. More are coming, and this bitch will die tonight. Our master Ralph will return to his rightful place and he will take us with him," the thing hissed at me.

"Who are you calling bitch, you beast?" the princess told the beast-thing as she came to life and grabbed his wings, twisting them with as much force as she could muster.

"Ahhh!" screamed our favorite hell-thing. He lost control of the princess and she rolled off his shoulders.

If Katrina was a super-soldier with killer tricks, Princess Genevieve was a full ninja. She did a quick combat roll, landed on her feet, and proceeded to deliver a round house to the head of hell-thing. I was pretty sure the hell-thing did not see that kick coming. He dropped to one knee and Shorty and his boys rushed down the steps to protect the princess. The hell-thing tried to charge at the princess and the boys, but I was on top of him. Before he could get up, I sliced off his head with the scythe. Ashes flew everywhere.

"That's what I'm talking about, boss lady." Shorty came over and gave me a high-five. I returned it with a smile.

"Are you okay, princess?" I asked my new favorite Kung-Fu warrior.

"Yes. Thank you," she answered, looking at me a few times over. "Please call me Genevieve."

"Isis," I told her, and we shook hands.

"Shorty over here with the triplets," Shorty told her as he pointed at the three men behind him. I was wondering if they were really triplets. They didn't look anything alike.

"Thank you. You are one of Death's Interns, right? Why is a Reaper helping me?" Genevieve asked looking around the place.

"Because princess, you are in Haven and the boss lady over there is in charge," Shorty answered for me. "Not to mention the boss lady is all about helping those in need," he finished. He looked like a proud parent or maybe a cool uncle.

"Really?" Genevieve asked in amazement.

"Long story," I told her.

"Too bad you won't have time to tell it," a tall blond man said to us. He was standing with two other men, all dressed in very expensive suits. They came out of Union Station.

I recognized these three from our visit to hell. They were also part of Ralph's entourage. Too bad their beautiful features didn't last long. In a matter of seconds, they morphed into a similar version of their friend. The sight of them disgusted me.

"Gross," one of the triplets said.

I nodded and stuck my tongue out, acting like I might puke.

"The price to pay for using the elevator," the former blond hottie told us.

"I'll make a note to raise the fee for future travelers." That stupid elevator was becoming a pain in my existence.

"Oh, no need. There won't be a next time," former hottie stated. "Give us the princess and we will kill you quickly." His words slurred together, his new fangs making it hard for him to talk.

"If death is our only option, we will go swinging," Shorty told the former blond hottie. "Fire at will, boys."

"Guns? Please," former blond hottie said. "Don't be absurd."

I was inclined to agree with former blond hottie. I was pretty sure bullets were not going to help us now.

I moved in front of Genevieve and took up my best fighting stance. The three former models turned hell-things walked towards us. Shorty and the triplets unloaded their entire clips on them. To my surprise, they actually filled them with holes. Smoke billowed out from the bullet holes and one of the hell-things got hit in the face a couple of times. He screamed mercilessly. I was pretty sure the former models were in more shock than me as they noticed all their injuries.

I decided not to wait for their recovery and rushed them. Shorty and the triplets followed. I took out the former blond hottie by chopping his head off. His buddy on the left was next as I sliced him in half. It was probably merciful since he was screaming nonstop from his burned hands. The triplets shot the third a few more times and Shorty chopped its limp head off with a machete.

"How?" I asked the boys.

"Big Bob told me bullets were useless against a hell-beast, so we decided to convert," Shorty told me, and the triplets nodded happily.

"You converted into what?" What was Shorty talking about?

"Catholic," Shorty answered, sticking out his chest.

Last time I checked, converting to Catholicism was at least a six-month process. We were obviously not talking about the same thing.

"Shorty, I have no clue what that means. Explain," I said as Genevieve joined us.

"We asked Father Francis to perform a baptism," one of the triplets said.

"I'm baptized, and I still got tossed around." What kind of holy water did Father Francis use on them?

"Not us, silly," Shorty said. "We asked him to baptize the ammo and the weapon. I figured if he can do the miracles with water, then lead should be about the same." Shorty and the triplets beamed with pride.

I was impressed. They were not helpless people, but resourceful soldiers on a mission. Bob's training had paid off.

"That was brilliant. You guys are awesome." I gave Shorty a fist-bump and high-fives to the boys. I needed to tell Constantine that a raise was in order—or at least some medals.

"I recommend you celebrate later. This is not over," Death said beside me. I actually jumped and so did everyone else.

"Death," Genevieve said and bowed her head.

"Genevieve," Death said and bowed back to her. "I see you met my Intern. Welcome to Haven," Death told the princess.

"This is truly Haven? I thought they were joking," Genevieve told Death. "How bad is it?"

"No need to fear. We've got this under control," Death told her.

I hoped she was right because five more model turned monsters were walking out of the station.

"We are changing the access code to that elevator and raising the entrance fee," I told Death.

"That's a great idea," Shorty told me.

"Boatman will take care of it tomorrow," Death told me. "Unfortunately, it's Halloween and too many rituals are taking place to give easy access to these men," she finished, looking at the group with pity in her eyes.

"Wait. People are trying to summon those things?" I asked Death. What the heck had happened to humanity?

"Their followers are paying for passage." Death pointed as three more arrived.

"I hope you have a plan," I told Death. We were outnumbered, and I didn't know how many bullets Shorty and the triplets had left.

"You need to get Genevieve to Reapers. She will be safe there until morning," Death told me. "The rest of us will cover you." Death stepped in front of us and cracked her knuckles.

"You know what will happen if you attack us," the leader of the hell boys told Death.

"Oh, little one. You broke the rules of Haven by having your beast attack my Intern," Death replied with such a sweet voice. Good to know that beating up the Intern was not allowed. "I'm only enforcing the law. You should have stayed in hell." Death's voice was cold and ruthless when she finished. I was afraid of her in that moment.

"You have condemned this town to die. We will destroy it all to get what we want," the leader told Death.

"You have one night to try to get it done, but first you have to go thru me," Death finished with a smile. "Isis, when I give you the signal, go," she told me as she stared down the hell-things.

"Okay," I said, looking around frantically. "Shorty, I need your truck," I told him. It was probably a horrible idea, but if the princess died here, hell itself would open up on us.

"Boss lady, get to Reapers and don't look back," Shorty told me as he tossed me his key.

"Thank you," I told him and grabbed Genevieve. I really didn't want to leave them.

"Boss lady, focus," Shorty told me. "We got this." Shorty faced a platoon of demons and he was sure they had things under control? God, I wished I had his spirit.

I gave him a nod.

"When Death gives the word, you climb in and stay low to the floor board. Got it?" I said.

"I can fight," she replied.

"Yes, and so can I. But you heard Death. That is not our mission," I told her, and she understood.

"Now, kids. This is your last chance. Head home or pay the consequences," Death announced to the hell boys. None of them moved. "I tried," Death said as she took a deep breath.

Death raised her hand and blew a fine powder in the direction of the hell boys. Two got covered in the weird mist. They tried to shake it off, but the powder stuck all over them.

"Goodbye," Death told the two hell boys as she made a fist and crushed the two into ashes. "Isis, now," Death told me.

Genevieve and I ran to the truck and climbed in as quickly as possible. Fortunately, Shorty's truck was an automatic and easy to drive.

"Shorty, clear a path for them," Death ordered Shorty.

Hell boys were coming from every direction. Death made a scythe out of thin air. Unlike mine that was silver, Death's was bright-gold like it was made of pure light. There were too many bad guys, though. I really didn't have a clue how we were going to get away.

"Arthur, you take the right side. Iason, go left," I heard Bob giving orders from my headset. An army of deadly elves and vampires were charging to Death's aid.

"What took you so long?" Shorty asked Bob.

"Those stupid hell beasts just kept coming," Bob replied, pulling a machete out.

I tried to maneuver the truck, but we were stuck between allies and enemies. This was turning ugly. I heard a thump behind us and two hell boys landed on the bed of the truck.

"Damn!" I yelled. Before I could do anything, I saw Katrina running at us at top speed.

Katrina jumped on the hood of the truck and somersaulted towards the bed. She had two machetes in her hands. I turned in time to see her delivering one huge beating to the hell boys right before they started smoking. I was trying to drive, but we were moving too slowly. To make my job even better, two hell beasts blocked my way.

"Isis, hit the gas. We'll cover you," Bartholomew said over the headset.

I turned around to find him and Father Francis waving at me from the bed of the truck. Katrina had dispatched the two hell boys and was leaning on the side of the truck, daring anyone to jump in.

"Baby girl, send them back to hell. We got you," Katrina told me, tapping the side of the truck.

I made the sign of the cross and prayed to God I didn't get us all killed. I hit the gas and channeled my inner Shorty. The beast launched at us and the boys hit them with holy water before they reached the truck. The beast jumped to the side, avoiding the water. We didn't have time to slow down because I had my foot to the gas pedal as far as it would go.

"Constantine, we are clear. They are all yours," I heard Bartholomew say over the headset. In true Constantine fashion, he let it rain bombs from his drone and blasted the beast to pieces.

"Isis, Eric has traffic cleared for you. Just followed the sirens," Constantine told me in my headset. "We will take care of the rest."

"Thank you, Jesus," I said out loud as I drove like Shorty down the streets of Texarkana.

"You have some amazing friends," Genevieve told me as she climbed back to the passenger seat.

"So do you, princess," I told her, not taking my eyes off the road.

Chapter Thirty-Four

Death was right about sending us to Reapers. Our headquarters had turned into a full military compound. Constantine had rifles on two sides of the building, shooting at anything that moved. We rushed inside after taking out two more hell beasts. Were any of those demonic creatures even left in hell?

I pulled in the parking lot, not bothering to park Shorty's truck with the other vehicles. Instead, I left it in the middle of the lot as we all rushed up the stairs.

"Constantine, what's the status?" Katrina asked first.

"Those demons are unleashing hell on us," Constantine said with an evil grin. "Feeling bad for your boss. He is missing the war of the year. Die you fools." Constantine grimaced as he pressed some buttons in his controllers.

"Let's avoid that conversation," Katrina told him. "What do you need from us?"

"Genevieve, please have a seat," I told the princess. I wasn't sure how you handled a pregnant elven princess, but I didn't want her to pass out on me.

"I'm not fragile, Isis," Genevieve rolled her eyes, obviously offended.

"True, but you are pregnant," I replied.

"Let me explain something. Pregnant does not translate to invalid. Now, how can I help?" Genevieve snapped.

Okay, then, I thought. I think I better just keep quiet from now on.

"Well, now that we settled that, we have a battle to finish," Constantine announced. "Isis and Katrina, you two are on the roof. Father Francis, I saw your amazing work downtown. We need you to bless a few more things for the girls." Constantine pressed more buttons, an almost too-wide smile planted on his face.

"When I took my vows as a priest, I wanted to lead people to God and fight the forces of evil," Father Francis told Constantine, a little out of breath. "I never expected I would be fighting it in hand-to-hand combat." He shook his head.

I grabbed a few bottles of water from the fridge and passed them around. Katrina and I were used to the hard days of being a soldier. Poor Father Francis was a priest, and not even a Chaplain in the military. This kind of lifestyle was totally new to him, but he was holding up really well.

"Let's get moving, children," Constantine said. "Genevieve, I need you to take the controls for the South side. Those fools keep trying to break in our door. Bartholomew—"

"Way ahead of you, Constantine," Bartholomew interrupted as he passed out earmuffs to Katrina, Father Francis, and me. "Here. These will protect your hearing but will also make it easier for us to communicate. The headsets kept cutting off for some weird reason." He took up his position at the computer station. "Ladies, I'll take the North side, you two get East and West. Give them hell." Bartholomew put on his headphones.

"You guys ready?" Katrina asked Father Francis and me, and she looked like a kid on Christmas morning. I had never seen her so excited as she bounced on the tips of her toes, ready for action.

"As ready as we are going to be," I told her.

"This is a whole new level of exorcism that nobody ever covered in seminary," Father Francis replied.

The three of us rushed around the corner towards the bedrooms. The emergency ladder to the roof was at the end of the hallway. My hands were shaking in fear of what we would find on the roof. I had to take several long breaths to calm myself before I found myself puking in the hallway.

"Isis, give me ten seconds," Constantine said through my earmuffs. "Let me clear the roof for you." I totally forgot Constantine was still manning his drone. "Clear!" Constantine yelled, and we rushed out the door.

I had no idea what those demon things were throwing at us, but the roof was covered in some weird slime. I avoided it like the plague. Katrina took over the machine gun on the East side and I rushed to the one on the West. Father Francis did his prayers on both sides as fast as he could, and we were lucky he did because before we knew it, the enemy had started coming from every direction.

"Father, stay inside," I told him. "When we need you, I'll call."

After a nod, he ran back to the door.

"Isis," Katrina said, looking over her shoulder. "Kill them all..."

"And let God sort them out," I finished the motto.

Katrina opened fire on the incoming demons. I was pretty sure God had given up on that group. There was nothing to save here. I took the safety off the machine gun and started firing at the beast that was scaling my side of the building.

I couldn't believe it, but we fought all night. Many times, we had to reload the drone as well as the machine guns. When the drone was down, the beasts took advantage of it and landed on the roof. It wasn't fair that they were able to fly. In those occasions, I was grateful for my scythe. More than one of those beasts turned to ash due to a swift cut. The fighting continued until sunrise. It was the most beautiful sight I had ever seen. As the rays of the sun came up, the beasts evaporated back to hell. I wanted to cry tears of joy for that.

Katrina and I climbed back into the building, looking like we had been run over by a train. Father Francis was waiting for us at the foot of the stairs. He wasn't looking much better, but he was smiling brighter than the sun. He gave both of us hugs, then he led us back to the loft.

"Nice job, ladies. Father, if I consider converting, you are the man I'm going to," Constantine told us. I had no idea how that cat was so fresh and relaxed.

"Can I pass out now?" Bartholomew asked, and I realized he had dark circles under his eyes and his face was paler than I'd ever seen it.

"Isis, I'm ready to be an invalid now," Genevieve told me. She looked exhausted, but still better than the rest of us.

"I second that," I told her before I dropped on the couch beside Katrina.

"Please tell me they are gone for a while," Katrina told Constantine. "Even my eyelashes are tired." Katrina dropped her head on my shoulder.

Everyone was too tired to move. I don't remember when I passed out, but I was sure it didn't take me that long. I woke up in my bed under my covers. I didn't care who brought me, but I was so happy they did. I had no clue what time it was, but I didn't want to move to find out.

"Good morning, Isis," Death told me.

I guess boycotting to get up is out of the question, I thought.

With a groan, I turned the lamp on my night table on and tried to adjust my eyes to the light.

"How do you feel?" Death asked, scooting the chair she sat in closer to the bed.

"Like I was run over by a bus, at least twice," I told her, trying to stretch my sore muscles.

"You had a rough couple of days, but you did well," Death told me.

"No, the team did well," I corrected her. "I could never have pulled that off by myself."

"I'm glad you realize that," Death said. "You are part of a team. Most Interns feel they have to do everything on their own. Don't let that be you." She smiled at me and got up. "I do recommend getting up. You have a lot of people waiting for you." Death adjusted my hair and kissed my forehead. I wondered if moms had the same power over their kids. All my pains had disappeared, and the soreness was gone.

"Thank you," I told Death with a sigh of relief. At least I could move again. "What time is it?" I asked her as I enjoyed being pain free.

"Eight in the morning," Death told me with a smile.

"Really? I have only been asleep for an hour." That was amazing. I was pretty sure sunrise was around seven.

"Eight in the morning on Friday, dear," Death told me. "You have been out for at least twenty-three hours."

"What?" I screamed as I tried to jump out of bed.

"Relax, Isis," Death told me. "You weren't the only one. Most of your friends are still in bed. I just needed to give you a message from Jake." I stopped pacing my room like a maniac. "He says thank you. It appears Ralph's little coup lost its fire after sunrise. Jake is doing a little house cleaning of his own. He owes you one."

"Do I want the devil to owe me a favor?" I asked Death.

"Sure. As long as you never use it. Claiming that favor will open a whole Pandora's Box we are not ready for," Death told me.

"Good to know." That was one thing I didn't need in my life.

"Constantine has set you up a final mediation meeting with the vampires and elves," Death told me from the door.

"What am I supposed to tell them?" I really didn't want to meet with either one of those groups.

"I'm sure you will come up with the best course of action for everyone." Death winked at me.

Not the advice I was hoping to hear. We found the princess, but what was I supposed to do now? I couldn't turn her over to either party. It wasn't like Genevieve was a sack of oranges with no say in the matter. I really didn't want to think about it, but I had no choice. I headed for the shower and prayed inspiration would hit me between the shampoo and conditioner cycle.

Chapter Thirty-Five

The loft was deserted. After all the commotion we had the other night, the quiet was almost eerie. I walked to the fridge and found a simple note on the door from Bob. Get an Eric shake from the fridge and meet me at Abuelitas for part two of mediation. I grabbed my shake and decided to drink it at home before heading out. The way my days were going, if I left the house, I might never have a chance to finish it.

The door opened, and I figured it was Constantine since I didn't see anybody else. I had no clue how that cat got the door open.

"Why are you still here?" Constantine asked me as soon as he made his way around the kitchen island. He hated talking to humans from the floor, so he jumped on the kitchen island and glared at me.

"Decided it was safer to finish my shake here before tackling the world," I answered as I sipped my shake. The flavor today was passion fruit and it was pretty yummy.

"That is actually not a bad idea," Constantine replied. "You still better hurry. Your meeting starts at nine. It would suck for the host to be late."

Was Constantine kidding? Why was I the host?

"Why are things never easy?" I looked at my watch. I had ten minutes to get to Abuelitas, so I gulped down the rest of my shake and ran out the door.

It was a blessing the meeting was only at Abuelitas, or else I would have never made it on time. I pulled into the parking lot to find a large tent set up in the back. I guessed Abuelitas was not big enough for everyone's ego to fit. I parked Ladybug next to Bob's truck and went around the building to the back. I had no idea why we needed a tent this big, but I didn't care. As long as we were finishing this here and not in Kansas, I wouldn't complain.

"Well, it's about time you joined us." I was greeted by the lawyer representing the vampire's emperor. Lovely, just what I needed, the lawyer-puppet show.

"What can I say, gentlemen? I like making an entrance," I announced to all the lawyers staring at me.

The inside of the tent was dark, and it appeared it was sun-proof. The only things giving off any form of illumination were tiki torches and white Christmas lights. This was a huge fire hazard, but as I walked to the center of the room, I understood the need. We had another large stage in the middle of the room, and Arthur stood on the right side. He was a brave vampire. That boy risked turning into a pork rind for the sake of love.

On the elven side stood Iason with his dad's lawyer. I guess I should be grateful the heads of each house stayed home instead of creating another war in my city. I crossed the room and climbed the stage, wondering how my godmother had handled the pressure last time.

I looked around the tent and saw Katrina and Bob standing across from me. Genevieve stood between them, looking as regal as any queen. I smiled and waved, not really knowing what proper regulatory proceedings were, and I didn't care. I just wanted to put this silly war to rest.

"Can we start now?" The vampire emperor spoke through his lawyer. It was creepy to hear his voice come out of this poor human.

"Yes, we don't have all day," the elven King added. I didn't know when he had connected with his lawyer, but it was definitely his voice coming out of the lawyer's mouth.

"This is a great start. At least you both agreed on something," I told them. "Going to be a fabulous meeting." I clapped my hands together like a cheerleader.

Katrina covered her mouth with her hand, and I knew she was hiding her smile. She shouldn't have tried. Arthur and Iason had no problem showing off their smirks.

I grinned. At least I knew who my fans were.

"Reaper, get on with things," the emperor told me.

"Fine, fine," I told them. "Don't die on me." I flashed him another smile.

He rolled his eyes at me. The nerve.

"Like we promised, here is Princess Genevieve," I told the group of men and pointed at the princess.

"She is coming home with me," the elven King yelled.

"No, she is Arthur's betrothed," the emperor jumped in. "Obviously, after last night, you can't protect her."

That got both parties yelling at the top of their lungs. Each side called the other one names I was afraid to repeat. They were vicious, throwing insults that I considered completely inappropriate. I put my fingers to my mouth and whistled at the top of my lungs. That got them quiet.

"Well, that was exciting," I told them again with another smile. If I kept that up, I could apply for Vanna White's job. "I'm sorry to inform both of you, but I really don't care what you think should happen here," I told them, and they glared at me with hate in their eyes. "Yeah, yeah. You both can get as mad as you like. Genevieve almost died because of your pride and failure to communicate. She is not a thing you get to decide what to do with. Genevieve has a choice here."

Both lawyers and their representative rulers stared at me in shock.

"Genevieve, please come up here," I asked Genevieve and she joined me on the stage. "This is your life we are deciding. What would you like to do?" I wanted Genevieve to pick her own future.

"Father, I love you," Genevieve started, her voice shaking with emotion. This was not a good sign. "David, you have always been nothing but gentle to me. I love you, too." Wait, the emperor's name was David, who knew? Genevieve took a deep breath. "But I can't go with either one of you."

My mouth dropped open. "Wait. What?" I slapped my hand over my mouth. I hadn't meant to say that.

Genevieve turned around to face me. "Isis, if you let us, we would like to stay here in Haven."

The whole room was looking at me now.

"Here? Why?"

"Now that the world knows I'm pregnant, there is no safe place for me and my child," Genevieve answered, rubbing her stomach. "Anywhere we go, war and destruction will follow. After last night, nobody will ever dare to attack Haven again. Not with Death herself leading the troops."

"Fair enough. But you don't need my permission. Haven is open to everyone," I told her.

"Yes, but Arthur and I have another request to ask." Genevieve looked me straight in the eyes. "Would you be our child's godmother?" Genevieve waited, hope lighting her eyes.

"Of all the people in the world, you want me?" I blurted. "I know nothing about kids and I'm a walking disaster everywhere I go," I told her.

"The Reaper has a point there," Emperor David told her.

"Genevieve, the Reaper is also mortal. Are you sure about this?" the elven king asked his daughter.

He was right. The facts didn't lie.

"You were raised by your godmother, right?" Genevieve asked me, and I just nodded in answer. "Kids don't need perfect parents. They need people who will love them unconditionally. You would die for your friends, Isis. I want someone that if something happens to Arthur and me, they would love and protect our child that same way. I can't think of anyone as unselfish and loving as you."

Genevieve took my hands in hers, and I couldn't hold back the tears. I was such a wimp when it came to this kind of stuff.

"Yes, I promise to love and protect your child as my own. Like my godmother did with me," I told Genevieve, my voice cracking and raw.

It didn't matter how angry I was at my godmother. I knew she would kill or die to keep me safe. I wanted to be that person to someone else, and now I could.

Genevieve hugged me. We were both sobbing when we parted.

"Emperor, I ask your permission to relocate with my family." Arthur fell to his knees, begging Emperor David.

"Get up, Arthur. I wouldn't expect anything else," Emperor David told him. "I'm going to be a grandpa, the old-fashioned way. Who would have believed that?"

"Does this mean we need to ask permission anytime I want to see my grandchild?" the elven king asked me.

I rolled my eyes. "I guess we are all family now. You can come and go as you please," I told both sides. "Just make sure to obey all Haven rules so Constantine doesn't turn you all to ashes." I might as well be honest with them. Constantine would shoot first, ask questions later. I didn't need any special guests dead in Haven.

"Thank you, Isis." I got another hug from Genevieve. "By the way, thank you for saving Noah. He is a good kid and will be staying in Haven as well," Genevieve whispered to me.

I was glad she mentioned him because I needed to add Noah to my list of people to check on. That boy was going to need therapy.

Arthur stepped over and stood beside Genevieve and me, and an awkward moment passed while we tried to figure out how to act with each other. I didn't want to hug him because his vampire nature still made me uncomfortable. In the end, we settled for a fist-bump.

"I guess that means we will be seeing a lot more of each other," Iason whispered in my ear and I almost fell off the stage.

"Why?" I asked him, not understanding the meaning of his statement.

"Don't look so offended. My feelings are hurt," Iason told me, putting his hand over his heart with mock sadness.

"Whatever. Just answer the question," I told him, not falling for his theatrics.

"I'm not only going to be an uncle, I'm also the godfather," Iason told me.

"If you are the godfather, why do they need me?" I was sure Iason was perfectly capable of protecting this child against the world.

"It is our custom that the women raise the kids. Hence the godmothers have the most important jobs," Genevieve told me as she embraced Arthur.

"That sounds a little sexiest, but who am I to judge?" I told Genevieve and she laughed. "Guess we will be seeing a lot more of each other. If you try that glamour thing, though, I will impale you with my scythe." Magical creatures were a pain in my neck and I was done with games.

"I'm charming without it. You won't be able to resist me," Iason told me with a wink.

I decided to walk away before I poked Iason in the eyes for being cocky. I didn't care if he was flaming hot. Humble men were a lot sexier.

I made my way around the crowd and let them all discuss details of visitations and who knew what else. Katrina and Bob were deep in conversation with somebody I couldn't see from my angle.

"Can we go home now?" I asked them as I approached.

"Honey, you did great," my godmother told me from behind Bob and Katrina. I rushed towards her, wrapping her up in the biggest hug I could manage.

"I love you so much. But if you ever lie to me again, I'll punch you," I told her, crying again. My godmother never married or dated in order to raise me. She had sacrificed so much, so who was I to judge her?

"I love you, too, dear. I'm so proud of you." Godmother wiped my tears away. "We have a lot to discuss, okay?"

"Okay. When did you get to town?" I asked her after the shock of having her here wore off.

"Constantine called. He said it was his version of a peace offering," Godmother told me, shaking her head. "He was letting me audit your work. I'm glad he did." Godmother hugged me again after she finished.

"Nice job, girly," Katrina told me and gave me hug as well.

"You are too giddy. What's going on?" I asked Katrina, a little wary.

"War forgave me, and I have my full rank back with all my privileges," Katrina told me, doing a happy dance. "That was after Bob punched him," Katrina added the last part as an afterthought.

"You punched War!" I yelled at Bob. Thank God all the supernatural creatures were busy in their own discussions.

"Long story," Bob told me, trying to blow me off.

"Right. I want full details later," I told him with a glare.

"What's the plan now?" my godmother asked, changing the subject.

"Guess I'm going house hunting," I told them. "Reapers is not big enough for an elf, a vampire, and a baby."

"Thank God," Bob told me. "Let me makes some calls. We need to fix this fast." At least Bob and I were on the same page.

It seemed I was going to be spending the rest of the day shopping for houses with the new members of my family. Our little motley crew just kept expanding.

Chapter Thirty-Six

It was seven o'clock by the time I walked into the loft of Reapers. My feet were killing me, and I never wanted to see another for-sale sign in front of a house as long as I lived. Katrina was the only one in the loft.

"There you are. What took you so long?" Katrina asked me from the leather couch.

"It was awful," I told her. "Give me a squadron of demons any time," I finished as I dropped into one of the kitchen chairs, propping my feet up in a chair to my right.

"It couldn't have been that bad," she told me as she made her way towards me.

"It was worse," I said as I watched her take a seat next to me. "How can two people be so different and so in love?"

"You know what they say. Love is blind," Katrina told me with a smile.

"Blind, deaf, and a bit senile," I told Katrina and she started laughing. "Arthur wants a mansion in the middle of the city. Genevieve wants a hacienda in the country. They want land but security—blah, blah, blah. I hate house haunting. If we ever move, Bartholomew and Constantine are in charge of relocation."

"Did they decide on something?" Katrina asked, enjoying the situation at my expense.

"After hours of wandering, they finally decided they should build," I told her, frowning. "They are getting land on a vacant section of Mitchell Ryan in Wake Village. Actually, they bought the entire block to build their dream home."

"That's a good thing, right?" Katrina asked as innocent as possible.

"Yes. It is within Haven limits and close enough to us that we can be there in less than ten minutes." I was thanking God for small miracles. "In the meantime, Genevieve is staying at the Hilton with her family. That was another thirty-minute discussion. They made my head hurt." I dropped my head on the table.

"Do I want to know what the discussion was about?" Katrina asked.

"Not at all," I told her. "By the way, where is everyone?" Reapers was never this quiet for long periods of time.

"At Abuelitas," Katrina answered happily. "Abuelita convinced Constantine to let her use the tent and chairs overnight, and she is doing a luau." Katrina was almost bouncing off her chair with excitement.

"Does Abuelita know she owns a Mexican restaurant and not a Hawaiian one?" I asked her, confused.

"Are you planning to tell Abuelita she can't do a luau?"

Katrina was right. Nobody in their right mind would tell Abuelita what to do.

"Good point."

"So, let's go. The boys are waiting for us for dinner." Katrina stood up and waited for me.

"Katrina, I'm not in the mood to go out," I told her. "Just go without me." It took me a while to realize today was November second, and that happened to be my birthday. Nobody had said anything, and I was grateful for it. I still felt guilty for celebrating when my parents were dead. I just wanted to hide in my room.

"Isis, this is my last night in town. You are going to dinner with me if it means I have to drag you." Katrina crossed her arms and mean-mugged me.

"Do I have to?" I really didn't want to go out, but I was sure Katrina would have carried me if I refused.

"Yes, you do. Go comb your hair so we can go," Katrina told me.

I dragged myself out of my chair. No sense in arguing with a super soldier. I just worried how bad my hair looked.

My hair, my face, and the rest of my body were a hot mess. I jumped in the shower for one of the fastest showers I've taken since leaving the military. In less than fifteen minutes, we were out the door and heading to Abuelitas. Katrina was in a fabulous mood, and I figured it was because she no longer was in trouble with War. Bob still hadn't explained why he hit War, but I hoped it was hard. War had it coming for messing with people's minds the way he did.

I pulled up to Abuelitas and struggled to find a parking space.

"Who would have thought a luau at a Mexican place would be this popular?" I told Katrina.

"Maybe they heard she was making Kalua pig," Katrina told me.

"What is that?" I asked her.

I made my own parking space in the grass. "It's a smoked pork and from what I hear, it is to die for," Katrina told me as we climbed out of Ladybug.

"I have a horrible feeling that dish won't be appealing to either one of us," I told Katrina with a smile.

"Who cares?" Katrina told me and grabbed me by the arm. "I'm sure we can find a blue Hawaiian cocktail to make up for the pork."

Katrina was almost dragging me to the tent. The tent's door was closed. I wondered why Abuelita wouldn't put the flaps up so people could walk in, unless she was afraid of bugs. Granted, it was November and the nights were a lot cooler.

Katrina opened the tent's door and we walked in. The place was pitch black.

"Are you sure we are in the right place?" I asked Katrina.

"SURPRISE!" voices yelled from everywhere.

I tried to bolt, but Katrina held me by the waist. I never realized how much stronger she was compared to me.

"Don't even think about it," Katrina told me, and I stopped struggling and faced the crowd.

"HAPPY BIRTHDAY, ISIS!" the crowd screamed as tiki torches and the little white tea lights came on. The place looked beautiful. It looked like a Christmas wonderland, definitely not a Hawaiian luau. Abuelita even had ice sculptures spread around the room. Curious enough, some were in the shape of cats. That was probably Constantine's doing.

I waved to the crowd, trying to find an escape exit. One-by-one, all my friends came up to wish me a happy birthday.

"You honestly didn't think we forgot about you," Eugene told me when it was his turn.

"I wish you had," I told him. He hugged me again and moved down the line to get food.

"I'm so happy and proud of you, sweetie," my godmother told me when she came up.

After a good fifteen minutes, I was sure I had said thank you and hi to half of the world. My cheeks were starting to hurt from faking the smiles. I knew everyone meant well, but I felt horrible and undeserving.

"Happy birthday, Isis," Death told me. "Please come with me, I have a surprise for you." I followed Death across the room and out of the tent. I knew better than to disobey her.

We walked into a beautiful pergola that I had never seen before. It had purple wisteria covering it and beautiful white lights creating a soft glow. In the middle, a couple stood holding hands. They turned towards us and my heart stopped. It was my parents. I stopped and stared at Death. Had I died during the battle and nobody told me?

"Relax, dear. It's the Day of the Dead, remember?" Death told me, and I nodded, afraid to look at my parents in case it was a trick. Death pointed at my parents before talking. "You made a Haven, Isis. During this night, the dead are allowed to come to Haven to visit with their families. On this night, those who believe will actually see their loves ones. Every year, you will have hundreds—if not thousands—of people making the journey here. In the meantime, go and make peace with your past." Death gave me a little shove in the direction of my parents.

At first, I barely moved. But when my parents started walking towards me, I ran. I wrapped my arms around them and cried. I was doing lots of crying today, but I didn't care.

"Oh, Isis, you are so big, honey," my dad told me, drying my tears with his hands.

"You are so beautiful," my mother told me, holding my face and kissing my forehead.

"I'm so sorry," I told them. "It's all my fault. If I hadn't been playing in the car, the accident would not have happened."

"Shhh," my mother cut me off by covering my mouth with her finger. "Never again will you blame yourself for what happened. It was not your fault. Do you hear me?"

I heard her, but I didn't believe her.

"Baby, it was our fault for not preparing you better for the things coming your way," my father told me. "But you were so young. You are doing so well." He kissed my forehead.

"Honey, we love you and we are so proud of you. Please remember that," my mother told me. "We want you to be happy. Not to spend each birthday mourning for us. We are in a good place, honey. Promise me you will move on." She paused, and I said nothing because I didn't want to promise her that. "Please, Isis, we need to know that you will be happy." Tears rolled down my mother's face.

"I will," I finally told her softly. It was breaking my heart to see her cry.

"That's my girl," my father told me. "We have to go, sweetie. Our time is over, but we will see you next year." My dad held me tight, and for the first time in forever, the pain in my soul lessened.

"Next year?" I asked them.

"Next year," my mother told me.

"Happy birthday, our precious Isis," my parents told me as they disappeared back to their afterlife.

"Are you ready?" Death asked me as she slowly made her way towards me.

"Thank you," I told Death. "That was the best present I have ever received."

"They missed you as much as you missed them," Death told me. "Everyone wins tonight. Now let's go back before Constantine sends out a search party for you," she told me as she wiped my tears with her handkerchief.

Death and I walked back inside the tent and the party was getting started. The negotiation stage had been moved to one side, and a dance floor was put in the middle. A DJ booth rested on top of the stage and Bartholomew and Constantine were managing the music. That was a sight to remember.

"Scratch-Master-Flex on the mic and DJ Mighty-Flow on the turn tables will be hosting the night," Constantine told the crowd, and, of course, they went wild.

"What's in the punch?" I asked Death. This crowd was too lively for this early in the night.

"You don't want to know. Eugene and Angelito were in charge of drinks," Death told me, eyeing the punch table on the far right.

"Good to know. I'm sticking with water," I told Death with a smile.

"Here you are," Katrina said as she rushed at me.

"Sorry, Death. We are stealing her," Eugene added right behind her.

I got dragged to the dance floor by them, each one holding one of my hands. I looked over at Death and she waved at me.

"Birthday Girl is in the house," Constantine announced, and cheers exploded. I needed to have a talk with Eugene and Angelito on responsible cocktail making.

"DJ Mighty-Flow, let's party!" Constantine shouted, and Bartholomew started playing Bruno Mars's Uptown Funk.

Katrina and Eugene got the party started. They pulled people from their chairs and dragged them to the dance floor. Even Bob and Shorty were jamming in the back. I couldn't believe all these people were here to see me. For the first time in years, I wanted to dance on my birthday. As an Intern, I never knew what my future would look like. That hadn't changed, but one thing had. I had a family, and today, I was going to enjoy them.

Oh wow- this was a wild ride, even for me. But I'm ready for the next one.

The next installment in the series, **Unstoppable Famine** is here. The last Horseman is making their appearance, and the Reapers' Crew is not ready for Famine. Don't forget to grab your copy.

Acknowledgments

Dear Reader,

I would like to start by thanking you for reading this book. I'm so grateful you have made Isis and the team a part of your life. Thank you and I truly hope you have enjoyed the adventure. Our world is so busy and sometimes so full of negativity. If I could bring you a smile for a few hours, I have accomplished my mission.

This series get more exciting with each book. Being able to introduce you to new Interns and new characters, is absolutely so much fun. Katrina, the Boat-Man and even Godmother, all added to the joy we called the Reapers' Universe. I'm still blown away by the huge support and all the love The Intern Diaries has received. This series is a project of love and I'm so humbled by all the people that have joined the family.

I would like to thank the amazing Mr. J. Patton Tidwell for taking on the challenge of being my beta-reader. Thank you to my family, my best friend and better half, and even my cat, for putting up with my crazy schedule. Thank you to the fabulous Ms. Cassandra Fear and Michelle Hoffman for helping to polish this work with their editing talents. Absolutely, it takes a village to get this done.

If you enjoy the story, please consider leaving a rating and possibly a short review. Your reviews help others find

the books you love.
   With love,
   D. C.

About Author

D. C. Gomez was born in the Dominican Republic, but grew up in Salem, Massachusetts. She studied film and television at New York University. After college, she joined the US Army, and proudly served for four years.

Those experiences shaped her quirky, and sometimes morbid, sense of humor. D.C. has a love for those who served and the families that support them. She currently lives in the quaint city of Wake Village, Texas, with her furry roommate, Chincha.

Also By D. C. Gomez

In The Reapers' Universe- Urban Fantasy Books

The Intern Diaries Series

Death's Intern- Book 1

Plague Unleashed- Book 2

Forbidden War- Book 3

Unstoppable Famine- Book 4

Judgement Day- Book 5

The Origins of Constantine- Novella

From Eugene with Love- Novella

Rise of the Reapers- Novella

The Order's Assassin Series

The Hitman- Book 1

The Traitor (coming soon)

The Elisha & Elijah Chronicles (UF and Post-Apocalyptic)

Recruited- Book 1

Betrayed- Book 2 (coming soon)

Humorous Fiction

The Cat Lady Special

A Desperate Cat Lady (coming soon)

Young Adult

Another World

Children's Books

Charlie, What's Your Talent? – Book 1

Charlie, Dare to Dream – Book 2

Devotional Books

Dare to Believe

Dare to Forgive

Dare to Love